Copyright © 2019 A R Pliley

All rights reserved.
No part of this book may be reproduced in any form or by any electronic or mechanical means, including information storage and retrieval systems, without permission in writing from the publisher, except by reviewers, who may quote brief passages in a review.

Cover design and images by Rebecca Main
Editor Pauline Harris

Printed in United States of America & countries supported by Amazon Kindle Publishing

Published by A R Pliley through Amazon Kindle Publishing

Email: heritagesaga@gmail.com

Visit https://heritagesaga.wix.com/mysite

A R PLILEY

Dedicated to my beautiful daughter, Kaylee, for whom this book was originally written.

PROLOGUE

In BloodHene the wondrous hills of green and yellow had been watered daily with fresh blood, burned by catapults and crumbled to dust under the feet of so many soldiers willing to die for Kings, most had never met.

The pure white snow that started to fall during that winter had quickly been stained dark red, like the ground under it, from strong, determined men on either side. As the battle reached the pinnacle when either kingdom could have changed the outcome, all the fighting was suddenly halted.

After almost eight years of hard, constant fighting a peace treaty was created. The contents of the treaty were kept a secret from everyone, except those who were present on the snowy mountainside for its signing. The men, women and children from both kingdoms rejoiced at the cease fire and the soldiers quit the battlefield without any resistance. Everyone felt such a sense of relief due to the fighting being over that even the gruesome task of collecting the fallen was completed with a feeling of hope for the future.

Yet even though the treaty was signed both Kings knew it would only be a matter of time before war would strike again. While one King reveled in the idea of a breach, the other prayed the day would be postponed as long as possible.

Not for his own sake but for that of his only child.

BARRELS

"My lady!" Lance's dark blue eyes narrowed on his serious face in anger as he yelled scowling as Princess Katherine Caltrek, the only heir to the kingdom of Maltesh, who dodged passed the last player on the opposing Barrels team in between her and her target.

At that particular moment the bullseye she was aiming for was an overturned barrel with a line of fabric wrapped around it indicating which teams it was for. Kicking the leather ball filled with ragged cloth into the barrel on the right side of the field she made a goal. The goal caused the crowd to yell out in excitement drowning out Lance's complaining. He could do nothing but watch the barrel she hit twirl around in a circle from the impact until the keeper boy who Katherine had dodged at the last moment, managed to get it back under control.

"I'm sorry Lance. I tried to stop her," Lance looked down from his six foot two height, at the young woman with bright blue eyes, who addressed him from the side of the player's bench that was closest to him. Her clothing made her stick out terribly as the others were dressed in ragged and dirty cloth, while she wore a beautiful pale gown and delicate slippers.

"It is alright Carey. I know how she can be. Were the guards at least in place ahead of the game?" Lance's eyes scanned the field, the lines of people surrounding the four sides and the floor space between the wooden stand and the players on a bench.

"Luckily for us yes. There are two by the Kitchen staff's barrel, two by the Bakers barrel, and three on each side of the field and then there are those two," her arm stretched out and pointed to guards in black standing on each side of the player's bench.

"Any injuries?"

"Only exaggerated ones. You know how they get when they see her running down from the palace. She took the place of the first one who approached her and he's been jumping up the highest since," Carey smiled a little as the man a few seats away glanced nervously at Lance and then averted his eyes as Lance's returning scowl caught his attention.

"She is a great player," one of the players added under his breath yet loud enough for them both to hear.

"That she can play is not the issue," Lance's voice went higher in volume causing a few people close by to turn around. "The point is she is not to play until she has been dismissed and she was not dismissed by her teacher or the King. My Lady!"

Lance used the pause in the game to shout loud again to get Katherine's attention. His look of disapproval clear as she continued to play completely ignoring him. Lance was of medium build and taller than her, by almost a foot. He had a long face, short dark wavy hair and an expression that was always set in a stern look.

"Yes boy!" She yelled scowling back trying to play while shouting towards him.

"You know the King's rule about playing this game," he continued in the same tone, "You are to complete your studies and wait until the guests leave before you participate. You are putting yourself at great risk and as heir to the kingdom you must never come here alone. You know you have to stay beside me at all times. I cannot protect you otherwise. Something could have happened to you or Carey."

She had been caught again.

Katherine rolled her eyes towards the sky taking her eyes from the field as she ran towards the goal, once more remembering a time not so long ago where she could have played her favourite game all day, every day and no one would have cared. Everything had changed so quickly and it had started during a similar Barrels game that had resulted in her sporting a monster of a black eye and then the dreaded meeting with her father the

King that followed. In fact thinking back on it now she also remembered it was the same night that she had first met Lance.

*****

Four years earlier Katherine had snuck out of the palace avoiding a meeting with yet another suitor that her father had set up with a local Duke's son, who she thought was a complete bore, even before actually seeing him.

The game was an exciting one. It was all tied up with Katherine playing in favour of the Palace Guard, an excuse to the King so they could keep watch over her at the same time, against the Pier staff. One of the female servants from the opposing team had stuck out a foot tripping Katherine as she had charged towards their barrel, preventing her from scoring at the last second. In a rage Katherine had attacked the young girl without thought and they had begun fighting with all regard for rank forgotten.

To Katherine's dismay she had been seen by her matron of sixty, Mary. She had been a old plump woman who delighted in gossiping to the King about everything she would do against his wishes. Mary had located her at the game, seen the fight and ran from the field to report her. She had the counsel rushing back to the field with the King in tow only minutes later. They had all turned the bend at the end of the grounds from the courtyard onto the grass just as a beautiful right hook hit Katherine directly in the left eye.

Her purple black eye shone like a beacon all through dinner that evening. Katherine could feel several guests and servants alike watching her and arching their necks in strange ways trying to get a better view. As she tried to avoid eye contact with everyone, her father, King Henry Caltrek of Maltesh, had remained completely silent. While everyone ate, the other high council members, the Duke, his family and the other nobles were left to the idle chit-chatting.

When the meal was winding down a smirking servant placed a small white envelope on her now clean bread plate. It was by this short note that Katherine knew the night would not end in her favour and even though the letter contained very few words, she could feel his disappointment and anger in each stroke of the quill.

Private meeting quarters promptly following dessert.
And I mean promptly

Walking to the private counsel room that evening seemed to take seconds, even though she had taken the longest route she knew. Passing through the great hall, strolling down the path that curved around the private garden and counting each of the doors in the guest wing could not halt the enviable.

It seemed like with only a few short steps she was standing in front of Henry's large wooden desk. Henry was sat in his favourite large red chair, with his personal guard Calzar standing directly behind it, and once she was permitted to enter he looked her over without speaking. His eyes only stopped for a brief moment longer on her swollen left eye. After many minutes of silence he spoke with a mixture of frustration, sadness and anger.

"So what do you have to say for your disgraceful behavior today?"

"I'm so sorry father," she mumbled quickly. This was her automatic response when being caught and Henry had heard it so many times it no longer had an effect on him.

"Are you really?" He shook his head keeping eye contact with her. He was old, almost sixty, yet held the demeanor of someone in their forties. His bright blue eyes shone like new and his face kept a somewhat youthful appearance with shoulder length white hair that was always in a long braided ponytail and a well-kept thick, short white beard.

"I wonder if you even realize what happened today. Well, do you?" He continued in a calm steady tone. Thinking for a moment she answered slowly.

"I left before meeting Prance-a lot...I mean Duke Pracon's

son, Geffrey and fought at the game,"

"Yes, beloved that is all true and sad, but you also caused so much more trouble. The young woman you fought with, did you know her name? Did you even attempt to ask for an apology before your temper took over? Did you remember the breathing exercises you were taught to calm your temper?"

"So you know she tripped me?" Katherine was surprised about how much he knew about the game, but then again he was the King and able to gather information quickly with less hassle than herself.

"I know that your anger led to that poor girl being beaten for attacking a member of the Royal Household. Do you feel any remorse for her at all?"

"Of course I do," in truth the reality shocked her and she felt a little bad.

"Explain to me how much Katherine? Do you feel as if you should track her down to apologize? Do you feel that you should have taken the punishment for her?"

"Not that," she responded quickly without thinking, "She struck first,"

"And that justifies your attack on her?"

"Well..."

"No, Katherine it does not," he stared at her with such intensity she could not help looking away after a few seconds, "I have told you many times that your temper will create more problems than solutions and today only proved it further. Did you stop to think that maybe the girl did not know who you were and that due to the nature of her days labour at the pier she had never seen a member of the Royal family before?"

"No, I didn't father," she was surprised a second time as she had never once thought that anyone in the kingdom would not know her by sight alone.

"No, you did not. I spoke at length to her and believe it or not, she had no idea who you were. Sadly I had no choice except to carry out the law upon her and she suffered because of a childish act by you. You must understand that you are not a child anymore. You are becoming a woman and there are new responsibilities that come with that,"

"How do you mean father?" She asked not sure as to what was being said, except she could sense it was important. Honestly Katherine had only heard parts of what he was saying and though she worried about the girl, it was more about what she would say about Katherine and that she deserved punishment for tripping her up. Yet now as Henry continued speaking in a calm and serious tone, it was clear she also would be punished. He never once looked away from her as he spoke.

"You remember the stories about when I became King?"

"Certainly. You became King after Grandfather was killed on a hunting trip by a stray arrow,"

"Good then you should also remember that I was just a few short years older than you are now when that responsibility was passed to me. Not by choice, but because it had to be as there was no one else. I was not prepared for a life of service to my kingdom and was not expecting to have it for many years. The task suddenly became mine to unite a kingdom suffering from my same grief and keep the peace with other kingdoms that wanted to intervene," he stopped for a moment, "I am only telling you this because I feel I have done wrong by you,"

"No, you're a great father and a brilliant leader," she always loved to smile at him as she played innocent. Though she spoke the truth it usually helped her case to flatter him. This time however it did not work.

"Listen to me beloved," he interrupted raising his right hand a little, "I have been letting you do what you wanted to make up for my past and the restrictions that I had to go through to rule the kingdom. Everything you wanted I gave as I never got a chance to have them, and I thought that by doing so I would be giving you more. Today I realized with great sadness that I was terribly wrong. What if that young girl had been a spy sent by Mischelle? What if she would have carried a knife, not just a fist? Mischelle and Staton will stop at nothing to have both Buletis and Maltesh under their rule. It would only take one small simple act from them to start another war,"

"Father…" to her own ears she could hear the doubt and almost whine of hearing about their rival kingdom for the hundredth time.

"Even though we are not at war, does not mean that they will keep the treaty forever. You are the only child and living heir to the throne. Killing you would ensure the downfall of our way of life. There would be no one to take over the throne once I am dead,"

"But father…"

"No, I am not finished. All the skills you have been taught so far will benefit you well in the years to come, I have no doubt, but from this day forward your schedule will change. Please send him in."

Henry motioned to Calzar, who walked passed Katherine giving her the usual stern express as he opened the heavy brown door behind her. Calzar was almost the twin to Henry. Yet where Henry was light, Calzar was dark. Dark eyes, dark hair and a more weathered look. However those bright blue eyes matched Henry's almost perfectly. To Katherine he had been almost an uncle aside from Henry always coming first for him, above all else.

With the door open Lance walked in and Katherine had not known what to expect, however she could still remember every detail about him. He had been twenty four at the time, yet he looked closer to fifty. She could tell her had seen people die as he carried the same expression that men did returning from battles. His face was pale, drawn and dark blue, green eyes looked as if they would never smile again.

"This is Lance Mabelle. From this day on he will be your shadow as Calzar is to me. He is to be your personal guard and constant companion. Every day will be scheduled as it is for myself and Lance here is ensure you are present at every single thing on your list. He is also there to protect you with his life at all times. Starting today you are no longer a small child. You are sixteen years old and a woman. You are the only heir and the next ruler of Maltesh. You will be schooled and trained in the running of the kingdom. From this point on you are to devote every waking moment to studying, devotion to the people, your King and the kingdom," he ended in a tone of such authority that Katherine did not know what to say. Through all the years of carefree activities and trouble she got into never once had he used such a tone towards her. It was the tone he used for conducting business and settling disagreements with the people. She could not find her voice no matter how long she stood there.

Thankfully Lance spoke for the first time breaking up the silence that followed the King's last words. "Your highness, if I may speak?" His voice deep and his tone serious yet respectful.

"Certainly Lance, what is it?"

"If I may sire. The hour is getting late and since the Princesses new schedule starts in the morning I should escort her to her room for the evening,"

"Yes, you are right. Beloved I will see you at breakfast. Goodnight and sleep well my daughter," she could say nothing except.

"Goodnight father." And was still in shock from what just happened. She would no longer be free to do as she pleased. Everything she ever loved doing would no longer be permitted.

Katherine had never noticed before that the corridors were cold as ice. They had walked down the dark passageways in silence as neither knew what to say to the other. Lance again spoke first as they reached her quarters.

"Is there anything else I can get for you tonight, my lady?" She looked into his eyes for the first time still unsure as to what to say. After another awkward moment she just replied softly.

"No thank you Lance. That will be all."

And with that her life had changed, for the worst in her opinion.

"Highness look out!" Someone close by yelled bringing

her mind back to the field and her current barrels game. Seeing the threat, a short man from the opposing team running towards her, she was able to fake a direction, go around him and score causing the crowd to erupt in cheers. Still she could not escape Lance's watchful eyes.

"My lady, if I have to tell you once more I shall call the Royal Guard," Lance yelled as his patience wore thin. Their years together had caused him to know exactly which tone he could use towards her, without fear of the King's wrath. Katherine did not listen at all if he was in any way subtle or unclear.

"Kat, for once listen to him. You can play again next time." The voice came from Carey. Carey Bernett was Katherine's newest companion and had been for over a year. Henry had decided she needed a female companion since the passing of Mary. Someone as the King stated, "Slightly older. Someone you can look up too."

At this announcement Katherine had simply, nodded smiling. Of course this change could not have possibly had anything to do with people in court talking about the future Queen only even being seen in the presence of a man.

Once Carey found out she had been chosen they had become fast friends, even though they mimicked the King and Calzar in being completely different in appearance. Carey was a brilliant blonde that hung straight down to her chest when loose. Most of the time she had intricate braids that formed a circle on the back of her head. This caused it to be out of the way of everyday things. Before they had known each other a week they were as close as sisters. This made life harder for Lance as he had become responsible for them both, but even more fun for Katherine as she could tease him about something else.

At this moment Lance was still waiting impatiently for Katherine to leave the Barrels field. His posture stiff as a statue leaning on the large wooden stand. The Barrel stand had been created at Katherine's request in the very center, on the left side of the small field that held the game every week during the spring and summer months. During the winter months it was used to house the city cattle. Katherine had insisted that if she could not play every game she would not miss a single second, of any she could attend. There were five rows of wooden seating as well as several small dirt piles that people used on the ground if they had a spare blanket.

A specifically made platform, higher than the others, was made for Katherine. The platform had six individual wide seats, each with its own cushion. Lance and Carey had been included in its design. To ensure she could watch in any weather Henry had also placed a roof and three sides, low enough that their heads could be seen, yet high enough to block any unwanted wind. There was also a small staircase that reached from the ground level all the way to the top for easy access.

UNEXPECTED AND UN-WELCOME GUESTS

Finally leaving the field after ten more minutes, Carey joined Katherine's right side as she always did, vacating her usual seat up front. The ladies walked briskly passed Lance continuing their previous conversation regarding the Royal ball that was to be held at the palace that very evening.

"It's a shame that such a tragic event is cause for celebration," Carey nodded slightly in Lance's direction as they passed him. He returned the gesture yet Katherine did not even notice the exchange or even acknowledge that he was there.

"I've told you before Carey, it's their way of forgetting about it. Think about what happens at the ball every year. There's the toasts, the dancing, the food and I did I mention the toasts," she chuckled. Carey joined in and laughed a little.

"How can I forget? I swear each year they add another ten people to speak,"

"At least we get to drink each time they stop talking. I seriously think they need to bypass the sadness and get to the fun parts,"

"A lot of men died, its hard to think of having fun at times like that,"

"The ball is in celebration of the treaty, not the battle of BloodHene itself. I mean really father's is not heartless,"

"I didn't mean..." Carey stumbled on her words, not in any way wanting to excuse the King of anything.

"I know you didn't. We just have to focus on the positive. The war ended fifteen years ago today and thanks to that we get to have a huge party and drink a lot," Katherine laughed louder this time and Carey joined in.

"And what about the dancing with the suitors?" Carey smirked a little as Katherine made a sound at the back of her throat.

"Oh no, I completely forgot that on purpose," she made a face, "Each song I must endure countless fools professing their fake desire and interest in me. It's exhausting,"

"I'm sorry for you. I know its hard finding someone who really cares about you,"

"All they hear are the words Princess and coins and then they think they need to agree with everything I say or at least pretend to listen. Ever since him I just can't trust anything they say," Katherine glanced over at Carey with an almost sad expression and she knew exactly what to say.

"At least you were able to see through his deception before it was too late,"

"Who are you kidding? I know it was all you," Katherine smiled widely at her

"It wasn't just me Kat," Carey shifted her eyes to Lance as he caught up with them. Lance followed their path off the field, down several streets and passed the marketplace heading towards the palace. He had reached them as they started taking the steps into the palace grounds, two at a time and turned left towards the Royal living quarters.

"Playing again, my lady?" He walked as stiff as he always did, speaking in a disapproving tone. Katherine could not help herself. He was such a pain and asking for it.

"I don't believe anything I do is your business boy,"

"Kat, please don't do this again," Carey pleaded knowing full well where comments like this had led before.

"Me! I didn't start anything. He did! He has nothing better to do so he has to find pleasure in ruining my day!" She yelled at Carey upset that anyone would ever blame her for anything.

"My lady," Lance suddenly barked moving in front of them, halting both their tracks, "My job is to make sure everything is done as set by the King. I am to protect you from harm and keep you out of trouble. This can be done two ways. Easy. Or. Hard. I do not mind which but I would appreciate a small amount of courtesy from you during our short time together,"

Katherine stood amazed and in shock. She a Princess being treated like a common servant. Instinctively Carey took a step back as she watched the volcano inside Katherine erupt.

"How dare you! If it weren't for me you would have to fend for yourself as an outlaw or something! My father's kindness has kept you fed, watered and clothed for the past four years! You ungrateful.." Lance interrupted cutting her off in a steady, yet stern tone.

"With all due respect my lady. The King is my master and to him I am eternally grateful, something you would never know anything about. He has been a great inspiration to me for many years. But my job does not mean that I must endure, constant belittling from you," he remained calm only raising his voice a little at the end to get his point across. Katherine shrugged slightly, smirking as she responded.

"Sorry boy, I didn't take you for a woman," she openly mocked his show of emotion, laughing a little at him.

"Show me a man who does not embrace his emotions and I will show you a man with no heart or soul,"

"And you are saying that you have both?" She scoffed at him doubtfully.

"A wise man once told me that without a heart capable of love and a soul capable of good, everything you do means nothing,"

"Ha, what old crackpot told you that rubbish?" Katherine asked with only a slightly changed tone. Lance held a wide smile on his face as he spoke two words loudly.

"The King."

Carey chuckled a little as Katherine's face went more than a tiny bit red at his words. While she could not speak her eyes glared at both of them in shame and anger.

As the sun was beginning to set in the west, the light rested on the back of Lance's head for a moment as they had come to a standstill in front of a large window inside the palace. Katherine was struck for a moment on much older he really was. Only a few years by birth yet decades in his experiences. She studied him closer than ever before, then she realized they had at some point begun walked towards her quarters again and had already reached her private room.

Outside her quarters stood three guards dressed in the Royal uniform of red and gold. They were showing proudly the Royal symbol of a bright gold griffin sitting up in the centre with two swords crossing above his noble head, embroiled in dark red and outlined in gold. The guards were located on both sides of her door and one was standing against the opposite wall, facing her wooden double doors.

As the three guards heard footsteps approaching they immediately straightened up. Lance stopped at the doorway and bowed towards the ground as etiquette required before the women.

"Will that be all, my lady?"

"Yes boy." She replied turning her back on him and entering her chamber without looking back. A quick final nod to Carey as she closed the door behind herself and he was gone.

Carey's heart felt like the weight of the world to her. For all the riches in the world could not make a person like Katherine feel anything apart from in anything done to herself. Since her schedule had changed Katherine had turned the injustice she felt towards the servants of the palace, but most of all towards Lance. For the past year Carey had been stuck in between them and even though she was making small amounts of progress it was not enough as far as Lance was concerned. She could not take the heartache any longer.

"Why must you treat him so?" Carey asked in a low questioning tone as the sound of the door closing echoed around the room.

Carey would not have considered Katherine's quarters merely a room. In terms of quarters here were more like a private wing. She had a large bedroom complete with four wardrobes, two side tables to her four poster bed and large washing area where her specially made luxurious bathtub sat surrounded by stand up curtains, which matched the brightly coloured ones around her bed. On the opposite side of the bedroom was a large wooden desk with a picture of a beautiful woman, in her early fifties, above it in the most elegant frame. Above all her possessions this picture was Katherine's favourite. It was of her mother, Anna, and had been painted for Katherine right before she had been born to show the strong grey haired lady who loved her unconditionally and would always watch over her in spirit. At this moment though Katherine was not looking at her mother's calm and gentle face.

"What?" The reply was showing how oblivious to everything else she was as Katherine was already shredding her common clothes for a white dressing gown and rummaging through her third wardrobe that contained her formal dresses to find a gown for the ball that night.

"Why do you torment him? He is only trying to help you,"

"Oh calm down. This is Lance we're talking about. He knows how to take a joke," she responded still not turning to face Carey.

"It's not a joke to him Kat. He really cares about you, but you're so wrapped up in your own world that you don't see it. I sometimes wonder if you notice anything at all," Katherine was taken back by her words and turned around to stare at her.

"How dare you! Why do you speak to me like that? You have no right to take such a tone with me,"

"What right do you have to treat any of the servants like you do?" Carey replied raising her voice to match Katherine's

"I'm of noble birth! Royalty! Not a common maid from the city!" A small chuckle emerged from Carey's throat as she smiled back with no humour in her eyes as she responded.

"And what of me? I'm from a common family. A common maid from the city. Chosen out of hundreds because you wished it, not because I'm any different. Tell me honestly, if I hadn't been selected, would you treat me like that?"

A flashback came to Katherine's mind of the woman she

had fought with all those years ago and the beating she had suffered at her hands. Seeing Carey's eyes and the tears that she was fighting back had Katherine shaking her head quickly throwing the image of Carey in her place out of her mind.

"Never. You know you're like a sister to me. I have never looked on you as a servant..." she paused as the tears finally started rolling down Carey's face. Carey lowered herself on the end of the bed and looked at the ground as she continued speaking.

"That's why you don't understand," her shoulders moving as her head turned away from Katherine's face, "Even though I'm like a sister to you I'll always be a servant and nothing more just like Lance,"

"Carey I..." Katherine was interrupted as Carey continued by standing and heading towards the doors. As she reached them she turned to face Katherine and spoke quickly and to the point still filled with emotion.

"Sorry Kat, but I must make ready for this evening. Do I have your leave?" Katherine knew she was almost as stubborn as herself and made the choice not to argue. She simply nodded.

"Yes, you may. I'll need you here in around four hours... if my sister will still like to accompany me to the ball." She added the last sentence at the last moment hoping Carey would understand she knew what had been said was true and that because of it she would try to be nicer to the servants. It was not lost on Carey. She smiled knowing her words had finally shown an impact on her friend and was secretly hoping that the feeling would last throughout the night.

It was time to go when Carey knocked lightly on Katherine's door a while later. The doors opened slowly to show Katherine in a delicate purple ball gown. Her gown had no sleeves, clung to her chest and midriff, fanning out a little at the waist. Small purple flowers lifted small arches of cloth around the base of the gown and enhanced the top. A little trail of the satin cloth was following behind, making her look even more elegant as she started to walk towards Carey.

Her dark blue eyes shone brightly in the torch light, while her hair was in a beautiful twist with a few loose curls of the light brown hair that were hanging around her oval shaped face and neck. Stepping into the hallway she wrapped her matching shawl around her bare shoulders and glanced at Carey, who was in awe standing next to Lance. The dress certainly made a change from the common cloths she had worn at the game that afternoon. Common brown trousers with a basic white cotton shirt.

Carey on the other hand always looked amazing in the dresses she wore every day and this evening was no exception. Carey wore a plain yet elegant, bright yellow gown that matched her beautiful locks that hung down to her shoulders. Her hair almost covered the slightly puffed up sleeves that covered her upper arms. Lance wore his official uniform that closely resembled the guards, with the only difference being the minimal change in the way the jacket was cut. This was due to Lance being required to dance, if the occasion arose during the dinner.

"Oh," Carey smiled widely at her, "You look just beautiful Kat," Lance stepped forward quickly.

"You might want to start using her full name. Do not let the King hear you calling her that in front of the guests,"

"Do not worry, my dearest boy. My sister understands what is expected during such an event and be reassured that both she and I will be on our very best behavior," Katherine spoke in her official meeting the guests tone and voice, then took her place beside him and accepted his slightly offered left arm.

They began walking in the direction of the great hall and the ball, which according to the music they could hear, had already started. Katherine started to speak noting quickly his more than usual serious expression. He clearly had not yet forgive her for the events of earlier.

"Boy...I mean Lance. I wanted to say that I'm sorry... about before." Apologizing was never something that she liked and rarely did yet Carey smiled at her proudly for at least trying to make amends before Lance interrupted her by replying with a short response.

"Thank you, my lady." And if Katherine was not mistaken he even cracked a small smile towards her.

The Hall of Ages looked fantastic. The dull grey stone that usually would have dominated the once elegant location was draped in the most beautiful white satin cloth. The long pieces of material hung down the entire side of each wall from the vaulted ceiling above. The setting looked perfect for a celebration. In every direction Katherine could see white satin bows of all sizes used to decorate hundreds of small square tables and candles by the thousands. The middle of the hall was large empty space, which was reserved for when the dancing began.

As they approached trumpets sounded so Katherine's name could be announced officially. She mumbled to herself while waiting at the entrance to the hall to make her appearance.

"It would be faster if they would just let me start walking in." The herald spoke in a clear loud voice to her right yelling, "Her Majesty Princess Katherine Caltrek of Maltesh."

Carey and Lance were added as a last thought as her 'Royal Highnesses personal guard and companion'. All three were required to walk down a specifically laid out path through the middle of the event towards the main table to make sure all eyes were watching them. As much as Katherine loved the gowns and the attention, making a grand entrance at every single even grew tiresome. If she admitted it to herself it was not just making the grand entrance, the decorations or the constant stares.

It was the rumours.

No matter who she spoke to or danced with rumours about a relationship always surfaced once the night was over. She was once forced to dance with a foreign Prince, who was only twelve years old and the next day the court was a buzz with wedding details. And with rumours came the gossip, scandalous glances and speaking behind hands or objects or both. Events like this one were a guaranteed annoyance for Katherine as she had to endure it.

Henry had already made it clear to her that no one would be punished or executed for this type of behavior, when she politely made the strong suggestion, and she could not take matters into her own hands. As once again as Katherine began the long walk, seeing the looks and hearing the comments about who her potential husband could e, she clenched her teeth in a smile to hold her tongue tightly.

"It's not right for someone of her age,"
"Twenty years old and not yet married. Such a shame,"
"Surely someone here would be suitable,"
"If she doesn't pick someone soon, no one will want her,"
"Do you think she wants to be married?"
"Maybe she doesn't want to marry."

Katherine was not completely against the idea of marrying someone. It was just hard to know whether they really liked her or just the idea of becoming King. Thanks to one particular Duke's son she was maybe a little more cautious than she should have been, yet she was in no rush and did not care what anyone thought. Ignoring the chatter they reached the main table smiling and Katherine immediately embraced her father playing the part she was trained for perfectly, smiling and laughing without fault.

The celebration was a great success.

As King Henry made an amazing speech about the battle of BloodHene and everyone raised a glass to the fallen soldiers, Katherine and Carey were able to take extra sips of wine when no one was looking. After a couple more toasts Calzar, Henry's personal guard, had removed their goblets and talked to the servants so they would not be offered any more.

Katherine and Carey were having a wonderful time meeting people from all over the kingdom and learning about different cultures once all the toasts were over. Katherine was almost positive that she had even seen Lance smile more than once during the night.

The only part of the even that she hated was being handed around to dozens of men she did not know and having them gloat to her about all the boring things they had achieved, while they swirled and twirled around the dance floor. In truth most Princesses are destined to marry a Prince, just like in the stories, yet the Prince around was not even an option to consider for either Katherine or Henry.

This left her in an awkward position of having to be married, if she ever agreed, to someone below her station. Over the course of the evening she was introduced to many Lords and Dukes from all over, yet none of them had made a good impression on her. In fact most had made it hard for her to walk by the end of the ordeal.

Finally after what seemed like an eternity to her, it was time for the feast to begin. Katherine smiled at Carey and whispered to her as they took their seats at the head table, away from would be suitors.

"Finally," she exclaimed, "I didn't think I could last much longer with all those buffoons,"

"Lord Cerb is certainly making his interest known," Carey laughed

"Tell me about it. I swear if his wandering hands had gone much further I would have pulled a sword on him," Katherine muttered under her breath angrily regarding the short, Lord with a long curly moustache, "I will never be one of his conquests. I don't care if he's the last Lord in the entire world,"

"At least you have options. I'll be lucky if I can even find someone to take notice,"

"Carey, don't be so naïve. You know how beautiful you look. Believe me people have noticed." Katherine indicated to a group of young men, barely in their teens, smiling and whispering in Carey's direction. She chuckled and whispered back to Katherine.

"So it's either children or creepy old men? Wow, I'm so

lucky." They both laughed.

Carey thought quietly to herself that she was lucky to have Katherine in her life. Katherine had shown her that not everyone had to act as part of their station. Katherine embraced life and was not afraid to show who she really was to the world. At least in part while attending events such as these. She refused to go without eating or eating very little just to please the person she was supposed to be entertaining. She also refused to dance with every man in the room simply because they were wealthy or offering their hand in marriage. Carey understood the reasons for her cautiousness, especially with men like Lord Cerb in the mix. Servants were usually not too lucky to avoid or even cause disinterest in such men.

Luckily their thoughts were soon redirected as everyone was seated and people started filling their pates with the delicious looking feast. As the music lowered to a dinner time sort of humming, loud voices and shouting could be heard from the other side of the halls great wooden doors.

Suddenly a group of men wearing black uniforms entered the great hall uninvited. Lance, Calzar and the King were immediately on their feet as the soldiers around the inside of the hall converged towards the centre, blocking any path to Henry. The group was being led by a man well known to the kingdom.

"Staton! How did you get in here? What is the meaning of this?" Henry slammed his right rist on the wooden table shouting as loud as he could, causing the entire room to fall deathly silent. The tall, slim, dark greasy haired Staton Macton, ruler of the rival kingdom Buletis, did not answer until he was standing only a few feet from the table, which was as close as possible with the guards in his way. He wore the same black uniform as the other with a slight change at the collar. His expression was one of humour at everyone else's shock.

"I were merely upset at the thought you would have a celebration regarding the treaty and would not invite us...your friendly neighbours," he smirked a little as the word left his lips.

"Friendly!" The King roared," Friendly! How can you

even pretend to know that word? You did nothing but rage useless battles with us since you became King. If it were not for the treaty...you would still cause bloodshed,'

"Henry, you misunderstand me," he smiled walking around the two guards directly in his path to approach the table in front of Katherine, to Henry's right hand side. Henry indicated that he alright yet Calzar tensed next to him, placing a hand on his sword hilt. Staton continued smiling.

"I was merely testing your army and resources," Henry scoffed loudly and Staton pretended to not noticed, "Anyone here would tell a friend if they were in danger and I have discovered a way we can both win this coming battle," looking directly at Katherine he grinned with no humour showing. He briefly glanced her over like a hunter would his prey before striking. Her skin crawled from his expression. Katherine had heard about Staton, as he was a legend in Maltesh, for all the wrong reasons, yet had never seen him in person before now. She was glad of it.

"What are you talking about? What battle?" Henry's tone changed slightly yet still contained a hint of anger.

Facing Henry again, as was the disrespected King's intention he stated calmly, "I came in all honesty to warn you. My scouts to the far west have discovered a huge mass of northern warriors heading this way. If they keep their current pace, they will be at your front gates within the month, if not weeks," The King was taken back by this for only a moment. He knew Staton all too well.

"Why would you tell us this? What do you want in return for this information?"

"Henry," he smiled again widely, "It seems you know me more than I remembered. The force I speak of will in fact reach my kingdom sooner than yours. Maybe even within the next fortnight. To reach you they must first get passed me. I do have two requests to help us both. I would like it if you would permit me two garrisons of soldiers from your army to help me defend my kingdom,"

"And the second?" Henry responded immediately still in shock about the first as they only had close to four garrisons total.

"That my son, Lanell, be permitted to remain here as your guest until I am able to come back for him. All going well of course. I do not wish him to be involved in this fight,"

In the short time he had been speaking Katherine was certain that his concern for his son was the only truthful thing he had said. Henry took stock of Staton's overly dramatic expression and hand gestures as he spoke to gauge the truth. Meanwhile Katherine noticed that the person standing closest to Staton on his left side held an expression of upset.

At closer inspection she deduced that this must be Lanell. Looking at them side by side you would not have thought they were related. Lanell stood tall with a medium build, blonde hair and bright blue eyes. Lanell could not hold his tongue for long.

"Father?" Lanell leaned closer to him and spoke in a low voice yet everyone at the table heard him. Instantly Staton turned on him and back handed him across the face.

"Silence. I am speaking with the King," was all he said about it and faced Henry again. Lanell did not seem shocked by the reaction Staton had, yet Katherine could feel the tension as he gripped his hands into fists behind Staton's back.

"As you very well know Staton, such matters would need to be discussed with my counsel and deliberated," after a brief moment of pause he added, "Given the idea of such of threat could exist I will speak with them after the celebration, outside of that I offer no promises. You have my leave to stay in the city for the evening while we confer,"

"Thank you highness. May we also be permitted to attend this grand event?" He asked in a calm and indifferent tone.

"You may. But Staton I would have you know all conditions of your banishment remain intact and until you leave a guard will be assigned to watch your every move. He will also be reporting each hour. If for any reason, any reason at all, he is late or harmed in anyway, you will be escorted out of the kingdom without a second through. Are we clear?"

"Yes highness. We understand," Staton agreed bowing slightly and added facing his men, "Are we clear men?"

"Yes sir," they changed together as one. Before they could become silent Staton continued speaking to them in a serious tone.

"Good, but understand this all of you. Anyone that goes against him goes against me. And I swear by the almighty raging god Mesas, I will kill anyone of you that betrays me!" He finished almost screaming at them, yet his face was closest to Lanell's who chanted with the others.

"Yes sir," they echoed once more.

"I and my men are at your service, my neighbour King. Please continue with your feasting we have held it up too long already," Staton's tone was relaxed and calm as if he had been doing so the entire time. He then bowed a little towards Henry and walked back towards his soliders and Lanell.

"Guards, have extra tables and chairs brought for our new guests and please have the feast continue," Henry smiled lifted his arms into the air signaling the band to begin the music again. The music and talking began againt as a surprisingly fast pace thanks to the news of Staton and his men. With the atmosphere relaxing around them Lance and Calzar sat down at the same time Henry did, both of them did not loosen their grips on their swords. Katherine leaned over to Henry speaking in a low and panicked voice.

"Father, how can you even be thinking about helping that creep? He is up to something, you know it,"

"Please control yourself child. After the feast the advisers and I will discuss the matter and make a rational choice,"

"Sire, I understand your position but you must know that my lady is right. If the force, he is suggesting, were real we would have heard about it before now and certainly not from him," Lance added lowering his voice almost to a whisper as well as he spoke. Henry again stated in a simple tone.

"We shall discuss this later in private," frustration clear in his voice.

"But sire..." Lance tried to speak up again, however the King raised a hand to stop him.

"I understand your feelings on the matter Lance, and I agree he cannot be trusted. That being said we shall come to a decision later. Please contain your emotions until then,"

"Lance?" Staton's voice echoed across the table in a soft, almost seductive voice. He had worked his way around large room once more and was standing before Lance smirking, holding out his right hand for him to shake it.

Katherine was shocked from the reactions of everyone around her. Carey's mouth was hanging open with a fork frozen half way between her plate and her mouth. Calzar tense immediately and almost rose out of his chair, yet a restraining hand from the King caused him to remain seated. Henry appeared outwardly calm yet she could see his eyes narrow on Staton's face. Lance was the most surprising of all. He looked as if the hand reaching towards him had just thrust a sword into his chest. He appeared both unable to move or breathe. Before he could respond Henry spoke up in the same calm voice towards Katherine.

"Daughter, is it not time for you and Lance to dance? The night will be over all too soon," knowing full well that something was happening that she did not comprehend and sensing a deep meaning in Henry's words she quickly nodded. As she stood Staton's attention was taken away from Lance for the moment and without warning he grabbed Katherine's hand bowing a little. Lance tensed and stood up slowly with her, making sure she was close enough to reach for if necessary.

"Princess, I do not believe I have had the pleasure of meeting you. Truly it's an honour," Staton lifted her hand and kissed it gently. Though she had endured countless others performing the same task since the ball began this was different. He lingered, stroking his fingers across her palm and fingers. Never one to hold her tongue she could not help herself.

"Regrettably the pleasure is all yours Staton. If you'll excuse me," she pulled her hand back and stepped back, closer to Lance. Staton smirked at her and she felt sick to her stomach. Wanting to forget about him she grabbed Lance's left hand and led him away from them quickly. As they walked towards the dance floor stirring the crowd and the band to pick up the tempo she could not help but over hear her father speaking to Staton.

"Contact with him is strictly forbidden. You would do well to remember that..." Katherine did not hear or see the remainder of the conversation as they began twirling.

Lance's expression never once changed. He acted completely different than he usually would. At every other event he was serious, yet he could dance with such grace that Katherine was constantly reminded of a bird in flight. Now he was hard, emotionless and stiff. His eyes seemed distant, unfocused and after almost five dances Katherine could no longer remain silent.

"What's the matter?"

"Nothing my lady,"

"Something happened, didn't it? With Staton I mean?" His whole body tensed instantly under her hands.

"It is nothing my lady. The past is the past," his words though serious sounded strained.

"If it's the past, why are you acting like this?"

"Because sometimes it is hard to forget,"

"Don't you mean forgive and forget?"

"No, I do not," he looked down at her and something in his eyes made Katherine nervous. She would not be swayed from wanting to know.

"Fine," she shrugged, "Don't tell me anything. You know I can find out if I want too."

Suddenly they were whirling and twisting faster than the song towards the open balcony doors to the left of the hall that led to a private garden. Then without warning Lance stopped dancing and took her forcefully by the upper portion of her left arm and quickly led her out of the hall. He only stopped walking once they reached the balcony outside away from the prying eyes and ears of the other guests. The evening was cold with a little moonlight showing through the clouds.

"Release me!" She demanded trying to loosen his grip. However Lance continued to hold her firmly by her upper arms, which started to hurt slightly, and bend down slightly to have their eyes level. He pleaded to her in a low almost emotional tone.

"Highness, please do not use your tricks with this. It is nothing you need to worry yourself about. If you push this with anyone it will only cause more pain, do you understand me?"

"Of course not. You won't tell me anything,"

"Please my lady. Promise me it ends here. Right now. No questions. No bribes. Please this is important," Katherine knew she could obtain the information as she had before countless times, except she had never seen Lance in any kind of frantic state, and even though the whole thing intrigued her she felt like she owned it to Carey and Lance to keep quiet.

"It would cause more pain? To you?" Her voice quieter than before as she watched his facial expression.

"More than you can imagine," his eyes were already filled with so much pain she could not help but feel a deep need to protect him from further harm.

"Alright Lance. I promise," her tone was calmer while her mind was made up and determined to restrain herself.

"Thank you. You are indeed a rare treasure," he smiled for the first time since Staton's arrival.

"Only just noticed that, did you? You know for an old man you're not very wise." She laughed out loud smiling back at him. It was also the first time she had ever looked at him as a man and not an annoying boy.

From that point on the rest of the evening flew by. Instead of returning to the main hall and the uninvited guests Katherine and Lance had stayed out on the balcony. They had spoken about things they had seen and childish pranks they had done to guests at passed events. Before too long Carey came looking for them. As she approached the balcony she could hear their laughter and saw them both making fun of a boys nervousness as he spilt his drink on the girl he was trying to talk to in a huge garden below them. An extra step by Carey made her shoes hit the grey stone floor and brought the two back to the reality. They both knew as they saw Carey waiting in the wings that their night had reached its end.

"It seems your matron has waited for you long enough, my lady," he laughed.

"Lance. Hey while you two have been hiding from the guests I've had to dance with everyone and let me tell you Lord Cerb is still not a gentlemen," Carey snapped smiling as a matron was the head servant of the entire Royal household. The matron alone would be responsible for every servant in the house and due to their usual firm and strict demeanour they were usually not well liked.

"Carey, you know it was only a joke. My lady," he spoke turning to Katherine holding her right hand in his, "You will never know how much this meant to me. Without you I may have made a fool of myself and the King," his tone was first happy, then sad and then ashamed.

"Thank you Lance but you could never make a fool of yourself or my father. It's been a pleasure spending the evening with you too. It could have been me dancing with Lord Cerb," she chuckled at Carey's expression.

"Kat, we must take our leave." Carey seemed anxious that the King may see her still up at the late hour.

One last look into each other's eyes and Carey pulled Katherine away from Lance towards the great hall once more. Ensuring they were not seen by Henry the two women and Lance sped like lightning out a secret doorway that was hidden behind the same staircase they had entered and began running down the semi-dark corridor towards Katherine's quarters.

DISCOVERY

The nearby clock chimed midnight as they raced down the hallways and around each corner laughing. Rounding one of the last corners both women came to a blinding halt, that almost had Lance slamming into them. Blocking their way stood Staton, Lanell and two guards. They stood in front of the guest quarters, which Katherine needed to pass in order to go to her quarters coming this way. The men had not heard them approaching and from what she could tell Staton was saying goodnight before staying outside the palace with his men. Lanell's expression showed he did not want to stay. Katherine walked casually around the corner, after composing herself, as if she had never even noticed they were there. Lance followed behind with Carey, his hand on the hilt of his sword as they approached. Staton instantly smiled and spoke to her in a hopeful tone.

"Good evening your highness. Off to bed are you?" Staton's eyes flickered over to Lance yet he did not address him directly.

"Yes, thank you Staton. The hours does grow late,"

"It seems strange to me that such a beauty, would retire without having a suitor accompany you to your bed?" Lance tensed and Carey gasped at his suggestion, yet Katherine was quick witted.

"I appreciate the compliment on my looks, yet I do not need a suitor to come to my bed. I already know not one of them is worthy of such a prize,"

"Could it be you have yet to meet a suitor of suitable quality?"

"I do not pretend to know every suitor, everywhere so it is possible,"

"Give it time highness. I have a feeling you will meet someone to your liking soon enough," Staton smiled and she could feel a chill in the air.

"We will see. Good evening to you," her tone remained calm and steady except that her hut was running amok with butterflies. She knew enough about Staton to be cautious.

"Oh and your highness," he called out again as they took a few steps passed them.

"Yes," she paused turning slightly to face them once more.

"If you would be so kind. My son is not used to living in such accommodations. You see in my kingdom just because you are born into priviledge does not mean you are treated any differently than the soldiers. Do you think your father would object if he stayed outside with me tonight?" Knowing he probably had another reason for wanting Lanell outside and no longer wishing to speak with him, she simply stated.

"Since it is my father's decision I would suggest that you speak with him, not me,"

"We already tried your highness. Sadly he left the celebration early to gather the counsel for my proposal,"

"I guess he would have. In that case I would have Lanell just see if he can put up with our level of comfort for just one night. Lanell, what do you say? It is after all just for the night," she looked Lanell directly in the eyes and for a moment she could have sworn he had smiled at her.

"Of course highness. One night would be fine," his voice was soft yet serious.

"There you have it. He will face the challenge. Problem solved. Now I bid you both a good night." She turned and continued walking away without even looking back. Although as she turned another corner she thought she heard a noise that sounded like laughing, except she could not be sure.

When the women left Lance at the doorway as usually and walked into Katherine's quarters Carey was more than a little troubled. Since her second encounter with Staton, Katherine had been silent all the way to her room. They arrived at her room just minutes after hearing the clock as they usually did yet Katherine did not seem to notice. She was deep in thought about everything she had heard and seen since the disturbance at dinner. She had been learning about the kingdoms history in one of her classes and had started learning about Staton but had not considered him to be anything more than a person in their past.

She felt so naïve.

She had discovered in her lessons that Staton joined the kingdom army before he turned twelve years old, lying about his age which worked since he had looked old enough. He quickly earned a reputation for being brutal in battle by killing as many enemies as possible. In the beginning he was commended, awarded for his acts of bravery and decisiveness. Then he began disregarding orders. He started running off in a different direction that he was ordered to, killing women, children and even any pets or live stock of the enemy. He was once recorded in a disciplinary counsel and quoted as speaking in a harsh tone.

"Any enemy is an enemy to his core. Everything that belongs to him must die for him to be truly dead."

There had even been rumours that he tortured, raped and murdered people in his own garrison for reasons so ridiculous that he was never arrested or charged with anything. He had been banished from the kingdom for treason against the crown as he was caught plotting to kill the King, Henry, and take the crown for himself. Which according to reports he had achieved later in Buletis, when Queen Mischelle's husband died mysteriously and she named her present lover as King. It just so happened that Staton had been the current man in her bed.

Katherine's mind ached from trying to connect Lance to him and too much dinner wine. Carey was assiting her into bed covers when she whispered.

"They hid the truth from almost everyone and changed the records about Staton's banishment. The fact is that all the servants knew," she lowered her head as Katherine sat up in bed curious.

"Carey, please tell me what happened. If I'm to be the next ruler. No, it's more than that. I hate seeing Lance so upset," she asked, "Why does Lance hate him so much?"

"It wouldn't do any good. You would never believe me. You need to see for yourself," Carey started muttering to herself more than Katherine.

"See what?"

"Sleep now. I'll come early in the morning and collect you. He can tell you, if he wishes," she sighed, "I don't understand what is going on with Staton being here, except I can tell difficult times are ahead of us. You will need to know." At that she said goodnight and left. For how many thoughts rattled inside of Katherine's mind she fell to sleep quickly and slept soundly.

What seemed like only a few moment later Carey was leaning over her large bed with one small candle on the bedside table gently waking her.

"What time is it?" She mumbled as she noticed it was still dark outside.

"An hour before dawn," Carey answered quickly gathering some plain clothes for Katherine as she prepared for them to leave the room, "We must hurry. The change in the guard will arrive soon. Dress quickly."

Carey continued passing clothes to Katherine, who was still half asleep and not even realizing what she was wearing and within moments they had left the royal quarters and were walking towards the servant's wing. Silently they walked at a fast pace deeper into the servants quarters. Once in a while they could hear voices floating up from the kitchen as the bakers began their bread making for breakfast.

Katherine had never wanted to go into the servant quarters before so it was all new to her as they walked down three identical looking corridors. Dark shadows and countless doors on both sides gave an uncomfortable closing in feeling to Katherine. It seems the call for breakfast would ring in advance of them reaching their destination, when suddenly Carey stopped in front of a single door on their right. The door did not seem special in appearance any more than the other fifty or so they had already passed by. However when Carey knocked on the door a familiar voice spoke up.

"Who is it?"

"It's Carey. I really need to talk to you."

For a moment Katherine was shocked to see where Cary had led her. After the shock came a strange thought of why Carey had not mentioned that was she standing beside her. It was then the plain light brown door opening to show Lance topless, wearing only a pair of dark brown pants.

Once the shock subsided, embarrassment came over her seeing how he was not dressed, then after only a quick glance at his naked chest she could not tear her eyes away. What made her stare was not his defined muscles or his slight tan she had never noticed.

It was his scars.

Hundreds of them were covering his entire torso and every part of the bare skin she could see from the neck down. A moment seemed to last for hours as her eyes constantly moved from one faded scar to the next. Suddenly Lance's loud yelling snapped her out of her own thoughts.

"Carey, what the hell is she doing here?"

"She's going to be told sooner or later. You need to tell her what happened,"

"Like hell I do. You promise my lady. Does your word mean nothing to you?"

"What?" Katherine was shocked at the entire situation.

"You asked her to bring you here, didn't you?" He shouted in her face. The time of day and rank forgotten. Surprising, even herself, she replied calmly, quickly and in a serious tone.

"I swear to you I didn't. I kept my promise," her throat caught at the idea that someone had hurt him so badly. He turned away from them both and Katherine saw that his back matched the front being covered in countless scars. Carey continued speaking as if they had not.

"Look if Staton is trying to convince the King to send him anything, something is going on that he is not sharing. She will need to know. Maybe she could help," she paused then added, "Would you prefer her to hear about it from Staton or Lanell?" At his name Lance stopped and faced them again slowly. Katherine spoke up again in a confused tone.

"Lanell? What has he got to do with anything?"

She glanced from Carey to Lance and neither of them returned her gaze. They only stood motionless staring at each other for the longest moment. Lance's expression was sick, almost to the point of fainting at any given second. His whole body seemed to physically sag in defeat.

"Fine, we'll tell her." His tone matched his posture, while Carey just nodded knowing there was no victory from winning this argument.

Lance put on a shirt while Carey led Katherine inside the room and to his bed, which was one of the four small pieces of wood furniture in the small room. The small room held a chest of drawers, a small wardrobe, a desk and the single bed they were walking towards. As Carey and Katherine both sat as she explained.

"Before we tell you the story, you need to understand why I thought you needed to know. Since the history of the kingdom began men have always ruled. From your studies you know sometimes we had kind and generous Kings, like your father. However there have been several rulers from the past that decided the only way servants would stay in their place would be by using cruel and inhuman ways to keep them in check,"

"What Lance is about to tell you is from a time, not too long ago, that was kept out of your lessons and we feel as future ruler you must knw the terrible past, to avoid it in the future. Your father is going to need your help in the days to come, I can feel it, and you need to understand Staton's past in junction with the kingdom. You heard about how your father became

King?"

"Yes, grandfather was killed during a hunting trip with father," Katherine wondering tone was not missed as she wondered why it was important and how she had recalled talking to her father about it just yesterday. Lance moved from his position next to the closet to Katherine's left side on the bed while Carey remained on her right as she continued speaking calmly.

"There is a part of that story covered up, which is why the King was panicked the day you were hit on the barrels field. At the time of the hunting trip, your grandfather was King, a heartless ruler who treated servants like his own personal entertainment, yet he was not a fool. Staton's cruelty had already become legend and he was still only in his early twenties at the time. Everyone knew he had bigger plans that just a solider, no matter how high of rank he achieved in his career. During a formal morning of business, Staton made a request to have a title. He declared that for all his years of loyal service he was owed something in return. The King simply laughed at his request and stated that while he was King, no lowly peasant would be given a title of such honour. Later that same day your grandfather was out hunting, bent down to make the first cut in the beast they had shot as tradition states he should when a knife hit him directly in the back and killed him,"

"Did he kill my grandfather?" She gasped.

"No one knows for sure. But rumours spread that the person killed during the struggle that followed, declared that Staton would soon become King, right before he died from the counter attack," Lance indicated he would continue from that point.

"I am sorry about the way your grandfather died, but he was not the great King your father is today. Your father became King overnight and although it was sad for everyone to lose your grandfather, your father became a beacon of light where Staton created nothing save darkness. When I was eight I lived in a small village outside the main town. Having not received the title he thought he deserved Staton wreaked more havoc on the world. Everywhere he could. Everyone whispered his name," he almost spat speaking his name yet continued in the same unsteady usually emotional tone.

"Anyone who stood up to him was punished in public as an example or disappeared. Back then he was in charge of all the Maltesh Royal household servants, plus a garrison or two. My mother worked for the Queen counting close to ten years. Every day I was hurt deeper seeing her return with fresh cuts, bruises and red marks all over her body…if he saw something he wanted he just took it without thought. He raped and tortured the servants for his own pleasure," Lance paused for a moment catching his breath, giving Katherine the break she needed to explode with emotion.

"I'm sure if father had known he would have stopped it," Lance simply shook his head, took a deep breath and continued speaking with emotion clear in his voice.

"Any time word reached his ears Staton would somehow make the person pay for trying to have him stopped. He told the King that it was just rumours and it was so crazy that they were jealous of his success. He made sure no one would believe the servants and always had people who stood behind him, giving him perfect alibis as to where he was every second of every day," his voice became calmer.

"But your father started to realize over time that something was wrong. He could tell Staton was manipulating everyone around him to say whatever he wanted so the King arranged a secret meeting with Staton's knowledge. My mother was among the few that spoke up telling him everything that had happened to her and some others she had seen. If she only knew what would happen next I'm positive she would have remained silent. There was a spy,"

Katherine could not help but gasp as the implication of those few words. Carey's eyes were wide and teary it was clear that she already knew what happened next. Lance added.

"Once the meeting was over we were dismissed to our home and your father confronted Staton in front of the court for his crimes. While Staton was being sentenced his warriors known as the Black Tide came and swept the rumours away. They rampaged through every house killing all the people who had spoken up against him. I was among twenty five children taken to his secret hideout after they forced me to watch...they killed...my family...my sister was only...three," a pause came as uncontrollable tears ran down Lance's pale face as unwanted memories flashed in his mind forcing him to remember every detail of the worse night of his life. Carey continued as she knew for the moment he could not. Katherine reached out and grabbed a hold of Lance's hand and squeezed it tightly.

"Staton was never released from his cell. He was sentenced to death, but he escaped with help from Mischelle and the Black Tide," as they both fell silent Katherine did also. She began thinking about everything she had heard so far and after a moment or two asked the dreaded question.

"Wha...what happened to the children? What did he do to you?" Even as the question left her lips she was not sure whether or not she wanted to know. Carey answered quickly so Lance would not have too.

"They were kept for over a year in a cell barely big enough for a few adult men," Lance motioned he would continue as Katherine squeezed his right hand with her left again. His voice strained a little as he spoke.

"It was a daily occurrence. They would select a few and do as they wished. The girls were taken and beaten, while the boys were forced to endure hours of torture. We were...burnt with hot pokers...whipped until we could no longer stand. If we tried to fight back it only made things worse for everyone. We were then nursed back to full health and just as we were ready to fight back, they would begin all over again...and again...and again," another pause so he could catch his breath, "There are other things that happened but I will never speak of them...not even on command,"

Katherine nodded now realizing the hate that had developed against Staton, as a boy of eight had endured countless acts of violence due to a mother's plead for help from a King. She was suddenly struck with a wave of hatred towards Staton.

"Our salvation finally came from a travelling man from Saconer. He passed by our prison and by some act of the gods had witnessed our misery without being seen. The man was named Davis. He saved our lives by informing the King our situation. The King's army rescued us as soon as they heard where we were," Lance smiled a small grin in memory of the daring rescue as Carey added.

"He makes it sound simple. Once the Black Tide figured out what was happening they turned on the prisoners and began slaughtering them. Lance became your protector because the King, himself, was there fighting with his men, fighting like an animal trying to clear a path for the children to escape. He saw Lance in a corner surrounded by five fully grown men and despite his injuries he had grabbed a short sword from a fallen guard and was waving it around to keep them back. The King saw a little girl behind him. He wasn't fighting for himself, he was fighting for her. The King jumped on two, another guard took out two more and Lance killed the last,"

"I did what anyone would have done," Lance answered in a serious tone, brushing away any note of being the hero he was.

"Are you joking?" Carey continued in an excited and proud tone, "You did wonderfully. Do you know once the King brought him back to the castle he refused help and insisted that everyone else get help first. The only reason he was finally able to be helped was when he fell unconscious from all his injuries and lack of food," Katherine looked over at Carey with a confused expression, the complete opposite to the almost giddy one of her face.

"When did Lance tell you about all this?"

"He didn't at first. My uncle was the guard that killed two of the men trying to kill Lance. He was interviewed for Staton's trail that sentenced him to banishment from the kingdom forever,"

"I heard about that trail, of course now I know that a lot

of details were left out. Several soldiers, five children and two of Staton's own men spoke up against him," she remembered the history lesson on his betrayal and exile in detail.

"There is something else you would not have known," Lance added, "Those children were the last of the ones taken and everyone who testified against him was killed or mysteriously disappeared, except one...me,"

"You? You testified against him?"

"Yes, and I would do it again without a thought."

He smiled a none humorous grin. Katherine still had Lance's hand and squeezed it as hard as she could. She had never thought of a regular man being so cruel and now she understood what they were trying to tell her. Staton longed for absolute power and would stop at nothing to achieve it, even if that meant killing the whole population of their kingdom to do so. Both Carey and Lance had remained silent for a minute allowing Katherine to absorb everything. Lance was the first one to speak.

"When the King realized the people who spoke out were being hunted I was brought here as part of the household staff. I worked my way through each position and as soon as I could I signed on with the soldiers. After the battle of BloodHene, when I was almost eleven I worked in the kitchen and even with the treaty in place with Buletis, Statons men had been trying to find a weak spot in the border and had been causing trouble for people travelling to the kingdom and stopping our supplies. I was accepted at sixteen, after going to the training academy and served in the army for many years. It was then I received a close encounter with a broadsword and joined the night watch while I recovered. I had only been there a year when I was chosen to be your personal guard by the King himself,"

"Well, that explains it," Katherine laughed a little and when they both pulled confused expressions she added, "When we first met I thought you looked pale. No sun for an entire year, that would explain it." this broke the tension that had been felt in the room since their arrival.

Reluctantly Carey mentioned that they should be heading back. Katherine held Lance's hand until they reached his door and still she did not break eye contact with him. For the longest moment they stood in the doorway staring at each other as Carey started to walk back towards the royal quarters.

"Kat, come we must go," Carey turned around again. Katherine released Lances hand yet could not bring herself to move away.

"I swear I will kill him for you," her voice was shaky, yet cold and serious. Lance reached for her hand again and smiled a little as he replied.

"My lady, nothing would give pleasure than to see him dead but I wouldn't want to place that burden on you. Thank you for offering."

"Kat!" Carey started walking back towards them.

"Goodnight Lance."

"Goodnight my lady."

Their hands were released and the women departed from the servant's quarters quickly. Katherine could not help looking back towards Lance's room as they distanced themselves from it. Lance stood in the doorway for the longest moment watching her go. Things were never going to be the same.

HISTORY

Katherine's mind was raving with everything she had heard as they walked back to the royal quarters. She hardly noticed that the sun had risen above the garden wall. They had both remained silent until they approached the doors. As soon as they came into view one of the guards outside her door stepped forward ready to block the way if necessary.

"Halt! Who goes there?" His voice harsh and serious as he demanded to know who came closer while starting to draw his sword.

"Put that away. It's just me," Katherine smiled slightly as he looked at her in a bewildered and confused expressions. He put away his sword quickly as she asked, "I've been away from my room, is that a problem?"

"Not at all, my lady," he moved back into position when Carey spoke to Katherine.

"I'll leave you to your thoughts for a while. If you need us send one of the guards and we'll come as soon as we can,"

"I will Carey. And I know it wasn't easy for either of you to talk to me, yet I'm glad you did. So thank you," she paused a moment, "And tell Lance I said thank you too. I know it must have been extremely difficult for him,"

"I think he feels better with you knowing. Besides you really should thank him yourself,"

"Maybe I will," she smiled as they embraced and then Carey turned leaving her to enter her quarters alone.

Entering the room slowly, she closed the door and lent on it with her back as if her legs no longer wanted to support her. Slowly looking up she glanced around at all the luxuries she had at her disposal and everything she could see only seemed to add to how terrible she felt.

How Lance had managed to stay his hand at dinner she

did not understand. Then again thinking about it more she could. Unlike Staton, Lance was not someone who would kill for pleasure, revenge or pride. Which is why he did not want her to kill Staton for him. This knowledge made her think of Lance more of a man and less than the boy she had insisted on treating him like.

Looking back on all the times she had been mean to him made it hard for her to breathe. She did not feel like a Princess today, instead she was one of the slave traders from centuries ago who were finally overcome by their deeds of evil that they killed themselves to be rid of the guilt and shame.

That is how she felt.

That is how she deserved to feel.

Overcome with remorse for the things she had done to her one and only protector. Burdened with the knowledge that if she could have only been nicer to him, he may have trusted her with this information sooner. Crushed by the fact that she was a spoiled, selfish child who thought about no one except herself. She felt sick to her stomach to the point that she needed to sit down quickly and sank to her knees with the door at her back.

Wanting to take her mind away from her remorse and sadness she decided to do a little research. Katherine had all her class books in her quarters since her lessons were held in a large library just on the other side of her extensive bedroom, connected to her own private garden at the back of the palace.

The garden and library had been made specifically for her as Henry believed having windows in the direction of the barrel field would give her more motivation to complete her lessons. Even after this proved false, in fact it encouraged her to leave earlier, she insisted it remain part of her quarters. No one else she ever head of had an entire library to themselves.

Katherine had always like things that were made for her, it made her feel special, on any other morning she would have been thrilled to enter her huge library and marvel at how much she was adored by her father. Today instead of smiling at her own private library she refused to even glance upwards as she raced to the pile of books on a large table in the centre of the room and quickly found the one she wanted.

Feeling the familiar history book under her finger tips she instantly before searching for something. At first she was not sure what until she found a servant schedule for the year of Staton's death sentence and then banishment. Reading it in more detail then the first time she had barely glanced at it, she was shocked to discover a name on it that she knew.

"Macy, Lanell. Born twenty eighth day of the second month. Mother Macy, Margaet. Mother died in child birth. Father unknown," she spoke out loud reading the text, "Could that be the same Lanell?" She asked herself.

Reading more information about this person she discovered that Lanell's mother had been a servant for the royal family for years, around the same time as Lance's mother, and had lived with a man she claimed was Captain of the guard before her death. It was documented that after her death, Lanell had been taken in by the palace staff and was later given the rank of paige. During that same time Staton had achieved the rank of Captain through his victories in battle.

"This was years before Staton's true self would surface," she muttered to herself, "It's him. Lanell Macy is Staton's son, Lanell. He was servant for the royal household when his father reached the rank of Captain. I would guess that he somehow found out he had a son and used him to gain information on the staff,"

She checked the list of staff and people that were part of the trail for Staton, while viewing all the other court documents. "He's not mentioned once and it doesn't say why. It was like he just vanished days before the trial began." Instantly Katherine was up on her feet and heading for her bedroom door. She flung open the double doors and yelled at the nearest guard.

"You! Do you know where my father is now?"

"Yes, my lady. They are still in counsel about Staton's request," he answered quickly in a shocked and nervous tone.

"As soon as I'm ready you will escort me there. And you," she yelled to another, "Fetch Carey and Lance and bring them to us as fast as they can,"

"Certainly, my lady," before closing the door to get ready she remembered the terrible night and muttered quickly to them, "And thank you for your help. All of you."

As the doors closed behind her she did not see each of the guards glance at each other with expressions of shock clear on their faces, before one guard left quickly to find Carey and Lance in their quarters.

Katherine dressed as fast as she could and hurried with one of the remaining guards to her father's counsel chamber. As they approached the corner just around from the room her heart stopped in time with her feet. Quickly waving away the guard she listened harder without revealing her presence. She could distinctly hear Staton's voice and it sounded happy.

Very happy.

"Thank you highness. You will not regret this decision I ensure you. We will leave as soon as your men are ready,"

"They will be so within the hour. I will meet you in the main courtyard at that time." Hearing Henry detail the actions that were to come chill Katherine to her bones. Something was not right.

"*I must have heard wrong.*" She insisted to herself as she risked a quick peek around the corner.

At that same moment she saw Staton and Lanell bow towards the counsel room door. Light from the two huge windows opposite caused their sword hilts to glisten and their kingdom symbol on each of their uniforms to sparkle in the morning glow. After their quickly bow they both straightened up and left in the opposite direction to Katherine. Once they had gone out of ear shot she turned the corner slowly in shock of what she had just heard. Quickening her pace she hurried to the counsel room door and without stopping burst in.

"Father!" She gasped.

Henry, who had been walking back towards the table,

Calzar who had been leaning against the far wall behind Henry's chair as usual and his three council members, who were still seated in their chairs, jumped up in shock as the door exploded inward admitting her. Calzar was instantly ready for a fight and seemed to magic his sword straight into his right hand from its hilt without touching it. Realizing the situation was not a threat had Calzar quickly replacing his sword and smiling a little at her while Henry spoke in a tone that was both annoyed and slightly amused.

"I am happy to see you up so early child, but I am afraid you are a little late for a lesson in negotiation,"

"What?" She stared in awe as she noticed the other counsel members gathering up the papers that had been scattered on the large wooden table. The table was one of three pieces of furniture in the room and it took up most of the space. The wall were Calzar leaned was grey and bare, like most of the great hall on an average day, but unlike the great hall this room had no windows. Bright torches cast a light around the room that seemed to enhance Katherine's feeling of dread. The only picture on the wall was a medium sized one of Anna that Henry liked to look at while he was thinking. It showed a proud, older woman with a round, soft face, ivory coloured skin and long grey hair, which was always worn in a braid from what Katherine had heard.

"The decision has been reached and settled. We have granted Staton's request,"

"No!" She yelled loudly as Carey and Lance both appeared at the doorway behind her, which had remained open, "How could you? He's nothing but a monster!"

"Katherine, please restrain yourself. You may also join us inside," he motioned to the two hovering in the doorway behind her.

Carey and Lance had remained still as they were unsure as to whether or not they should enter or not. With Henry beckoning them forward the counsel members saw it was time for them to be on their way, gathered their papers quicker and were passing them on the way out as they approached the table.

As the doors closed behind the counsel members Henry motioned for everyone to take a seat at the table. Many candles had been lit showing the King's troubled face as he sat on a cushion in his larger wooden seat at the top of the table while Katherine, Carey and Lance positioned themselves on smaller ones close by. Calzar remained standing behind Henry.

Katherine could not remain quiet a second longer.

"Why did you agree to aid Staton knowing full well what he is capable of?" She sounded disgusted.

"First of all," Henry snapped a little in a serious and firm tone, "Let me explain something to you for the last time. Until you are crowned Queen any decision I make is final. No one, least of all a woman, will ever undermine my authority in public again, do you understand?"

"Yes father. I'm truly sorry," she replied in a sincere tone. She knew the scene she had caused entering the room and disagreeing with him openly had been extremely disrespectful to him. If it was thought that the King changed his mind about a serious situation because the Princess was against it, it would not only cause problems for his reputation and honour in the eyes of the counsel, but could also risk a way as the people would think he was not strong enough to rule. He continued to speak in a slightly softer way, yet still holding the serious tone.

"I have told you many times before, the first thing you must learn as a ruler is to never show any emotion when dealing with an enemy. You must master control over these strong feelings beloved. They will show to be a weakness as you give your enemy a power over you," she opened her mouth to speak yet seeing this, Henry indicated with a wave of his right hand that she was to remain silent for the moment.

"I know you were away from your room last night and that you were studying in your library this morning, so I can be certain that some histories were shared. I do not approve of the timing, except I am glad you know since you may understand my decision. Even if you do not agree with it," he paused as he glanced at Lance and Carey with a disappointed face, then back to her serious expression.

"I am only telling you this so you will try to comprehend. Our main focus is the need to know whether the force Staton claims to exist does or not. I know more about what he is capable of, than any of you and I will never tell you. I am no ones fool. I did grant his request, however with only a quarter of the men he wanted and with one man reporting back every few days with an update. If indeed he is telling the truth the remaining force will join then,"

"My lord, please forgive me but how do we know the force, if there is one, is foreign and not one of his?" Lance spoke up hesitantly as Henry simply smiled as he replied.

"Again it seems you underestimate your King. You need not worry. I have given specific private instructions to be passed on to the men that will ensure we get all the information on this before we act in the slightest,"

"And what of Lanell? Is he staying?" Carey piped up in a concerned tone.

"Yes, he will stay with us. But it was agreed that he will be under constant watch. If for any reason our riders or men do not return his life is then forfeit,"

"My lord, I would proudly be his watch while he remains with us," Lance instantly stood up bowing as protocol dictated. Katherine was shocked at his request, while the others in the room did not seem to find it out of the ordinary. Henry could not help himself and chuckled as he responded smiling.

"Yes, I am certain you would love any chance to watch his every move. No, sit down my boy. It was already decided that you would serve the kingdom better if you were still protecting Katherine, especially with an enemy among us. I have no doubt that there is a larger plan here than him just staying for his own safety. As such I want constant watch on you as well," Henry looked directly at Katherine who seemed shocked by his remarks.

"Me? What would he want with me?"

"I knew you hated to study but did you ever pay attention? Even once? You are the only living heir to the whole kingdom of Maltesh and nothing comes to your mind," he chuckled again, "A word from you and our whole way of life could change. If someone like Lanell somehow manipulated it who knows what could happen,"

"Manipulate me!" She snapped loudly, "You think I'm so oblivious that I'd have anything to do with him. Especially after everything he and Staton have done!"

"Child you try my patience!" Henry snapped back at her in the same tone, "Will you at least attempt to control yourself! We mean in no way that you are weak. He has been trained since he was very young to get to anyone and right now you may be a strong target," he reassured her in a softer tone as his fists clenched turning almost white at her outburst.

Katherine bit down on her tongue hard trying to restrain herself from saying anything further. She did not want him any more upset with her and even though he had never once laid a hand on her she knew he could take it out on the others, if she continued.

"You are not being restricted in more ways than before. However both Lance and Carey will accompany you to all your scheduled events, every day, not just Lance," the women became slightly excited by this and tried really hard not to show it.

Usually Carey was sent back to the servant's quarters during Katherine's lessons or meetings she was to attend. It had been meant to prevent further distractions. Seeing a brief smile on both of their faces Henry quickly elaborated.

"I want all three of you to remember that we now have enemies amongst us. Until such time as the threat has been removed be cautious in everything you say and do. And I mean everything,"

"Do not worry highness. We understand. You can count of us," Lance smiled secretly hoping that he could count on Katherine as well.

"Thank you Lance. Now after talking all night I am ready for some food and rest. I imagine you are all as well. Let us go to breakfast shall we?" With that all four of them walked out of the counsel room, down the stairs and into the private dining room. All the while Katherine held onto Henry's arm tightly.

Something about the entire situation did not feel right.

The soldiers had been ready to leave within an hour of Henry's instruction and the entire party had left from the main gate before lunch was served.

Four days had passed since the meeting with Henry without any trouble. Yet knowing Lanell was inside the palace walls seemed to put everyone on edge. Lance seemed unusually tense and even Carey, who was usually relaxed, could not remain sitting for a long time.

On particularly hot and sticky afternoon Katherine and Carey were having cool drinks on her balcony, overlooking the private palace garden when Katherine's curiosity got the best of her.

"Carey," she looked over at Katherine's troubled expression as she struggled to find the right words.

"What is it? You looked concerned,"

"Not concerned, just curious. Why does Lance hate Lanell so much when it was Staton who...you know?" She could not keep the pain out of her own eyes as she asked the question. She was secretly thankful that he had been called away by the King for a moment so she would have time to discuss what she had been desperately wanting to know for weeks. Since the meeting with Henry, Carey and Katherine had not been left alone even once, and even now with Lance gone two guards were standing close by, but far enough that they were out of ear shot. At first Carey seemed to be frozen in place, a drink half way to her mouth, then she relaxed.

"How must do you know already?" Her tone was curious and her eyebrow raised slightly, knowing some kind of knowledge must have been found for her to ask.

"That he was a servant here in the palace around the same time everything happened,"

"It's true he was,"

"Didn't everyone hate him, knowing Staton was his father?"

"Quite the opposite actually. He was loved by everyone. No one knew he was even related to Staton until the banishment, and even then only because one of Staton's own guards told the King,"

"And Lanell kept it a secret. Of course, he wouldn't want people to know. I mean who would want to admit they were related to such a creature. And it would restrict him and put him under suspicion as well,"

"You have no idea Kat. When his name was listed as Staton's son during the trial…it fell so silent you could hear a mouse in the castle walls. He and Lance had become very close during the years before that and to find out…after everything that he was Staton's son…well, let's just say it didn't end their relationship in a good way,"

"In what way?"

"They tried to kill each other,"

"What?" Katherine sat up quickly in shock, "When?"

"During the trial when Lanell's name was called Lance wasn't there. He had only been allowed there long eough to give his account of things, and then he was ordered back to bed as he was still recovering. When he heard the news my uncle told me Lance was in a rage, like no one he had ever seen before. Still bruised and battered from his time with Staton he sought out Lanell, who was packing up his belongings to leave the kingdom, grabbed a nearby soldiers sword and tried to kill him,"

Katherine could not believe what she was hearing. Lance in a rage. Her mind could not picture him in such a way. A small child of nine or the adult he was now, but then she could not imagine the horror he had suffered at the hands of Staton.

"What happened?" She gasped.

"Nothing. Luckily for Lanell, Lance was still weak from

his orderal and a guard called out to him so he had time to move out of the way just in time. From what my uncle said it was a close thing, mere hairs away from that blonde head. The guards sent to watch over Lanell were able to take the sword away from Lance and restrain him long enough for the King to arrive, except it wasn't pretty. The whole time they were screaming at each other about friendship, trust, the horros and betrayal. Lanell had to be restrained when he almost hit Lance with a sword as his mother was brought up. When the King arrived they grew silent and he forbade anyone to harm Lanell, while he remained in the kingdom and Lance never forgave him for lying,"

"So he tried to kill Lanell because he didn't tell anyone he was Staton's son?" Her tone was one of disbelief that Lance could do such a thing.

"No, think about it Kat. He had been gaining everyone's trust and giving information to Staton. He may not have been the one hurting people but he helped do it. Not to mention he betrayed their friendship,"

"Does Lance know it was Lanell who gave Staton the names of the people who spoke up against him?" Finally the question she had been dying to ask came out.

"What?" Carey seemed completely shocked, "He gave..." she could not finish as tears came to her eyes.

Suddenly Katherine felt stupid.

Although Carye and Lance were close to the King they would never have seen the same documents that she had access too. They pieced together what they knew through people who were there but did not have all the papers to fill in the gaps. Katherine had discovered another secret that both Staton and Lanell had managed to keep from even Henry.

"I'm sorry Carey. Please forget I said anything. Please don't tell Lance,"

"There's no need to ask that. I'd never wish him to know. I don't know what he would do, especially with Lanell back in the palace," at that very moment Lance appeared close by smiling.

"Well, you two look busy," his tone happy and mocking their laid back appeared. He had not heard what they had said. Looking over them both he seemed to know something was wrong instantly. "Carey, what is it you look pale? Are you feeling okay?"

"Yes, of course. Just a little flustered from the heart. Maybe we should go inside for a while?" Carey pulled herself together quickly and Katherine was grateful for it. She did not want to be the cause of more trouble for the kingdom or for Lance.

"Well, it is time for your lesson. My lady, if you would care to follow me?"

"Lead on Lance." Katherine smiled quickly and followed him knowing full well the secret was safe with Carey.

Carey was gathering water from a bucket at the bottom of the Barrels stand as the day was growing hot when she heard the footsteps leave the cobble stone and start on the green grass. Looking up she saw a handsome man in full uniform walking towards them, then the sunlight highlighted his face and her breath was caught for a moment.

It was Lanell. And for a moment she had thought of him as attractive.

Noticing that she was watching his every move, in her light blue gown that enhanced her eye colour, Lanell smiled at her appreciatively. As he continued walking he lowered his head slightly down, indicating politely with his right hand by placing it over his heart with his palm flat to his chest and his fingers together.

Seeing the motion caused Carey to look away quickly. She was embarrassed that she had been caught staring at him. Carey turned around and hurried back up the steps to the box and took her seat, which was behind Katherine's and raised slightly so it still had a good view of the field. Watching her go Lanell noticed that Katherine was seated beside Lance, who was leaning a little closer to her than protocol dictated. He also noticed another empty seat next to Katherine on the left, which made his stride increase in length.

Hearing footsteps on the wooden steps close by caused Lance to turn expectantly, as he guessed who it could be. They all stood as Lanell was announced into the box, closely followed by his appointed companion Magel. Magel was a six foot four, mountain of a man with a chiseled face, big bright blue eyes and sandy blonde hair.

"A perfect choice to keep Lanell in check." Lance thought happily to himself.

Lanell bowed slightly towards Katherine and took up the empty seat next to her smiling broadly at Lance behind her back as they sat down. Lance's eyes immediately narrowed knowing his intent. He wanted to cause a reaction in Lance and had succeeded.

"Good morning my lady. It is a beautiful day," he spoke with a pleasant and friendly tone towards her, as if nothing had passed between himself and Lance.

"Yes, it is lovely. Of course being from a colder climate I am sure it takes some getting used to for people like you," she responded automatically returning her attention to the game.

"Who's winning?" He asked merely trying to make further conversation with her.

"Three to the kitchen staff and two the bakers," Lance answered for her smiling with a half grin as he did so. He knew full well that Katherine hated people speaking on her behalf and that she would have to restrain herself from comment. Risking a quick glance at her, she glared back angrily causing his smile to increase so much he had to turn away from Lanell a moment to compose himself.

"I heard a rumour you like to play this game yourself, my lady. Is there any truth to it?" Lanell stated smiling again.

"On the odd occasion," she smiled back hiding her surprise that he would have known that fact.

"I would bet the King absolutely hates the idea, does he

not?"

"He may have mentioned that," she answered smirking then adjusted her composure again as she caught a glimpse of something in Lanell's eyes as he watched her reaction.

"I do not blame him. If I had a daughter, as beautiful as you, I would never allow her to play such a violent game," the evidence of which was shown almost immediately as a fight broke out between two players, as one tried to trip the other as he attempted to score. Katherine could not help but stare uncontrollably at his side profile in reaction to his words.

His tone had contained no hint of comedy, flattery or sarcasm. He had spoken as if simply stating an obvious fact. At first Katherine did not know whether he meant it as a compliment or a comment about her being a woman and unable to defend herself. She decided on the latter.

"I can handle myself when there is need," she snapped back at him smirking without humour. He did not read her expression as Lanell had turned his attention back to the field once the fight erupted.

"What about you Prince? Have you ever played Barrels before?" Carey asked quickly distracting him while Katherine composed herself.

"Me? Certainly not. I do not play any game that is meant to empower servants and make them feel like they can achieve anything above their station," his tone indicated he was upset that anyone would even suggest such a thing. Lance could see his words hit a nerve with Katherine as she immediately tensed, clenching her fists.

"Without them, we would have nothing," she replied trying to control her tone.

"I agree," he looked back at her as he spoke, "Yet my father believes that servants should be treated differently," smirking he glanced over at Lance and continued, "Not badly necessarily, just shown their place in the world,"

"And what place do you think that is?" Her voice struggled to keep calm and without anger as she asked.

"They are called servants for a reason. They are hired to serve us. Each has their own specific tasks but they still serve, it is just in different ways,"

"Yes, for work and to provide for their families. It is not a life most of them chose. People do not wake up one day and decide to become servants until they die. They do so to enable future generations to become whatever they want to be," she finished speaking by glancing over at a stunned Lanell. A proud Lance smiled at her with Carey by his side, grinning for the first time since Lanell had appeared in the box.

"That may be true in some rare cases, my lady," his voice became soft, yet Katherine could sense a hint of danger as he continued, "Those some are proud of their past service but if you were given nothing, would you save all you earned for future generations? No, no one would. They need to buy food, clothing and pay for shelter. Those who have become anything have worked until death for many, many generations or cheated other people until they have enough for a decent way of life. You think there is a difference between the way we treat our servants my lady. You cannot deny that there is, for while being here only a short few weeks I have heard tales of your treatment of them and it rivals even my own,"

His words hit Katherine like he had smacked her in the face and she could not respond. She was stunned at his openness towards her and his advanced knowledge of her behavior towards others. After what felt like an eternity to her, she gathered up her thoughts and spoke calmly.

"I cannot deny it. In the past my actions towards the servants, and everyone else, has been ridiculously unkind, such as yourself," she added smiling a little, "Yet I have come to a realization that if you are about the people of your kingdom, then they in turn will come to care about you. This makes the kingdom stronger from within," Lance and Carey appeared to be smiling yet as Katherine kept eye contact with Lanell, who seemed to be at a loss as to what to say, she could not tell for sure. Katherine took the opportunity to continue, "So given the chance, how would you motivate servants to become more than what they are? Have them cheat other people? Beat them until they fight back?"

"No. I have found that simply telling them that they will always be a servant usually gives them enough motivation to improve their own way of life, in their own time,"

"Your father does not share the same ideas as you," it was a statement more than a question yet Lanell answered her anyway.

"He is very set in his ways that is certain. But he will not rule forever. Our servants will improve their way of life in their own time and telling them that they will remain in that station is all that is needed,"

"You really believe that telling them they will always be a servant will encourage them to become more than that?" She asked actually intrigued to know what he thought.

"Yes, I really do," his calm matter of fact tone made Katherine sure it was the only true thing she had ever heard him say.

"I'm truly sorry you feel that way," she replied in the same factual tone. Looking back at the field she could sense his gaze on the side of her face. As the final gong rang out Katherine, Lance and Carey all stood at one. Lanell stood slower facing Katherine.

"Thank you for joining us Lanell. I hope to see you at dinner this evening? You have been hiding in your room since you arrived,"

"My lady, I believe you will." He responded kindly glance her up and down once more. Bowing slightly, he turned and descending the steps again, closely followed by Magel who nodded his head a little in Lance's direction.

Katherine felt a sense of pride at having dealt with Lanell in such a cool and calm way, yet as soon as he had vanished around the corner of the field ahead of them Lance snapped at her.

"What was that?"

"I consider you my friend Lance and I respect you, so

please show the same courtesy to me while we're in public," her eyes glanced over at several people close by who had heard him and were staring, shocked that he would dare to speak to her in such a way.

"Forgive me, my lady,"

"Of course," she smiled widely at him, "Now regarding Lanell. If I have learnt anything from my father its never turn your back on a snake before it strikes. Facing it enables you to know when to move out of the way,"

"Are you telling me all of that was just an act?" He asked in a calmer, somewhat impressed tone.

"Not what I said. I meant every word. But just because we have one conversation doesn't mean he knows anything about me that he hasn't been told already by the staff. I thought about it last night. What would be a better chance to get to know our enemy than while he we have one right in the palace with us?" They started walking towards the palace, keeping a fair distance between themselves and Lanell. Lance had remained silent until they reached her quarters once more.

"You are playing a dangerous game my lady. In trying to know him he will be getting to know you, regarding of what you do or do not say,"

"Lance, do you in anyway think I'm weak?" She halted facing him.

"No one I have ever met is as strong willed as you and I doubt I will ever meet anyone half as stubborn. Yet you underestimate Lanell. He has been deceitful, ruthless and unfeeling since he was a child. He has survived solely on his ability to manipulate and use people to his advantage. Just promise me you will take extra care when you are dealing with him?"

"You fail to see my point,"

"What is that?"

"That you all seem to underestimate me. You forget while he was learning to manipulate through cruelty, I was already manipulating people to do my will using other methods. You worry yourself for nothing. Lanell met his match when he met me," Lance tense as she spoke and bowed quickly when she was finished for permission to leave, yet as he stood up awaiting her answer Katherine touched his left forearm gently looking him in the eyes.

"I promise. I'll be careful," he smiled a little as she continued, "Just promise me you will be too. Don't let any of his remarks bring you down to his level,"

"I promise to try my very best, my lady," she matched his smile, then a small chuckle escaped her lips.

"Lance?"

"My lady?"

"Will you ever just call me by my first name? You have been part of my life for a while now,"

"Only if I am ever taken out of your service,"

"Then I pray that day never comes." Katherine's smile grew bigger as he returned her glance, bowed once more and left towards the servant quarters.

Carey had been standing as still as a statue watching the conversation unravel. She had refused to speak in fear of breaking the spell she could sense in the air. Katherine was smiling as she turned to see Carey smirking back at her, watching her every move.

"What?" Katherine asked with the smile still present on her glowing face as they walked into her room.

"Do you mean to tell me that you have no idea what just happened?"

"What happened when?" The shocked response in Carey's tone caught Katherine off guard, and then she realized that the previous conversation was being discussed, "You mean with Lance? We were only talking,"

"True, but can't you see through the obvious. You are falling for him," she smiled widely.

"Falling for him! For Lance? That is ridiculous! He is barely a man," she shrugged off Carey's words while also speaking aloud, almost to herself.

"He is twenty eight years old. If he was working in the

fields, like his father, he would have been married for years already and maybe even had a few children by now," Carey stated shaking her head slightly at how naïve she was in the ways of the world outside the palace. Katherine thought deeply for a moment and shrugged again.

"Either way it doesn't matter. Father would never approve of him being a suitor for me. He would make sure I married someone with an office,"

"You mean like one of the boring Lords or Dukes you were dancing with at the ball?"

"Oh heavens no," she laughed, "But I'm sure it would be someone with a high standing in the kingdom,"

"Or someone else the King selects as his successor," she changed her tone seriously, "You're forgetting Kat, whoever you marry becomes the next King of Maltesh,"

"In that case I had better choose wisely." She smirked making light of her concern that had begun to surface at Carey's words. She suddenly realized that her father could decide not to wait for her and make the choice on her behalf. If he did she was not sure whether Lance would be accepted as an option or not. A fact she found strangely upsetting.

"I'm so bored," Katherine pushed a green covered book away from her chest and placed her head on her hand. She wore a simple purple gown with a green belt and Carey sat across from her reading an old children's fairytale book in a her favourite yellow gown.

"I'm having fun," Carey smiled.

"Only because you're new to this. Believe me with time you'll think the same as me,"

"So what do you want to do?" Carey calmly placed her book on the wooden table and leaned in.

"What did Lanell say to you last night at dinner?" Katherine lowered her voice to a whisper so that Lance would not hear from his position by the large window close by.

"What do you mean?"

"Since he started coming to dinner you're the only one he speaks to every night. So what did he say?"

"Nothing really,"

"Carey, I'm dying please tell me something," Katherine looked ready to explode. Carey could not help but chuckle at her.

"Not much. He just wondered if the weather was going to warm up soon,"

"The weather? He talked to you about the weather?"

"Yes," Carey answered quietly a little disappointed by it herself, "He seemed different,"

"How do you mean?"

"Since the week following the barrels game. He doesn't seem as arrogant and keeps more to himself. I don't know how to explain it,"

"I've noticed that as well. I wonder what his problem is,"

"You don't think it's anything to do with us, do you?"

"I don't believe so," Katherine thought back to the first week Lanell attended dinner and could not think of any behavuior that would have warranted his distance, "I thought we were all getting along extremely well. Lance was being almost civil to him,"

"That was something to behold," Carey tried to smile but it did not reach her eyes as she added, "Lanell just seems so sad recently. I hope he's not sick or anything,"

"I don't think so. I mean he's attended every dinner since then regardless of how he may be feeling. I'm sure he'll be fine," a knock on the door to the library caused all conversation to cease and Lance to straighten up. Katherine said it was okay to enter and a guard appeared, bowing low.

"The King requests your presence highness," his tone gave the impression that it was important and she immediately stood.

"Once I know what's going on I'll send for you," she indicated to Carey before leaving in a rush towards the counsel room with the guard and Lance.

As she entered all conversation ceased.

Being late Lanell, Henry, Calzar and the three counsel members were already seated and staring at a mud covered boy, near the doorway. He had patches of dried blood on his clothes and a large crimson stain marking the left side of his pale forehead as he stood shaking slightly. The small boy had glanced towards the door as it opened, the same time the men had. Yet now he turned away quickly once he realized she was there on purpose, slightly embarrassed.

She had heard stories about small children being used to carry messages yet until that moment had never truly realized what that meant. The boy must have been no older than ten years old. Henry motioned for Katherine to take a seat to the left of Lanell and for Lance to wait outside.

"David, please continue what you were saying," his tone one of calm reassurance. A small shaking almost squeak came out of him as he attempted to clear his throat and say what he had been telling them.

"We could see smoke rising once we reached Alkal. Staton planned to rest there but once he saw the smoke forced the company on," he swallowed hard as if the smoke was still clogging his little throat. His eyes began to tear as he attempted to carry on, "When we arrived at the first village everything was black, except a few small fires still burning. Staton called for the fires to be put out and ordered a thorough search for survivors. The search only lasted a few minutes when a solider called out. He had found…bodies," another pause as he tried to remember each detail he was trying to forget.

"They had killed everyone and set fire to the bodies," he mumbled with tears starting to fall uncontrollably from his red eyes.

"Barbarians!" Lanell spat the word and then asked in vain, "Was there anyone who survived?" David shook his head in reply.

"No Prince. Not in the four villages we searched," swallowing hard again he added in a whisper, "Not even the babies."

Katherine stood and before anyone could stop her, she ran to the child's side kneeling down so she was level with him and began hugging him, holding him close. Tears rolling freely down her rosy cheeks.

She could not help but think of Lance as a small child watching this poor child recall all the horrors he had seen. No one should have to experience such evil, especially someone as young as David. No one spoke for a few moments while the boy cried softly into Katherine's shoulder. It was Lanell who finally broke the silence. His tone soft, serious and a little emotional.

"David, what of the palace? What happened to my mother?" At this Katherine release the child and slowly returned to her seat, understanding that the information the boy carried needed to be heard. David cleared his throat once more after quickly wiping his face on his dirty sleeve before responding causing more mud to be applied to his face.

"I'm sorry Prince. Staton sent me back here to report before we had begun searching the palace," placing her right hand on Lanell's forearm as she sat down Katherine whispered.

"I pray that she is safe," he simply nodded slightly at her, unable to speak out loud without his emotions slipping through. Henry motioned to David.

"You mentioned four villages, yet I am certain Staton has five around the main city. Am I right Lanell?" Lanell nodded again, still not daring to speak. David mimicked him adding.

"Yes highness. Once we entered the last village a man came running towards us screaming, like I've never heard before. He was yelling for help and being chased by a small looking man. At first I was sure it was mountain man but he looked more goblin like. I heard one of the older men say a word I had never heard before, except everyone reacted like the little man was a god in the flesh,'

"What word?" Was asked by someone close by, yet Katherine did not see who. David almost whispered the word.

"Katzi," instantly all the men in the room took in a sharp breath at the exact same moment. Yet when Henry spoke he was still calm and steady.

"Please finish child,"

"That is about all highness. After a small scuffle with it," David raised his right hand towards the cut on his head without realizing it, "The creature died and the man that had ran towards us was heading towards Staton's tent to be interviewed. Your majesties personally chosen witnesses were told to meet there, when I was immediately sent to you to request more men,"

"Thank you David. You have done a great service for your King and the kingdom. Please rest, eat and have that cut looked at. Once we have a reply for Staton I will call for you,"

"Thank you highness," David bowed low to the table in general and left quickly without a second glance.

"Father, I don't understand. What is a Katzi? I've never heard of them in all my studies," she asked quietly. Lanell cringed in his seat at the name while Henry's first counsel man Jatas caught his breath and spoke.

"They are dark creatures. Legend says they were given to the god of the underworld, Tysis, as a gift from Katix, mother of the world. Katix rejected them as she did not want such evil beings on her beautiful world she had creature but Tysis was angry about being left in darkness so he rejected them to spite her. This left them with no place to go yet the realm of demons where they grew strong and later found a way to crosss over to our world against Katix's wishes,"

"That is ridiculous fairy tale garbage, told to keep children out of the Black Forest!" Lanell snapped to silence the old man. Everyone in the room jumped at the sudden outburst. Lanell kept eye contact with Katherine as he continued, "They are savages. They rampage through villages killing everything...and worse. My father is a bastard and has done many unspeakable things over the years. Don't believe that I'm such a fool not to recognize that, but beside these things," he paused again to take a deep breath. "They make his worst action seem like nothing more than a childish game. Among other things they eat human flesh…usually while their prey is still alive,"

Katherine swallowed hard as her throat became suddenly dry. Looking into his saddened blue eyes she spoke quietly.

"Don't worry, I'm sure your mother is fine," Lanell's temper was suddenly unleashed as he snapped at her without thought.

"What would a spoilt, selfish little Princess, like you, know of such things?" Without waiting for permission Lanell quickly stood, turned and left the room without another word to anyone. The door slammed loud and hard behind him. Katherine felt terrible knowing he reacted out of heart break for his mother.

Had she been wrong about him?

Could he be the complete opposite of Staton?

Was he capable of real feelings or just pretending?

Her mind was muddled and her feelings deeply hurt by his hard words. She did not know which was worse, that he said them or that she felt he was right.

"Please excuse me." She stated quickly realizing that all the eyes in the room were focused on her after Lanell's outburst. She was afraid that her voice would break with the hurt she could feel rising up inside as the words escaped her lips, except the men did not make any comments. Henry nodded slightly knowing that she was upset by Lanell's cruel words and needed to compose herself. A quick glance at the others and she rose from the table, opened the large counsel room door on the right and left closing it behind her as fast as she could without another loud bang.

She thought that leaving the room would enable her to breathe but after the door closed shut the last portion of air she had in her lungs was gone. Her throat constricted and her body began to shake. She leaned her back on the same door unable to move as unwanted tears ran down her flushed cheeks.

Time seemed to stop as she stood there.

She started to hear muffled voices coming from inside

the room as Henry and the counsel men decided not to wait for her turn and continued discussing their next move.

"Forgive me, my lady," suddenly Lanell's voice came from her left speaking in a slow apologetic manner.

"Not at all Lanell," she mumbled trying to compose herself quickly and use her small white handkerchief to wipe her eyes, "It's me that should apologize. You were right. I have no business talking about things that I know nothing about,"

"Even so my lady. I do feel that I owe you an apology. I understand now that you were only trying to comfort me and it was wrong to snap at you like that,"

"It appears then that we do have something in common. We are both sorry," a small laugh emerged from her lips closely followed by a heartier laugh from Lanell. They laughed together for a moment, suddenly seeing the silliness of their behaviour in a time that warranted more serious matters.

"Thank you for what you said about my mother. I really do appreciate your concern for her, my lady," Lanell composed himself first speaking in a calm yet serious tone.

"You're very welcome and Lanell, call me Katherine," she smiled as he offered his left arm. Happily taking it they continued to talk as they walked towards the royal gardens to the left of the counsel room.

A pair of angry dark blue eyes watched their back as they turned the corner without knowing they were being watched. Even with Magel following them Lance turned angrily away and returned to his quarters the opposite way faster than he had ever done before.

By the time Katherine left the gardens and strolled back to her quarters it was beginning to get late in the afternoon. Opening her bedroom door she stopped dead in her tracks leaving the light form the hallway on the floor in the room. She had come face to face with Carey and Lance who appeared to be fighting.

Katherine first noticed tears rolling freely down Carey's pale and drawn face, then a brown bundle in Lance's left hand

and his expression rage. Katherine was about to yell at them when Carey saw her and began shouting as loud as she could while running up to her.

"Tell me its not true Kat! Tell him its not true!" She ranted waving her hand in Lance's direction as she spoke.

"What? What's going on?" She replied quickly confused that they would think she was involved in whatever was going on.

"As if you did not know," Lance blurted out as Carey looked back at him with a tearful expression, "I can not stay I need to meet up with the others. Good bye Carey," he briefly glanced at Katherine yet did not speak. He gathered up his coat and sword that were on the back of a chair close to the door and left the room in a hurry.

"Lance please!" Carey tried to plead with him almost following him out of the door before he slammed it shut in her face.

"Carey, for the love of the gods. What the hell is going on?" Katherine asked concerned grabbing her by the shoulders and turning her so they could be face to face once more. After a moment of composing herself she spoke in an emotional tone.

"While you were in the gardens the King decreed that all able fighting men should report to the courtyard. They are being deployed to Staton's aid,"

"Impossible," she paused in shock, "But father said that Lance would..." suddenly it was hard for Katherine to breathe.

"He spoke with the King himself. The King thinks that he is needed more with the men. Magel and I are to be in charge of your protection until he returns,"

"That can't be. Father said..." her chest struggled for air as she began to panic a little. Sobbing a little Carey stated.

"They need everyone they can get Kat. There is talk that this battle will be as brutal as BloodHene,"

"But Lance? Surely father wouldn't allow Staton anywhere near him?"

"Their past is one of the reasons he was chosen. He knows

Staton more than most and can spot signs of his...old ways. And is the one person that cannot be bribed or silenced," Katherine muttered something under her breathe that sounded like "Preposterous!"

"That's not all," taking some deep breaths she added slowly, "He saw you with Lanell,"

"What does Lanell have to do with this? Did he say something to father to make him choose Lance? Because if he did I will kill Lanell myself," she looked both confused and outraged at the thought.

"Lance didn't argue with the King about any of it. He thinks that it might be better for everyone if he did leave with the troops,"

"That is utterly ridiculous! Honestly, the world has gone crazy. I speak with Lanell for a few hours and he thinks that I would fall in love with another man just like that. What kind of woman does he think I am?" Katherine grew so angry and ranted almost without taking a breath, not realizing at first what she had said. Carey began to smile as a large grin started to spread across Katherine's face.

"Kat, do you love Lance?" She asked directly.

"I don't know. I mean he is kind and handsome. Of course he is completely and utterly stubborn,"

"As are you. You still love him regardless, right?"

"What does it matter? He would never be accepted by father as a suitor," her smile faded slightly.

"The King doesn't matter in this. If you love him you need to tell him before he leaves. You can't let him go thinking you don't,"

"Does he love me?"

"What?"

"I don't want to tell him anything without knowing. What if he doesn't and I make a complete fool of myself?"

"After everything we have been through, how can you doubt? Believe me when I say that he does Kat. He loves you so much he has no idea what to do with himself. Seeing you speak with Lanell in a kind manner drove him crazy with jealousy," Katherine smiled as she thought to herself of all the times he had been by her side.

"I need to tell him. I need to tell him now," at that she began running towards the door with Carey hot on her heels.

"Hurry Kat. They are leaving any second."

As a very unladylike Princess sprinted through the palace servants scrambled out of the way, left and right, causing blankets, clothes and some fresh loaves of bread to fly into the air and crash to the castle stone ground loudly.

Katherine reached the palace courtyard as fast as her legs could carry her. Without slowing down to see where Carey was she passed the market place and finally rushed across the main yard area. Here her progress came to a sudden halt as hundreds of soldiers, granted to aid Staton, had already assembled and started marching out of the wide open main gate.

Her breathing was ragged and her face was flushed from all the running, yet her heart seemed to stop beating as her eyes searched each passing face rapidly, hoping and praying to any god listening that he had not yet gone through. Her gaze fell only for a moment on a large white tent that had been erected in the courtyard as a base for the important members of the counsel to watch the soliders leave and coordinate. She knew Lance would not waste much time there so there was no point even checking inside.

Suddenly as if one of them had heard her silent prayer a small path emerged between the serious soldiers. On the far side of the yard almost directly across from her, standing next to a beautiful black stallion stood Lance. His bundle he had been carrying was now secured on the back on the horse and he was talking to another guard who was already on horseback and appeared almost ready to do the same.

"Lance!"

Without thinking or caring about those around her Katherine yelled out his name as loud as she could to get his attention. Her appearance, voice and facial expression must have held some of the fear she felt towards him leaving, as without a second thought of their previous encounter, or looks from the others, he ran to her side seeking the cause of her distress. Katherine's breathing and heart rate slowed down the closer he came.

How had she ever doubted that she loved him?

She physically felt her heart expand in happiness as he finally reached her side, yet at the same time something strange happened. For the first time in her life she did not know how to act or what to say to this man she had known for the past four years.

She choked.

"What is it my lady?" After a few moments of silence Lance spoke up, unable to determine the problem. His tone was nervous and his hand gripped the hilt of his broad sword while his eyes still searched for danger. Carey arrived second's later and locked eyes with Katherine. She could see the words failing her so instantly started speaking.

"Oh good. You were able to stop him for me. Thank you Kat," Carey smiled widely, as she struggled to get her breathing under control, at Katherine's thankful expression and turned to face Lance's sudden anger.

"Please tell me you did not have a member of the Royal family run all the way down here so you could say good bye?" His nostrils flared as he spoke through gritted teeth in almost a whisper.

"For your information I didn't send her. She saw how upset I was and came herself so we could make up before you left," her tone was completely calm. Turning away from Lance slightly she winked at Katherine who still appeared frozen in place. Her lips cracked a small smile. Carey continued playing along, "I tried to stop her but you know how she gets," at this Lance relaxed his defensive position and instantly seemed to remember their previous conversation.

"There is nothing else to say," Katherine had not realized before how his shoulders sagged in defeat, yet now it was clear.

She wanted to reach out and hold him, but her feet still refused to move. Instead seeing his pain caused her voice to return in a matching whisper.

"I didn't come for Carey's sake Lance," he turned to face her, which made her stomach twist nervously.

"Then why did you?" His left eyebrow raised slightly.

"I wanted to tell you that…I think…well…what I mean to say is…" while she struggled to keep eye contact with him and find the right words, Carey shook her head chuckling a little. Finally it got too much for Carey.

"Will you just tell him already," she laughed out loud. At this Lance seemed to notice Carey's wide smile and Katherine's embarrassed and scared expression.

"Tell me what? What is going on? Don't you two know we have a battle to get too?" He could not help the smile even though he was not quite sure why. Upset at being interrupted Katherine's irritation got the best of her and she started ranting to the ground.

"Look, it wasn't my idea to run all the way down here, making a huge fool of myself just to tell you how much I love you. I was perfectly happy with the way things were. But no suddenly I figure out that I can't live without you and now I have to because you're leaving and you could die," as she caught her breath she looked up and for a moment could not understand the scene around her.

Everything had stopped.

Everyone, including the hundreds of soldiers nearby, were frozen in place and staring at her. Her eyes flicked from the widely grinning soldiers, to Carey's slightly damp eyes, who was in turn staring over at Lance, who was just as frozen as the others with a large grin on his usually serious face.

"Wait…" he grinned at her, "Did…did you just say, that you love me?" Seeing his beautiful eyes light up as he asked the question made Katherine change her automatic deny response that had begun forming in her mind.

"Yes, I do. I mean I did say that,"

"Really?" He glanced back and forth between the two women, his grin expanding with each passing second.

"Is that all you want to say to me?" She sounded both hurt and confused.

"Hmm," he did not know what to say while still in shock.

"If you have nothing else to say then I take it all back," Katherine spoke quickly feeling ridiculous and turned her back to him ready to leave when he spoke.

"My lady,"

"Yes," her response was impatient and her stubbornness refused to let her turn back around.

"I loved you from the first night we met," she could not stop as her body turned instinctively.

"Really?" She smiled back.

"Is that all you want to say..." he was cut off as Katherine ran into his arms and kissed him with all her might.

A deep male voice cut through the sound of the soldier's boots, as they were once again marching, bringing Katherine and Lance back to the terrible reality.

"Forgive me highness. Captain, we must go. The last of the men are ready to depart,'

"Yes, of course General," Lance replied regretfully as he pulled his lips and eyes away from Katherine for a moment. Katherine quickly composed herself and noticed a small scar through Lance's left eyebrow she had not noticed before. She knew full well that many people in the courtyard had both seen and heard everything that happened, yet no one seemed to care. They continued to embrace holding each other tightly as if afraid to let go.

"I have to go,"

"I know,"

"I'll miss you,"

"I'll miss you too,"

"I'll come back. I promise,"

"Oh Lance," she started getting a little choked up as she spoke, "I'm so sorry for everything I ever said to you. There are not words to express how awful I feel. I caused you so much pain. All the time,"

"I admit it was not easy, but it's in the past. Please don't think on it for another second. You love me and that is all that matters,"

"I hate this," she muttered to his chest lowering her head, "I just figured out that I love you so much and now you have to leave,"

"Only for a short while. I will return as soon as I can,"

"If you don't I'll come find you," she chuckled only half joking.

"You are a great tracker. Almost as good as me," after another moment Lance kissed her once more, deeply and then began moving away to follow the General. As he mounted the black stallion Katherine shouted.

"Lance, come back to me in one piece. Please don't try to be a hero,"

"As you wish my lady." He smiled urging the horse towards the gate entrance following the last group of soldiers out. Passing through the gate into the green and yellow meadows outside the walls, he turned again briefly in his saddle mouthing the words, I love you, and smiling broadly.

Katherine mimicked him with tears close to falling down her already red and flustered cheeks. She stood watching him leave with all the other wives and children of the other soldiers, and for once she felt their pain of not knowing if they would see their loved ones again. Their conversation was not lost to Carey who had stood in the distance close to the large white tent that held the King, the counsel men and Lanell.

While Carey tried to give Lance and Katherine their moment she had moved closer to the white tent. Doing so caused her to hear some of the conversation going on. Lanell could be overheard voicing his disappointment at not being allowed to leave with the soldiers.

"You know full well Lanell that part of our agreement with Staton is that you are to remain here. What kind of King would I be if at the first sign of danger I go back on my word?" Henry pointed out to him. Lanell seemed furious but finally agreed knowing it was his father's wishes and not that of the King.

"I do apologize sire. I'm only upset due to him telling me to stay behind and not fighting with him in this battle..." Lanell paused and Henry added.

"If we get any word at all about your mother I will let you know as soon as I can," Lanell's head hung down a little as Henry continued, "I understand your frustration and concern. After all I have been in the same position in which you find yourself today. This, however, does not alter your father's wishes," Henry remembered a battle long ago where his father had forbidden him to leave for a similar reason.

"I am willing to be content with your decision highness. May I be permitted to retire? It has been a long day,"

"Certainly Lanell. Inform Magel should you need anything at all. Know that since he will be watching over you and my daughter an additional guard will be present as well for both of your protection. I promise you should any news come in, I will notify you,"

"You are most gracious highness. Goodnight."

As Lanell left the tent he noticed Carey close by and glanced briefly at Katherine's back. She stood still as statue facing the main gate, while watching the last of the soliders leave. It was clear why she stared. At that same moment Lance turned his horse around as they reached the first turn in the road to face the gate with both a happy and sad expression in his smile. Turning back to face the road ahead he continued on towards Buletis knowing he had something worth fighting for.

Anger and resentment filling Lanell as he forced himself to look away. Making his way passed Carey and towards his room in silence. Seeing his expression caused Carey to avoid eye contact with him as he stormed passed.

Time seemed to stop dead in its tracks as Katherine

watched the back of the proud solider riding the black stallion in the opposite direction she wanted him to go. Her servant, her protector, her friend and her new found love. A silent prayer passed her lips hoping against hope that he would be returned to her safely. After several moments Carey relunctantly placed a hand on her shoulder to bring her mind back inside the palace walls. As she turned Carey could see tears only barely being held back from rolling freely down her heart broken face.

"Where is my father? I must speak with him." Katherine mumbled more to herself than anyone else. Without saying a single word a finger indicated to the counsels white tent in the far left corner of the courtyard.

A group of men could be seen through the open sides in a heated discussion. They were pointing and slamming their fists down on a large piece of parchment that lay out on a stone table. Most of the men blended together wearing either black for the counsel men or dark red for the Captains, only Henry stood out. He wore simple yet fine garb on his person, yet in times of trouble wore the Royal red tailed coat to ensure everyone knew he was present.

Still in a slight daze Katherine approached rather slowly and all conversation was halted as a guard slipped inside the tent, notifying them of her arrival. The eight white bearded men seemed to hold their breath until she spoke.

"I know you are busy and I hate to interrupt but may I speak with you in private for a moment please father?" Her voice was steady, aside from her eyes being close to succumbing to emotion.

"Of course child. Please continue gentlemen I shall return in a moment," he stated strolling out of the tent. Escorting her by his left side they began walking back towards the palace. Carey followed a short distance behind as was expected, closely matched by Calzar. Henry was the first to speak once they were out of ear shot of the others.

"Katherine, I realize how upset you may be with me at the moment considering how you feel about Lance. I was once in love myself, you know,"

"How?" She asked in confusion. Henry smiled at her sudden distress.

"People close to a situation can tell, yet sometimes the two people involved are the last to know," he chuckled slightly at her. He thought how much of a child she really was still. It took her a minute to shake off the shock of this revelation.

"Father, you know that it's not only my concern for Lance that troubles me,"

"I know child. What David said was cause for great concern enough, but it troubles me more to know that Staton commanded his return for more troops without completing the search of the palace and other possible survivors, almost like he knew there would not be any to find,"

"I have realized you are right about me. I still have a great deal to learn about many things but this entire situation, the coming battle, Staton, Lanell staying behind...it all feels wrong. My gut is telling me something isn't right," Henry smiled slightly as his eyes unfocused for a moment, while he responded.

"Your mother told me that each time I sent the soldiers to fight. Any fight, whether it was big or small. May she rest in peace with the gods,"

Katherine was stunned.

Henry rarely spoke of her mother as she had died at the same time she was born. A beauty from a foreign land, she had been barely in her teens when she came to Maltesh and almost in her forties when she gave birth to her first and only child. When Katherine took her first breath Anna took her last. Henry took the loss hard and it had taken days for him to even look at Katherine.

"Each time I see you I am reminded of her and her beautiful ways. During every battle she was in the chapel praying to each god she could remember, for each man that was killed, regardless of which side they were fighting for,"

"Father," she paused wanting to choose her words carefully, "I know that you are disappointed with me being born a woman. Not a strong young man who could lead your armies to victory for you," he was taken back by her words as if a sorrowful secret had been revealed, "Your treatment of me like a woman in public but in private I was a boy in a disguise. Riding, hunting, tracking and even learning how to use a sword. If the counsel men knew half of the things I was taught they would die from shock," she laughed as Henry chuckled.

"All this time and you never spoke of it,"

"To be honest I've loved every second of it," she smiled broadly, "It's only now when you're in need of men with my talents that I see how selfish I've been," tears again began to well up in her eyes as the reality of Lance being on his way to possible death made her breathing stop for a moment.

"From now on I promise I'll try not to act like a child. But you must promise to train me completely. I need to understand how to rule a kingdom well. Prepare me for my role as Queen and future ruler. Father, I'm ready," Katherine's head was held high as she spoke out loud the words that she had once feared.

"Dearest child," he paused looking into her determined, young, innocent face, "I had hoped that this day would never come but it seems I have no choice given the circumstances. You are ready so we will begin at first light."

ATTACK

Her training was to begin the very next morning, except the time for her lesson never came. Katherine was awoken to the sound of the doors of her bedroom being opened with so much force that they slammed hard against the walls causing a loud bang. Instantly she had a butter knife in her hand that had been hidden under her mattress for emergencies. Seeing Carey enter quickly closely followed by two guards who had their swords drawn she lowered it.

Glancing to her left and out the large window in her room that led to the balcony she could tell that the sky was still dark outside, however Katherine could see an orange glow rising from the ground. It appeared to be sunrise.

"We need to leave now!" Carey blurted out as Katherine sat up and placed the knife down.
"We're under attack highness!" A guard added grimly closing the curtains on the window and putting out all the candles in the room, except one torch they held between them.

Katherine did not need to be told what to do. As part of her tutoring she was all too away of what she was required to do in this situation. Evacuate to a safe location. As guards collected her emergency pack, which consisted a few travel clothes and common clothing, Carey helped her dress as fast as possible behind the screens in her room.

Within minutes she was speeding down the halls towards the same counsel room she had burst through and interrupted the King a month before. Her basic light brown gown flowed freely as they ran, yet this time as they approached guards opened the doors ensuring they could enter without hesitation.

Unlike last time no one looked up as they came in. All the counsel men, the head of the Royal guards and a member of the first garrison were present. All looked weary, sweaty and covered in dirt like they had been in the battlefield themselves.

Calzar, Henry's personal guard, was explaining their position using a large piece of parchment that was spread across the stone table. Henry was sitting in the chair at the head of the table on the far side of the room. He appeared to be a man torn between anger, sorrow, complete calm and utter chaos.

Lanell was also there pacing the floor behind the King and large group of men, closely watched by Magel, who stood to the side. Both of them seemed anxious and ready for a fight. From what she could tell the attack had been completely unexpected.

After a few slow seconds Henry looked up and his eyes focused for the first time on Katherine's worried and frightened face. He spoke like a man close to tears.

"My beloved." His loved his city, his soliders and all those dying outside for the kingdom. Yet nothing pleased him more at that moment than seeing Katherine's face. She appeared to be more concerned about him than herself for possibly the first time in her life and that warmed his cold soul. The counsel men looked up towards him as the King spoke, yet Katherine ignored them and immediately ran to his side.

"Father, are you alright? What happened?" She knelt by his chair, stroking his arm like a wounded animal.

"I am fine child," he nodded to Calzar indicating that he should explain the entire situation to her. His voice angry yet determined.

"It appears that a scout followed the boy, David, from Staton's location. Once they had us in their sights they led a company of around three thousand Katzi against us. They used the Devils Pass through the hilss to come at us unseen, until it was too late," he pointed to the map as Katherine stood to get a better view, "We had no idea they were coming until their first attack a few hours ago,"

Katherine stared at Calzar in horror at the news. Being close to sixty in age Calzar's hair and beard were closer to being white than the dark brown colour she knew it had once been.

Unlike Henry, Calzar still walked like a warrior even though she knew he had been retired from active duty for many years as the King had. He even spoke like he had been in many battles and suffered many injuries because of it.

"What of the pass patrol? Did anyone apart, from Tasis, survive?" She asked regretfully turning to face the tall, medium built man to her right. Tasis lowered his head and as his eyes reached the floor he spoke quietly.

"I am one of only two that live, your highness," she could tell he was clearly upset and somehow ashamed. Trying to help him feel better she replied in a gentle voice.

"I'm sure that you tried to save the others. You have nothing to feel ashamed about," he smiled back at her slightly knowing her intentions were good, while Calzar continued the account for her.

"So far we have lost at least two thousand men. Not including the men that could not be saved on the patrol. That makes it closer to two thousand and fifty. I would recommend for you to leave immediately. I am not sure how much longer we can hold them back," he was staring at Henry as much as Katherine while we spoke.

"What kind of King abandons his people in their darkness hour?" He asked in a weary and firm tone, "You, however, must leave now," he looked into Katherine's furious eyes.

"Father please…"

"Do not argue with me on this Katherine. You know full well why this must be done," he raised his hand to silence her before she could speak further, "Lanell, as your father does not wish for you to be in this battle either, I am sending you along with my daughter,"

"As you wish sire," he replied without further comment, even though his body tensed and his eyes shone with anger.

"I will send Carey, Magel and six guards along with you both. Beloved, look at me!" She had turned away upset and hurt about leaving him behind and not being able to fight alongside him. She looked back at him trying to hide her emotions.

"If you have not heard from the city within three weeks, you know what to do," she nodded as small tears began to fall from her sorrowful eyes, "Calzar, I would be honoured if you would escort my daughter and the Prince to the haven,"

"Sire?"

"You heard me clearly," Henry gave Calzar a small smile, which made him quickly reply.

"I wish to remain at your side, as I have always done highness,"

"I know, but right now she needs your help more than me,"

"If you wish it sire, I will guard them with my life,"

"I know that as well old friend. I entrust the choosing of the other five guards to your capable hands. You are to leave as soon as your men are ready,"

"Thank you sire. We shall leave within minutes," Henry stood to be face to face with him and shook his right hand. He knew that Calzar would do everything in his power to protect the future ruler of Maltesh.

Henry was no fool.

He knew this would be the last war he would see. This war would be his end and Katherine's beginning.

"Beloved, please come with me," he held out his hand towards his only living heir, holding her bewildered gaze. His request was so kind and gentle that she followed him without a second thought. He indicated they should be given only one guard, as they began walking so Lanell, Carey, Magel and Calzar could begin making the necessary arrangements for travelling.

Henry led the way down the dark corridors. The only available light coming from inside the palace as a small, single torch, like the one their escort carried as they walked. Katherine knew this was done so the enemy would not know where people were located in each building. If they enemy did not know where they were, they could not attack them directly.

For a moment at least.

When they arrived at Henry's private quarters he instructed the guard to wait outside so only he and Katherine entered. The first thing that she noticed about the King of Maltesh's quarters was the size. She had expected her father's quarters to be the biggest in the palace. She had been very wrong.

"You know," he smiled glancing back at her frozen figure in the doorway as the door closed, "When I first met Calzar in this room, he had the same expression on his face as he entered. We were both merely sixteen years old and he was to be my shadow. When I asked him what was wrong, do you know what he said?" She shook her head having not heard the story of how they met before.

"He said, I though your room would be bigger than mine, not smaller. I knew then that he and I would get along perfectly. Just like Carey and yourself no doubt," he smiled as she did.

"I was thinking the same thing," she laughed out loud, yet tried to control her volume. As she calmed herself, he continued.

"When I was nine your grandfather walked me out of my nursery and led me to every room in the Royal family portion of the palace. And just like I did with you each time we came to a door he would ask me if this room would be suitable for a King. Each time I would respond saying not this one, maybe the next. We finally entered this room and I instantly fell in love with its simplicity as it had the only things I felt I needed as a ruler. A simple desk, a comfy chair by a fireplace and through those doors a simple bed, a place to hold my clothes and enough space in between to pace at night if I needed to think,"

Katherine was amazed that the logic made sense to her. She was beginning to understand that a good ruler was not measured by their luxusirous quarters or belongings but by their actions before and while they rule. She was starting to understand her father. He continued.

"The day I married your mother I was so nervous on how she would take this. It is after all not what a regular Princess would be used to. I was almost certain that being from a different country she would hate it. Yet when she walked in for the first time her face lit up like the night sky, full of stars. She told me later that her room in the palace back in her home country was the same size. She absolutely loved it," Katherine felt a sense of love and joy to see her father's face become brighter just by speaking of her mother. She could only imagine the childish grin and red cheeks he would have had seeing his bride for the first time. His expression became serious once more as the faint noises of the battle reached them again.

"As you are going to the safe haven I must give you these," he pulled out a stack of parchment bound in a plain leather cover with the Maltesh symbol on the cover and tied with a simple knot. "These are my private journals and our family's history down to our last battle. If for some reason I do not join you, it will be your responsibility to continue it," she took them without saying a word.

These papers were about their people, about her people. Henry knew there was a chance he would not survive and he also knew the information would be safer in the hands of his daughter. It was a great honour to carry the burden of such knowledge and keep it safe, yet Katherine vowed that she would try to her best. Henry continued adding.

"I want you to know that your being sent away has nothing at all to do with your skill as a swordsman. I am so very proud of you regardless of who you are," he beamed at her. Of all his achievement's she was by far the most unexpected and the greatest, "I hope I am there to see what you become as I know you will be the best anyone has ever seen. With that being said," He paused again, "I wanted to give you these as well."

He reached behind his desk and pulled out a small lever, which when snapped into place revealed what appeared to be a secret drawer. Retracting his hand he passed her a pile of small decorative books held together by a collection of white silk ribbon, tied in a beautiful bow. At the centre of the bow was a small glass orb, which appeared to sparkle silver and held an intricate design of many colours within its shape. As Katherine took them she gazed up at Henry with a puzzled expression.

"There were your mother's personal journals. She started writing in them when she was sent here for our wedding. Once she found out about you she wrote daily," he paused again, "When she died I did not have the heart to let them go and I could never find the courage to open the first page. I know she would have wanted you to have them."

Tears of joy ran down her face as she felt the cover of the top book under the bow and orb. Lifting her head she smiled as Henry too was crying a little while trying to cover up his emotions. She placed the bundles of books and parchment to one side as she stood and hugged her father around the waist. Time seemed to stand still for a brief moment. The two stood locked in each other's arms both terrified to let go of the other. A small knock on the door made them separate and attempt to compose themselves.

"Enter," Henry finally stated boldly, hiding all of the emotion he had shown moments before. Calzar appeared apologizing.

"Forgive me, my lord, however we are ready to depart." Henry nodded and leading Katherine by the hand they left the room. Calzar being polite inquired as to whether or not she needed help in carrying her new belongings and knowing it would make travelling quicker she reluctantly passed over the bundles to him, however slipped the small orb into her pocket to keep it close to her heart.

They met back up with the others close to the counsel room and proceeded quickly through several corridors without stopping. For the second time Katherine could hear the battle and as they passed a large decorative window she caught her first glimpse of the chaos. She paused for a moment to take in what she saw.

From the high window in the palace she could see over the outer grey walls and see the giant mass of small black creatures waiting to enter the city. Dead bodies were scattered everywhere she looked. From the large catapult on the left hand side of the outer bailey to the armoury on the right.

Some Katzi had made it inside the cities outer wall however they were paying a high price for it. Boiling hot oil and stones were being thrown on to their bare heads from above the drawbridge. Somehow the drawbridge had been lowered and the main wooden gate rattled and shuddered as large amounts of pressure was thrown against it from the outside. A battering ram, Katherine was certain of it.

Then she got her first look at a Katzi.

One stood alone on top of the outer wall, having climbed to the top of some kind of black ladder. Seven or eight soldiers lay dead at its feet. It appeared short in height, being at the most five foot tall with similar features of a human. She could tell he was not one, however from his pointed ears, animal like eyes, large animal like pointed teeth and the strong feline type pose he held. It appeared as if he was about to pounce as his long claws scraped the walls surface.

She watched curiously as he seemed to be completely free of fear while smirking at the guards he had killed. As she stared loud explosions and sounds of fighting erupted around him, yet he remained in the same position undeterred. What seemed to her as hours later he caught sight of something on the ground. The Katzi's wide grin showed black drool oozing through his teeth and down his narrow chin. The creature slowly began to lower his head towards the nearest body, when suddenly Katherine was spun around by force.

For a moment her eyes were out of focus, and then Lanell's concerned face appeared closer to her own. He simply stated.

"That is something you don't want in your memory. Trust me."

He led her on to follow the others holding her hand tightly, afraid she would pause again. She was not aware that they were still grasping each other's hand until they stopped in front of a large beige stone in the dungeon and he needed to let go so he could help move it. It took all the men present to move the stone to one side revealing the black escape tunnel hidden behind. Henry spoke directly to Calzar once he caught his breath.

"Follow the tunnel all the way to the end. Remember it turns once in a while and gets steep in places so stay close together for the light and watch your footing. Once you reach the end you will see some horses waiting for you, they have been well provisioned. Katherine knows the way to the haven so she will give you directions as needed. If for any reason anyone, and I mean anyone, does not follow your instructions you have my permission to do whatever you must to ensure the survival of our kingdom. Is that understood?"

"Yes sire," Calzar changed with the other guards as he had finished by addressing everyone present.

"Beloved, do you remember the way?" He turned to Katherine who stood next to him shaking a little.

"Yes father," suddenly taking his face in her hands gently she spoke quietly with tears in her eyes, "Please, please come with us,"

"Please stay out of trouble," he smiled knowing her response to his teasing.

"I always do," she laughed choking back the tears as she released him. Hearing more fighting she had a hard time doing so.

"I love you Katherine," they quickly embraced and as the guards, Lanell, Magel, Carey and Calzar began walking briskly through the tunnel Katherine shouted back to him and waved with her right hand that held the small glass orb her mother had given to her.

"I love you too father!"

The last time she saw Henry was as she looked back briefly to see his smiling face for a second just before the tunnel entrance was sealed behind them and they were plunged into darkness.

No one spoke as they hurried through the silent, dark and damp tunnels. Only two torches gave out any light to enable them to see the way ahead. The occasional thud sound was the only noise except for their own footsteps on the dark stone ground. Several times Katherine stepped on something soft that had squealed and scurried away from the intruders, at which point she was glad she could not see the floor very clearly.

After the four miles of darkness they saw a small light in front of them. Peering from behind one of the guards Katherine could see the sun was still not up yet, though it was not going to take long. An hour, maybe two at the most, and the sun would rise above the surrounding mountains. They would need to be quick to get away without be seen. The guards immediately signaled for the women, Magel and Lanell to stay further back in the tunnel for a moment while they scouted the area for the horses.

"Katherine," Lanell turned to her and handed her a small beautifully designed dagger, "Take this." He muttered quickly. The blade was shining like silver with a blue hilt, which showed the symbol of Buletis in gold. Katherine knew its meaning was protection. She looked at him with both confusion and gratitude.

"It's beautiful. Thank you." She stated placing it inside her high riding boots. The side of which was high enough that the dagger became invisible.

Carey watched the exchange with a little uneasiness. She was still suspicious of him. Her nerves were already extremely high being outside of the palace without much protection while the city was attacked. Fearing for their safety was nothing compared to how she felt when she remembered her father and mother were both still in the city with the King. One of the guards returned to explain that the coast was clear and that they had found the horses with no problems.

"Follow me your highness." Katherine, Carey and Lanell

were led towards the opening by the guard.

Finally leaving the dark confines the tunnel caused Katherine to breathe deeply in relief. It was then she took the chance to look around. Calzar and the other guards were already altering the saddles for each horse, readying them to leave within minutes. Carey looked at each horse with concern. She had little to no experience with horses and the prospect of having to ride one for long periods of time did not appeal to her.

Once out of the darkness, Lanell immediately walked up to a horse and began changing the straps on the saddle as the others did, showing he was more a trained solider than used to living the Royal life. Glancing around at their surrounding Katherine realized where they were. They were to east of Maltesh and turning towards the west for a moment caused her breath to catch in her throat.

The entire city of Maltesh was in flames.

The outer bailey was completely engulfed in flames. The large white building that Katherine knew as the palace was black from the amount of smoke rising from the smaller building around it. Sounds of the battle could be heard even though they were far enough away to be hidden by the outline of the Blue Woods.

Suddenly a massive explosion knocked everyone to the ground and scared the horses away. Even from their location the blast caused their ears to ring for a moment. Katherine quickly looked up from the floor to see a large black cloud of smoke rising from a huge hole that had been create in the side of the palace, near where the great hall had been.

From their higher position they could do nothing except watch in horror as a large swarm of Katzi ran through the inner city and into the hole in the side of palace, like a black river of water. Katherine's first thoughts were to race back to aid her father. Yet as she stood Calzar was immediately at her side speaking loudly to her ringing ears.

"You can't help him! We must go! We're vulnerable here!"

Katherine stood amazed for a moment. It was as if he had read her mind or predicted she wanted to run the four miles back to the palace. Then she realized he must have been thinking the exact same thing.

"My lady, these trees do not provide enough cover! We must leave now!" Calzar spoke again pulling her left elbow back towards the horses which had been rounded up quickly due to the experience of the guard. Calzar continued saying, "Some of you will need to double. Magel take Carey, Lanell ride with Katherine,"

Both Lanell and Katherine looked shocked, opening their mouths to object made Calzar smile a cruel smirk, "Your highnesses will do as instructed or I will have both of you tied up for the reminder of our journey together and carried on the back of the horses like trophies, is that clear?"

"Yes sir." They chanted quickly at the same time with clenched teeth. It was difficult for them both to fight back the words of argument that came to mind. Without further conversation Lanell jumped onto the dark brown horse he had been preparing and turned to face Katherine. She was not staring at him. Instead she was glancing back towards the ruins of her kingdom saying a silent prayer for her father and all the others trapped there.

After a moment she signed deeply and turned to face him. Seeing Lanell take her seat near the horses head made her instantly angry, yet after everything that had happened weighed heavily on her mind she decided not to fight with him. At least not at that specific moment.

"We'll continue towards the haven riding in single file to hide our numbers. Lanell and Katherine you will be leading, behind me, guiding us. Carey and Magel you come right after. Everyone else you know the drill. Lead the way highnesses." Lanell helped Katherine onto the back of the horse as Calzar spoke and as they began riding he started to smile.

"Don't be ashamed to hold onto me tightly, if you start to feel afraid," she instantly laughed a little replying.

"If I do decide to hold onto you tighter, it'll mean that I fear for my life due to your riding skills." He chuckled back nodding his head a little in agreement. As they rode ahead Katherine took one last look back to see the smoking ruins and the large black and grey clouds still rising from the ground. Facing the forest she felt in her heart that her father was dead.

The first day in the Blue Wood passed in a blur for Katherine. All the woods seem gloomy, grey and unwelcoming to her, the complete opposite of why it was called the Blue Woods. It was so named as during sunrise and sunset the light hit the leaves in such a way that the entire wood appeared to be the most beautiful colour of blue. Most people called it calming and energizing, except not that day and not for Katherine. Only Lanell's presence seemed to make her feel better.

He was constantly talking. Anything that popped into his mind instantly came out of his mouth. Stories about when he was a child and the crazy things he was caught doing by his father. The story that she remembered the most has been funny and something she herself would have done.

"I was six or seven at the time and there was a huge feast that was being held in the great hall. Everyone had been forbidden to enter until it officially began, but of course being the curious soul I was I did not listen. The table that was laid out was incredible and had every type of food you can imagine. I noticed a small pie and figured since there was so many no one would notice if just one was gone so I ate it," he chuckled at the memory and then continued.

"I was found hours later during the festivities fast asleep under the King's table. I had been caught red handed with the remains of the small squash pie that the King himself had requested be made. The King was so amused by my courage and good taste that I had been allowed to attend the entire feast at his table."

Katherine laughed out loud at his story and then realized that she would have been at the same table, as she would have been only three or four at the time. She was too young to remember specific details though.

Aside from the stories the day was merely stating directions to their dark brown horse, Calzar and the emotionally strained travelling group that followed. Katherine remembered that they had stopped for lunch and to check the map although she had no idea of what time of day it had been or how long they had been riding. The trees grew so close together that the sunlight could barely been seen at times. They stopped a second time once Katherine led them to a clearing just as the sun was beginning to set once more.

Calzar instructed everyone to set up camp as they would rest for the night there. Knowing that all her privileges had gone up in smoke Katherine began helping Carey set up their tent without being asked as she knew how to do it from her outdoor training. Lanell noticed a small smile on her face for the second time.

"She knows how to camp. Who would have thought?" He thought to himself smiling.

Once the tents were up and the camp fire had been lit a soldier returned from the hunting with several grey rabbits. They were quickly prepared, cooked and eaten. When they were finished Katherine held a meeting in her tent around a small fold out table that had been packed with their supplies.

"We are here," she pointed at the map laid out in front of them. "We need to ride hard tomorrow south east bearing towards the Green Lake. Once the lake is in sight we continue east towards the Black Peaks to reach the haven. We'll reach the haven before the Peak's forest,"

"So we should arrive at the haven in about a month, then?" A solider asked quietly ensuring he was understanding her completely. Katherine chuckled a little at his embarrassed as she nodded. Calzar looked sharply at him and told him to wait outside. Only Calzar, Lanell and Katherine now stood in her tent as Carey was helping secure the remaining food from the forest predators.

"I know you wanted to place the haven somewhere secure away from any potential threat, but I don't understand why your grandfather had to make it so far away. What if we need help or the city needs us to return? Wouldn't it have been easier to make the haven closer?" Lanell stated plainly.

"For our enemies yes. The idea was to have it as you said far enough away from the city so that if it took a while to gain control back our lives would not be threatened and close enough that if they city is secure again, we can be notified and return without enemies knowing the location of the haven. I think it was brilliant,"

"I agree," He replied, "It's a great idea, but what if we run into trouble? We can't very well just stop and ask someone to aid us,"

"That is why I am here," Calzar piped up without smiling. Lanell quickly changed the subject.

"So a day's ride towards the lake and a few weeks to the haven, sounds easy enough,"

It will not be that simple," Calzar smiled showing no humour at his discomfort, "What about the swamp?" He asked Katherine directly. She thought for a moment before responding.

"This time of year it should be steadily rising yet still passable," she shrugged off his question like it was nothing.

"Swamp? What swamp?" Lanell was taken back by this new information.

"The swamp that we need to travel through to reach the haven," she smiled at him saying, "We should reach it about sunset tomorrow. It's located to the west of the Green Lake," her smile changed into more of a mocking smirk as she continued teasing him, "Whatever is the matter Lanell, don't feel like getting your feet wet,"

"You worry about yourself highness. I can hold my own," he teased back smiling.

"Focus both of you. If the swamp is not passable it will take us another week or two to go around it," Calzar sounded fed up of their back and forth, which had been increasing since they had left the kingdom.

"It shouldn't take that long, even if we have to go around but we need to ensure that we travel as much as we can each day," she added.

"In that case we leave at dawn. I will ensure we are ready. Goodnight Prince. Your highness," Calzar suddenly announced, bowed and left the tent without looking back. Katherine and Lanell were both shocked for a moment at being alone, in her private tent. Lanell was the first to speak after a few awkward minutes of silence.

"Katherine, I wanted to tell you that I'm sorry Lance was sent away to the battle,"

"Thank you, but I'm sure you had nothing to do with it so there's nothing to apologize for," she was taken back at his words and the subject. His eyes lowered to the soft cushions on the ground as he admitted.

"Actually I may have,"

"What do you mean?" She asked horrified that he would say such a thing.

"I told the King if he couldn't find anyone with my skill to help my father…that I would leave without his consent," she felt like she had been hit in the face and stepped back to sit down on the soft blankets near her bed. Lanell continued, "I swear to you. I thought they would choose Magel or one of the other soldiers. With Lance being your personal guard I didn't think they would even consider him,"

"You…why are you telling me this?" She asked trying to control her raging feelings.

"I want to become your friend, and to do so I need you to trust me and to know, without a doubt, that I would never harm anyone you cared about," he paused, "You know I hate to say it however sooner or later both our parents will be gone. It'll fall to us to rule a peaceful land. To do so I'll need your help and you will need mine,"

She had never seen anyone so serious at that moment.

Lance could be straight face and intense at times yet here stood a man who believed what he spoke with such passion that he could shout out loud to the world what he felt. As conflicted as she was Katherine knew that for the good of the two kingdoms he was right. It would eventually fall to this decision.

"I appreciate your concerned and kind words about Lance. I would be very happy for us to become friends,"

"In that case I shall leave you to sleep as we have a long day ahead,"

"Goodnight Katherine. My new friend,"

"Goodnight Lanell," with that he left almost bumping into Carey as he did so. Shock and confusion was on Carey's face as she realized that they had been alone.

"What was that about?" She asked suspiciously.

"Nothing Lanell was just saying that…" Katherine relayed the entire conversation to her. She sat with her arms rightly folded the entire time and an expression of concern.

"You realize of course that he is simply trying to snake his way into your life," she pointed out once Katherine had finished.

"What are you talking about? Did you hear anything I just said or what he just said? He just wants to be friends for the sake of the kingdoms,"

"That is what all men say to get close to you. Once he is close enough something will happen and you will end up liking him, more than a friend,"

"Oh Carey, don't be so dramatic,"

"Be friends with him 'for the kingdoms' if that is what you want. But you just remember I'll be here the entire time ensuring you stay just friends,"

"Great," she smiled, "That way you and Magel can spend more time together. Don't think I haven't noticed how you look at each other,"

"Goodnight Kat," Carey snapped back while smiling a little.

"Goodnight Carey." Smiles appeared all around.

It became night so fast, yet sleep did not want to come to Katherine. After a few long hours of staring at the roof of the tent she got up, wrapped a cover around her shoulders and walked out of the tent towards the camp fire. A second later a bright torch came running in her direction like a catapult revealing Calzar.

"Your highness, what is the matter?"

"Oh nothing, sorry if I startled you Calzar. I couldn't sleep," she replied embarrassed at her forgetfulness. He had taken the first watch and he would kill almost anything that moved once the tent settled down for the night.

"Forgive me your highness. I should have known it'd be hard for you to sleep," without realizing it Calzar escorted her towards the small camp fire and sat down beside her.

"How would you of known?" She inquired with a doubtful snap.

"I was barely twenty years old, as was your father, when we were forced to leave the kingdom the first time. A rival King's army began attacking the walls at sunset and the King was so angry about leaving without your grandfather that I needed to carry him through the old westward tunnel. Once we came out the other side I had to drop a bag of water over his head to calm him. We made our way into the forest and made camp after only a few hours ride as it grew dark. I was about to check on him a few hours before dawn, when I spotted him, as we are now, in front of the camp fire sipping warm water. I had never seen anyone look as sad as he did that night, worrying about his father in the city under siege...that is until I just saw you coming out of your tent,"

"Maybe I'm more like him that I cared to notice," she chuckled a little as Calzar nodded with her. Katherine could see he was hurting as much as she was to leave without the King and it made her at least a little glad that someone knew how she felt. Footsteps behind them made both their heads turn. Lanell came out of the darkness fully clothed. She could tell he had not slept either.

"It seems I wasn't the only one that couldn't sleep," he stated without his usual grin walking towards the fire. Calzar looked at Lanell with suspicion releasing his hand from his swords hilt.

"So it appears," he glanced back at Katherine as he continued saying, "Your highness. It was a pleasure speaking to you as always yet regretfully I must return to my post. Good evening Lanell. Good evening highness," he bowed towards her and left as Lanell took a seat close by.

"What's going on with him?" Lanell asked in a semi-serious tone.

"He misses my father. I think almost more than I do," her response was sad as she watched him disappear into the shadows.

"I understand that. The last time I saw my mother was three months ago. I went on a hunting trip with father lasted a week and when we returned he had me training all the time. I was training so hard that when I finally managed to sneak away all I wanted to do was sleep. The morning I got news to leave and warn Henry she was so busy helping organize everything that I didn't have the chance to say good bye,"

"You must miss her a lot. Do you miss Staton?" She forced herself to say his name in a caring way.

"Honestly, I'm not sure. He had never been the caring father. Everything is battle, scheming and war with him," he suddenly stopped speaking as if he had let too much of the truth slip out. Katherine smiled a little at his discomfort. He continued without emotion.

"I know how you feel about my father, so the things I say would make sense but he only does what he thinks is right," Katherine could not contain herself at his words. She exploded in a rage.

"Right! What about raping someone is right? What about torturing a helpless child is right? Nothing about Staton is right! He hurts people for fun and revenge! He finds amusement with other people's suffering! He is nothing but a monster!" She had stood as she screamed at him.

"You know nothing about him!" Lanell shouted back now standing face to face with her. She replied in a quieter voice choking back the hot tears.

"If I know nothing about him, you know less. Do you know what he did to…Lance?" He looked away from her unable to see her eyes any longer, "The truth Lanell. Do you know what happened to the children he took?"

"I heard rumours when they were rescued…not details," he answered slowly a few moments later still not facing her.

"I've seen his scars," she choked on some tears as she remembered, "Staton tortured a helpless child because his mother spoke up against him," Katherines eyes were now red from crying, "I know it was you that gave him the list of names," she turned away unable to control her tears any longer. The silence was deafening. Only her sobs could be heard for several minutes.

Calzar stood in the shadows close by stunned by this revelation. As far as the kingdom was concerned Lanell had merely been born to an evil man. He had no idea Lanell had been part of it. Lanell broke the silence by speaking in a soft, emotional voice.

"Katherine, please look at me," she turned slowly to see tears rolling freely down his face, "You're right. It was me. Except I was a child, younger than Lance, I didn't know what he would do. He convinced me that it was all lies. He told me people hated him for being so successful and so young. I gave the names to him and asked him what he was going to do. He just told me not to worry about it and sent me home," he paused as they both sat down again at the same time.

After taking a few deep breaths he continued, "A few days after he was arrested they brought news of the bodies. Hundreds of men and women were found dead in their homes and then suddenly he escaped from the dungeon. It was only after the search for him ceased that anyone noticed that the children were missing," he gulped trying to control his emotions.

"Some said they were killed and taken out of the city. Others said that they had simply been taken. No one knew what really happened to them but it didn't stop the rumours that it had something to do with father. Somehow I knew they were right and knew it had been because of the names I had given him. I finally asked my mother and she broke down. She explained that she knew that they had been taken and that he was so insane anything could happen to them. She was so worried for them. I tried to tell someone, anyone that he had taken them but no one believed me," his eyes focused on the fire for a moment as he took a deep breath.

"She didn't know where they were being held or what was going on. You must believe me Katherine. I swear to you. If I had known where they were I would have helped them," his plea came as he stared right into her eyes. His bright blue eyes shone with sincerity and a truth that came behind them.

"I...I believe you," she said in a calm tone a few silent moments later. Her gut twisting at hearing things from his point of view. She felt in her heart that her loyalty to Lance was being tested and her suspicious feelings towards Lanell were telling her he was lying about something, yet with this it was all true. Catching his breath he concluded.

"It was almost thirteen months later when rumours of their rescue began flying around. Stories of their terrible life were circling and father was recaptured, banished and stripped of all titles and lands in your kingdom. It was around that time when it was discovered I was his son and I was banished too,"

"Guilty by blood," she simply stated. No matter how suspicious she was of him her curiosity kept fighting her common sense. By her calculations it would have been around this time Mischelle's same husband died and Staton became King of Buletis.

"What you were both banished, is that when Lance tried to kill you?" He seemed to grow very still for a moment, shocked she knew of their fight.

"Yes, it was after father's hearing and the truth came out. Looking back I don't blame him for being furious with me. Although he didn't know I..." he paused suddenly realizing something, "Did you tell him it was me?"

"No,"

"Why? He has every right to know that I gave him up to my father. I'm the reason that his parents were killed and what they did to him. Why...why didn't you tell him?"

"Don't you think he has suffered enough pain and heartache because of what happened to him. What's past is past and I plan on keeping him from any further harm,"

"I don't know how to thank you," he almost whispered.

"I didn't do it for you, but you're welcome." She replied softly.

Silence wrapped around them once more. Lanell slightly touched her left hand that was placed on top of her knee and it disturbed her that she did not really mind. While they sat there Katherine began looking in more detail at her surroundings. They were heading further into the forest and up towards the mountainside so she could see a large patch of forest spreading across the ground like a dark green field. The sky was black with millions of tiny stars glittering down at them. She tried to look westward to see if she could see Maltesh but all she saw were trees. Lanell smiled slightly having regained his voice.

"Trying to see home?"

"I just wish I knew what happened to my father," she sighed deeply.

"He'll be fine. He's tough,"

"If not, you're in the presence of a Queen," she chuckled a little trying to make light of the situation. He remained serious as he replied.

"Would that be such a bad thing?" His eye brows raised waiting for an answer.

"Not for a friend." She smiled at him and he smiled back.

The next day of travel seemed to last forever. After talking so much the night before Katherine and Lanell were extremely tried and had very little else to say to each other. Every once in while Katherine would give a direction otherwise they stayed silent. Carey and Magel had both awakened during the shouting in the night and had remained hidden and silent, as had Calzar, to listen to what was said. Due to this they also kept quiet that day, watching the dark brown horse in front and its riders. Katherine usually loved riding but travelling this much was making her change her mind. She honestly thought the day would never end. Eventually, however, they climbed over a large grassy hill to see a far off view of the kingdom of Maltesh.

Smoke was only slightly rising now yet the damage could be seen clearly. The palace wall where the great hall would have been completely collapsed inward while most of the outer and inner walls were in ruins. Swarms of Katzi could still be seen camping around the city walls. Katherine quickly climbed down from the horse as they slowed, causing the entire party to halt. She staggered slowly forward her eyes tearing up, when suddenly she began vomiting to her right, then without warning everything went dark.

"What do you expect? She had had a lot to deal with the past two days. She may be physically in her twenties but she's still a child in many ways." A male voice spoke in almost whisper.

As Katherine began to open her eyes she saw a camp fire had been lit a short distance away to her left. Calzar and Lanell sat closest to her, while she could just make out the others on the opposite side of the fire setting up the tents for their second night outdoors.

It was then she was hit by the memory of what happened. She had seen the palace in ruins and the thoughts of her father laying dead on the ground while Katzi walked over him made her stomach lurch, causing her to let go of the previous meal. A sharp pain had erupted in her head and everything had gone black.

Remembering what happened made her feel ill again. Yet she fought it this time and propped herself up a little so she did not have to move much. She had fallen near a cliff edge and with a little leverage she could again see Maltesh. Lots of small camp fires could be seen from her higher location. She counted at least thirty fire below and at least another five large ones inside the inner walls. Calzar and Lanell had picked a great spot for their fire as they were far enough away from the ledge and down a slope so that none of the Katzi should have been able to see it.

"There are so many of them." She thought to herself. Her heart felt like it had fallen completely out of her body as it felt like ice. Only revenge filled her mind. One way or the other she would find the person behind this and they would pay.

Soft footsteps behind her indicated that Carey approaching. Seeing Katherine awake and not showing the others she sensed her reluctance to notify them just yet. That being so she spoke quietly as she reached Katherine's side so they would not be over heard by the others.

"Are you feeling any better?"

"Actually yes. Just a little thirsty. How long was I out for? Thank you," Carey replied handing a cup of cold water grinning as she sneakily drank it down quickly and then held out the cup for a second helping.

"For most of the day. We made camp for the night so you wouldn't have to be put on the back of the horse like game,"

"What?" Katherine suddenly realized that the sun was about to set and that was why she could see the camp fires so clearly.

"Kat, Lanell saved you," Carey paused as a look of shock and confusion crossed her drawn face.

"What? When?"

"When you fainted, you almost went over," she indicated quickly to the steep, rocky cliff face only a few feet away, "Lanell jumped off the horse as you lost your food and grabbed you back before the others even knew what was happening. I felt terrible that I hadn't even thought to walk next to you when you jumped off the horse. I know there is something weird about him being with us through all this, but since he saved your life I'm starting to like him," she seemed out of breath by simply describing the day's events.

Her voice lowered further towards the end as she admitted her warmer feelings towards him. Katherine laughed a little out loud at this, causing the men sitting close by to turn suddenly in their direction. Seeing that she was sitting up on the grass now smiling Lanell and Calzar walked over to her.

"I hear I owe you my life and thanks," she stood slowly as she spoke to Lanell directly. He smiled in return.

"Just try not to do that a second time,"

"Oh believe me, I didn't try the first time," she laughed, "How embarrassing,"

"It's completely understandable Katherine. You've had a lot to deal with the past two days," recognizing the male whisper from before she stared at him playfully.

"So you think I'm still a child in many ways, do you?" Her eyebrow raised suggestively.

"I simply meant that you have yet to experience real life as I have," his face clearly showed the embarrassment by her implications, which made Katherine chuckled more.

"I don't disagree with you. That is why I wish to learn as much as I possibly can about all the workings of a kingdom." she spoke for the first time as a ruler. She felt in her soul that she was to be Queen of Maltesh, if they should ever return.

Thanks to the incident at the cliff top they were behind schedule. To make up for her delay Katherine decided they should travel at night and tried to convince Calzar to take a short cut she heard about from Henry. This turned out to be more of a task than she would have liked.

"No," he insisted for the twelfth time.

"Calzar trust me,"

"I have already sent two of the guards ahead on this path,"

"This path to the right will be faster. My father put it on the map himself," she argued.

"Fine. We can wait for the scouts to return and send them up that way at that time,"

"They won't return until at least night fall, by then we could be passed the turn and further on the way to the heaven," she refused to back down.

"She has a point Calzar. From the look of this map it will take away half a day's ride, at least," Lanell stepped in looking briefly at the map that was spread out over the small table in Katherine's tent once more. The sun had only been up for a few moments but the discussion had started when the stars had been still shining brightly.

"Both of you will listen to me. I have been plotting courses and travelling in forests since before either of you could even crawl on your hands and knees," Calzar stated in a serious and firm tone.

"That is very true, Calzar. However you don't know the exact location of the haven. I'm the only one who does and I'm taking the path to the right," her tone matched his own and she gave each of them a look of pure determination.

"She does have a point there," Lanell smiled out of the left corner of his mouth at her spirit. Calzar rolled his eyes to the ceiling. His words were lost to him for the first time in years as he realized he would not win the fight on this.

"Fine, we will go down the right path. But when they return from scouting this path I want Mened and Carboz to go ahead of us. Until we are in closer range of the haven I want guards ahead of you at all times." Katherine nodded in agreement at the compromise.

The camp was packed up and they were ready to leave within an hour of the discussion finally ending. The scouts had not returned as Katherine predicted so they mounted the horses to take the right path. The sun had already begun to lower over the treetops. The pace was slowed as the path became harder to see in the dark but Katherine felt more at home.

She only needed to stop the group twice and check the ground for signs of a path.

They had been travelling in the darkness for hours with only the glare of two torches that were held by the remaining guard, which consisted of Nica, Ocsas and Magel, when suddenly a loud bang was heard coming from behind them along the their same path.

Instantly the torches were stamped on or thrust in the dirt to prevent smoke as everyone dismounted and moved in the surrounding foliage silencing the trained horses. From a sort distance back down the path they began to hear voices. Two were shouting as a third started weeping and begging for forgiveness.

"I never meant too! Forgive me!" An almost howling voice screeched.

"You blundering fool. Do you want them to find us?" The second man had a hint of fear in his voice.

"Maybe he does. That is why he keeps making noise!" the third and angry male yelled back. The first had not sounded entirely human. After a few minutes of silence three figures came into view. Two tall masculine men pulled a third short creature.

Calzar walked forward greeting them both and calling them by name, Mened and Carboz, the scouts that were sent up the other path. She was grateful to see that they both were still alive and appeared to have captured the creature without harm to themselves. Mened was shorter than Calzar, being around six foot and preferred to have a beard rather than being clean shaven like Carboz. Both men were of medium build and carried long swords, like the other guards.

Slowly Katherine moved out of the shadows towards the group. Glancing from each of the men she was caught in the gaze of the creature and a feeling a dread skimmed her soul causing her to shiver slightly. Seeing the creature in more detail she suddenly realized it was a Katzi.

A small smirk appeared on the hideous face as the Katzi

took a deep breath in and a black tongue came a small way out of the left hand side of his large mouth, lighting touching a pointed tooth. Seeing the brief exchange caused Lanell to lean in front of Katherine and pulled her roughly away from him.

"What are you doing?" She gasped in shock at him, while trying to release his firm grip on her upper left arm. When they were a good distance away he paused in walking, releasing his hold and spoke.

"There's something about the Katzi that clearly, no one told you. They're related to the Leludians,"

"Leludians? The descendants of Elves from the children stories?" She raised an eyebrow at him in denial.

"As crazy as it sounds yes. I found out a few years ago. All the stories about the descendants of the old races were based on some level in fact,"

"That is just ridiculous. Elves? Dwarves? Wizards?"

"Even dragons. I know what it sounds like to hear but I promise you I'm telling you the truth,"

"How do you know?"

"I met some Carvians when I was travelling with my father once and they can only be described as descendants of Dwarves. As for the Katzi, let's just say that I've seen first hand what these things can do and for some of it only magic can be the answer of just how," Lanell's eyes unfocused for a moment and Katherine remembered back at the palace when she saw the Katzi on the wall that he had said something about not being able to get some images out of your mind once you had seen what they do.

"The Katzi inherited an ability from their Leludian ancestors to use black magic. They have mastered a skill to lure their prey into traps. For them to achieve the deception they need to maintain eye contact,"

"Are you saying that he was looking at me to use magic?"

"Yes, and he will continued to try as long as he is with us. That is why we need to get any information out of him as quickly as possible and dispose of him," Calzar spoke out loud to them both as he walked over from the others.

"Highness, are you alright?"

"Fine, why?" She asked curiously as his question had come in an almost worried tone.

"That is strange that you felt no effect from him. You had eye contact for a few seconds, yet that is usually enough to warrant some kind of effect,"

"You really didn't feel anything looking at him?" Lanell asked interrupting Calzar.

"Dread. Hatred. Disgust. Is there something else that I should feel towards him?" She simply stated. The anger for his kind destroying her home and her life evident in her tone.

"If that is all you felt then you will be fine. Lanell, you and Magel will ensure that her highness and Carey are kept as far away from him as possible, at all times understood?"

"Yes sir." Lanell replied as a solider without a second thought. At least for the moment they agreed on something.

Katherine was furious at being told that she could not be present, while they interrogated the Katzi. Even with the information she had received during her last conversation with Lanell and Calzar her stubbornness refused to subside.

"Damn men!" She swore loudly indicating at the tent entrance where she knew Lanell and Magel were stood refusing to let them leave, "If I didn't know any better I would say that they were keeping us here for another reason,"

"Kat, they are keeping us here for our own safety. That creature is dangerous, even chained up," Carey simply stated trying to remind her of why they were being held away from him.

"So they say. I told you when I looked at him I felt nothing but hate. Why does that mean I need to be locked up like an animal? I did nothing wrong,"

"How many times do you need to be told? We're not being punished for anything we did. That creature is evil and will attempt to escape. Maybe even try to kill us the second he gets a chance. We need stay away from him so we don't put the others in danger,"

"The others could very well be as vulnerable as we are. Just because we're women they think that he only wants us. What if he could lure them as well? Did they think about that?" Katherine continued to rant while thoughts of mindless violence towards the creature swept through her entire body. Thoughts of Henry and Lance crossed her mind. She felt that Henry was dead for certain and as far as she knew Lance could have died already too.

"Yes, we have!" Lanell's voice penetrated the raised voices as he entered the tent without permission, "Do you realize that the entire camp can hear you and your childish rant?"

"What does that matter if they can?" She spat at him. A new target for her overwhelming anger.

"Calk, as he's called, is a low life creature but he is not in any way void of hearing. Hearing your feelings simply gives him ways to manipulate you,"

"Does every single person in the entire world think that I can somehow be manipulated?" Katherine looked shocked at Carey, who frowned, remembering the conversation she had had with Henry, "That creature doesn't mean anything to me in anyway and he certainly, no matter what kind of power he may have, will ever get any other kind of response from me. All I feel right now is hatred, anger and an overwhelming urge to gut him where he stands! Is that understood?"

Katherine was shouting so loud now that Calzar entered the tent in a hurry only to come to a complete stop seeing the scene that had formed. During her rant Katherine had walked right up to Lanell, pulled out the jeweled dagger he had given to her and was now holding it as his throat. Everything had happened so quickly that Lanell did not have a chance to reach for his sheathed sword. It lay motionless at his side as he stood rooted on the spot in shock.

"Kat!" Carey shouted jumping up from the cushions that lay on the floor of the tent, "What are you doing?"

"Is that understood?" Katherine repeated to Lanell, ignoring Carey, in a calmer more dangerous tone. Lanell showed no emotion as he replied slowly.

"Yes, your highness." Katherine stood erect as she back away from him, replacing the dagger in her boot. Lanell bowed and left the tent without another word. Calzar simply remained frozen in shock for the longest moment after the tent entrance became still once more. He started to move his lips as if he wanted to say something but changed his mind. Instead he also bowed and followed after Lanell without so much of a small glance back.

The following day passed without much activity. The appearance of the Katzi in the camp had made the decision to continue onto the haven a shaky one. The risk of danger was increased the longer he remained with them. Another discussion was held in Katherine's tent about their next step.

"We can not take Calk to the haven that much is clear. He would put more than just us at risk if he was somehow to get free," Calzar stated simply as Katherine nodded in agreement.

"I agree, however I don't feel it's a good idea to leave a group here alone with him either. As Carey said even in chains he is dangerous,"

"That is also true. So the question remains what can we do that would be best for everyone?" Carey piped up stating the question everyone was thinking.

"Simple," Lanell stepped into the tent, "We stay together here until we have managed to get all the information out of him we can. Once we do we kill him and leave," he locked eyes with Katherine as he spoke as if offering her the chance to kill the creature herself. She did not back down.

"We have been travelling for almost four days, when it should have only taken us, maybe two at the most to reach this point. We only have another few weeks for word to reach us at the haven. At the rate we have been moving it'll take another five weeks to get there. Whatever we decide must be done quickly. We can't delay in reaching the haven," she emphasized the position in which they have found themselves.

"That, at least, is something we can all agree on," Calzar smiled another humourless grin, "I think it would be best to combine both of your suggestions. Calk will be made to talk and no matter what happens or what he says we must leave this area by the time the sun rises again. Calk dies regardless by this time tomorrow, agreed?" He glanced from each face in turn, as they responded at the same time.

"Agreed,"

"I have only one condition to the plan," Katherine spoke up again before anyone could move, "I wish to have a moment alone with Calk to interrogate him myself. I'm not asking permission from anyone. I was simply stating what I plan to do out of courtesy. This condition will be met," both men took deep breathes in and stared at her. They regarded her young face with concern and anger yet both simply nodded their heads.

"Of course, your highness." Calzar was the one who ended the conversation.

After all the events of the day Katherine was exhausted and slept heavily. However her dreams held nothing like good tidings. For the first time in her life she saw images of a strange world with tall, majestic Elves, short scruffy Dwarves, powerful and frightening Wizards and Witches, and awe inspiring Dragons of all shapes and sizes. She stood on top of the biggest mountain she had ever seen and below her feet she could see a world in which good and evil lived in harmony.

Suddenly a huge war of fire, water, wind and earth raged between each race causing the entire world to die. Her final thoughts were of a single human male with long black hair tied in a long pony tail. He had dark red mysterious eyes and dressed in a light brown ancient ceremonial robe. He had been standing at her right side since the dream began, witnessing all the chaos and devastating scenes that had been displayed with her. Once all the scenes had ended and they stood alone looking down at a ruined wasteland he whispered to her one word.

"Drasio."

She suddenly sat upright in her bed. The thick white sheet that covered her was soaked through with her sweat. After a single moment of confusion her mind became crystal clear. Somehow she knew the Katzi would know the answer to her question. Grabbing her plain light brown clothes and her dagger she left the tent almost running to where she knew the Katzi was being held without being detected.

Turning the left around the last tent at the end of the camp, the small green creature looked up from his curled position on the ground. Had he not been dark green he would have appeared as nothing more than a sleeping man. As he came to a low crouch Katherine could see several bruises and cuts which showed the way the others had tried to obtain the information from him. The same humourless grin as before appeared on his swollen face and he spoke to her.

"I knew you would come to save me," then seeing the dagger in her hand his smile quickly faltered, "I would never harm you. So why do you come to harm me?"

"Do you know the word Drasio?" She spat at him ensuring that she was far enough away from him that he could not reach her with the chains length extended but close enough to kill him if necessary.

"Maybe I do. Maybe I don't. What brings the pretty woman to me with a silly word for?"

"That is none of your business. What is your business is that I have this dagger and that killing you would bring me the greatest pleasure!" She spat at him again showing him the silver blade as she flipped it around in her hand. He simply smiled at her unafraid and started swaying his head a little from side to side. His eyes became closed as he moved as if listening to something in the distance. His eyes came open slowly and the smile was removed from his face as he spoke in a deeper, clear voice.

"My brethren are coming to save me. They should be here soon. Release me and I promise they will not harm you,"

With one pounce Katherine was on top of the creature. Claws and teeth fighting the lighter woman, yet she was no ordinary woman as he thought. Years of horse back riding and training came to her aid and after brief struggle the Katzi lay under her pinned down by her knees on his hands. Katherine suffered a small cut to the left side of her head near her hairline and her shining dagger lay cold against Calk's throat.

During the struggle the entire camp had become alarmed and the voice of the men could be heard approaching from all sides. Calk squealed and squirmed under her, yet she held strong and shouted at him.

"I have no time for games! Tell me the meaning of the word or I'll slice you into little pieces for your brethren to find!" Calzar, Lanell, Magel and Carey came into view with the guards as he started speaking.

"I know the word pretty woman. Nice woman. He will tell you. He will tell you," she pushed harder on the dagger giving him incentive to continue, "Alador. The last dragon. Big. Red. Yellow. Ugly. It is said he tried many times to pass on his magic but failed. Legend speaks that he died in the mountains to the north, not long after the other first races did," he paused for a moment, then seeing the others began shrieking at the top of his lungs.

"Woman is evil! Take her away! She will kill me!" Katherine ignored his screams, pressed harder on the blade and shouted over him.

"Is that all?" He stopped and quickly replied.

"I swear it," Calk blurted out giving nothing further to the others behind her. Without looking behind at them Katherine called out, paying no attention to the creature beneath her.

"Lanell, when does the sunrise?" Shocked at being suddenly addressed it took him a moment to answer.

"About an hour. Maybe less,"

"Has he given you the information you wanted?" She simply stated without breaking eye contact with the creature.

"As much as we could get from him," came the reply.

Katherine smiled a little humourless grin at the green creature that lay still under her. He smirked up at her once more as his eyes rolled backwards slightly revealing the white, then suddenly his voice changed sounding deeper as he spoke.

"The people you care about most in this world will suffer the greatest pain before your journey ends. And all of it will be because of you."

A hatred like nothing she had felt before filled her heart and soul. Katherine was hit by another moment of clarity. It would come down to him or them. Her face became blank with no emotion and her voice lowered to almost a whisper as her face lowered extremely close to his. Speaking in a calm, steady voice she said, "This is for the people I care about." With one swift motion she slit the Katzi's throat from ear to ear.

Everyone stood frozen for the longest moment.

Katherine was the first show life as she pushed away from the dead creature, stood up and walked towards her tent. The blood stained dagger still clenched in her white knuckled right hand. Her light travel gown had several black marks of Calk's blood on it from her swift motion that had killed him.

As she walked passed him, Lanell watched her in utter silence. Her gaze was distant and her features hard. It was an expression Lanell knew all too well. It was the look of pure power, anger, sadness and guilt that only came over someone once they had killed for the first time.

Without being asked Carey followed Katherine to the tent and started gathering water for a bath while she undressed slowly. While she bathed no voices could be heard above a whisper from the rest of the camp. Carey stayed at her side in silence helping to remove the black blood stains off her skin and clothes.

Once Katherine was clean and the water black she pulled her knees towards her chest, wrapped her arms around them and became deathly still. Out of the corner of her eye Carey watched her closely.

As minutes ticked by Katherine remained in the same

position barely breathing. Carey was about to yell at her as loud as she could when suddenly Katherine's shoulders began to shake uncontrollably and large unwanted tears started rolling freely down her cheeks. Carey was instantly by her side sitting on the floor of the tent. While they held each other around the shoulders all the confusion and frustration about earlier events were forgotten as they sat side by side. Finally all the emotions that had been built up over the days since the attack were released.

Neither one of them spoke as time seemed to stand still and Katherine was all cried out.

"Are you feeling any better?" Carey spoke first releasing her hold only slightly.

"Yes, thank you," her response came in a quiet, almost withdrawn way. Finally letting Carey go so she could see her face she continued, "I had a strange dream and needed some answers. I don't know how but I knew only it would have the information. Holding the blade to his throat, I thought of nothing but my hate towards them...then how they were the reason I'm not at home with father...and Lance..." she took a deep breath as the tears threatened to overwhelm her again.

"Kat, you don't need to explain yourself. Especially to me,"

"I know. I just feel like you needed to hear it," her voice sounded like it was on the verge of breaking once more. Her emotions were barely holding as she spoke however her words camt out without any tears managing to fall. Feeling a little better Katherine got out of the now cold tub and dressed quickly. When Carey returned from dumping the water she stated softly.

"The camp is almost ready to leave,"

"Well, I guess we should do the same then. Really Carey I can't thank you enough for being in here with me,"

"What are sisters for?" Carey smiled at her before they embraced again for a moment and then set to sorting out the tent. Not looking forward to seeing the others Katherine insisted on doing most of the inside clearing and packing herself.

Yet the time came all too soon when only the outside needed to be taken down. Stepping outside the tent to finish packing it up Katherine remained silent and avoided eyes with everyone except Carey, who tried to smile reassuringly at her in return.

Once the camp was packed up and ready to go Carey motioned to Lanell to come over. When he reached them it was Katherine who spoke in a firm, serious tone.

"Carey shall be riding with me from here. You can ride with whomever you wish,"

"I would strongly advice against this Katherine. It would be easier on the horses if each woman travelled with another man," he replied hastily focusing on the logical reason to have kept together.

"I appreciate your concern for the horses. However the travelling arrangements will be adjusted according to the will of the Queen of Maltesh, is that understood?" Her voice stayed calm at Lanell's outburst but it held a hint of danger as if she was daring anyone to try and argue with her about what would be best for her camp. Calzar had appeared at her side as soon as the conversation started without being asked as if detecting trouble.

"It shall be done as you wish highness." He stepped in before Lanell could retaliate with another comment. Lanell simply nodded to her slightly without saying another word and walked away towards the other guards.

Carey, who had been silent during the entire exchange, simply looked at Katherine with a surprised yet extremely happy expression. She and Katherine had never been allowed to ride together before. Carey smiled a little feeling like a child who had found a gift that was not to be opened until a specific occasion.

After hearing the brief conversation between Lanell and Katherine no one caused a stir when the time came to leave and Carey was saddled on the horse behind Katherine. Riding in silence was torture to Carey as thousands of questions still lingered in her mind about the events of the morning, however it was only when they stopped for a quick break hours later that she was able to ask them.

"Are you going to tell me why you're making Lanell ride with Carboz?" Katherine took a deep breathe in as if smelling the air.

She knew sooner or later during the day she would need to explain herself, she had just been hoping for more time. Glancing over to where the men were sitting she sighed a little. Sensing her mood was still shaky they had chosen a spot a short distance away. She guessed they were probably speaking about her and what had happened earlier. As she started thinking about Lanell, he glanced over and when he noticed she was looking over towards them he avoided eye contact.

"When Lanell is around me I feel...I feel like I'm somehow being tested in my love for Lance. I can talk to him about everything and not feel embarrassed or ashamed," she paused for a moment to see Carey's reaction, thinking she would be shocked by this news, but instead to her surprise Carey was simply nodding her head.

"You think it's okay for me to feel this way?"

"Yes and no," she replied, "No one is questioning your love but you. You're in love with Lance, we know this, but you're being forced to spend time with Lanell. Lanell, who is a Prince and who has showed you that he is charming, kind and handsome, if you like that sort of man," she chuckled a little, "Any woman in your place would feel torn. You can't think badly about yourself for it,"

"So you understand now that with everything that happened today I needed to be with you on the horse?" Her question sounded more like a plea, hoping she would not need to go into more detail.

"Of course I do. After an event like that everyone wants to share the experience with someone who is close by and no doubt you feel that if you had been sharing a horse with him, instead of me, after this morning it would bring you closer together. And again since you love Lance you don't want that to happen," Katherine smiled slightly for the first time all day.

"Wow, I'm both shocked and glad you understand. You know sometimes I forget you're older than me," she leaned over for a moment, placed her right hand on Carey's left shoulder as she continued, "I honestly don't know what would have happened if you had not been here with me through all this,"

"Now Kat, don't get all sentimental on me. We have to keep these men in check," Carey smiled when Katherine laughed out loud causing the men to glance over at them quickly.

"I know you feel that your love is tested when you speak with Lanell and I know that his father being who he is makes you suspicious of his intentions. Yet how will you know what he is really like you don't give him a chance," she stated in a serious tone. Katherine was shocked at her lack of thought for Lance.

"Of all people to say that I never thought the words would come from you," she replied opened mouthed, "I thought you were the one that couldn't wait for me to admit to Lance that I love him. Why do I need to give Lanell a chance when I have found the one I love?"

"Two reason. One he is right in saying that sooner or later both your parents will be dead and it will be up to you to rule. It would be better to have him as an ally than an enemy. Second and you'll never know how much I hate to say this, but you know as well as I do that Lance may already be dead. And as Lanell is the heir to Buletis, he would make a logical choice as your husband," Carey paused knowing her words may have had a negative effect on Katherine.

A deep emotional expression came over Katherine's face, although her eyes held a look of resolution. She replied slowly with resolution and seriousness in her voice.

"I feel in my heart that Lance is still alive and until I know for certain he's not I'll never falter," her tone held a hint of sadness. A part of her agreed with Carey, he could already dead and yet another part refused to believe it.

Holding on to the faint hope that he had somehow managed to bypass the battle or at least to have survived it was the only thing he had left. She hated the fact that the part of her that believed he was already dead held Lanell in high regard. A thought that at this specific moment that made her physically sick to her stomach.

"Since he was...is my closest friend I appreciate that. Just know that once you know for sure about Lance, Lanell will be waiting for you. I want you to just promise me that if the time comes you give him an honest chance," Carey ended her sentence ensuring that Katherine understood the point she was trying to make. Only with a true chance would they discover whether or not they were meant to be. As much as Carey hated to admit it she also felt that Lance was dead and could see Katherine's attraction to Lanell as he was handsome, charming and intelligent. Yet she too still felt a little suspicious of him.

A month after leaving the palace on that awful night, the emotionally shaken group finally arrived at the swamp. A discussion was in process about which way they should go.

"The fastest way to the haven is straight through but we don't know if the way will be blocked by flooding and that could force us to back track this way. From all accounts it appears that the safest way would be to go around," Katherine stated as she looked down and pointed with her right index finger to the weathered map they had rested on the ground.

They stood at the edge of the swamp. As they had approached the swamp the trees had started to band closer together, as if keeping each other warm, and their top most branches grew thicker than they had ever seen, so no light from the sun could reach them on the path. The closer they had gotten the more animals running around the trees or through the roots.

Before they reached the fork in the road a strange white mist had appeared making it almost impossible to see the way. Even the men seemed uneasy about the place but the women physically shuddered at the thought of going closer. To Katherine the mist seemed to cling to their clothes and steal their breath, causing her to feel as if she was in small box with no visible way out. She would never admit to anyone that she was afraid of a place like this, but almost admitting to herself was unspeakable.

"What's so dangerous about travelling through the swamp?" Lanell asked in a reluctant tone. The guard Michael answered before anyone else could.

"You mean apart from this forsaken mist," a guard close by chuckled in unison as he continued, "There are the vast amounts of marsh land and man-size pits of plant filled watered that can drown you in seconds. Also the poisonous bugs that can kill a grown man with just one bite and the little flying insects that not only bite you but bury themselves under your skin and lay eggs that hatch painfully later," a slight pause came as a deep breath was taken in, "But the worst thing about this place is the Tisna people, if you would call them 'people'. They live in solitude in the mist but are always on the prowl for new flesh to ravage and eat. It is said that they worship the god of lust Tisnameshi and once they ravage the flesh of anyone who enters their domain, the person is offered to the demon Meshi, who it is said lives among them,"

"Ridiculous made up nonsense!" Katherine snapped as everyone in the tent fell silent, "My father travelled through the swamp many times during his life and never once spoke of such a people or any creature,"

"Begging your forgiveness, your highness, but did your father tell you every detail of what he did on all his travels?" Michael the guard, who had spoked up replied harshly before hitting the ground hard. Calzar had stepped forward and punched him on the right side of his jaw line.

"You disrespectful..." he paused realizing that he should not use bad language in front of Katherine, "Get out! I'll deal with you later!" Calzar barked at him half pushing him out of the ten when he stood back up. Calzar turned to face Katherine who was in shock from such a display of violence on her behalf, "My humble apologies highness,"

"I don't now, nor will I ever, hold you responsible for anyone else's actions," she smiled a little at him to ease his nervousness and anger.

Since she had killed the Katzi, none of the men were sure whether or not her pain had died with him or was still on edge. She continued speaking as if nothing had occurred. "Any messenger who is sent to bring news to the haven will not travel through the swamp, they would go around. It may taken them an extra few days but none of them would risk the other road. I see no reason to force us to do any differently at this point. Everyone get some sleep. We start travelling around the swamp in the morning."

The night passed slowly as every small noise kept everyone in the camp awake. The small amount of sleep was matched by the darkness around them and the dark thoughts that continually crept into their minds.

Lance was being beaten. Badly. Staton's voice could be heard over the loud thudding that came each time his fist landed on Lance's naked upper torso.

"Doesn't this bring back the same wonderful memories for you, Lance?"

Thud. Thud.

Staton appeared to be wearing his same black uniform trousers he had been at the ball but he had removed his coat and shirt. He was now wearing nothing but a sleeveless white undergarment, which was now covered in blood. Dark red blood covered Lance's entire body. He had numerous cuts and bruises on his body and parts of his lower thighs, shins and his feet that were visible. His left eyes was swollen so bad that it looked as if it was about to close.

"Go to hell!" Lance spat back at him as Staton paused to wipe his blood soaked hands on his shirt. Lance's breathing was shallow and he spoke like it hurt to even lift his head to do so. A deep evil laugh came to her mind as Staton brought his mouth to Lance's left ear and yelled loudly.

"You and Your Bitch First!"

Thud. Thud. Thud.

Katherine awoke covered in sweat, crying and in an upright position.

The blood. The anger. The sadness.

Had it all been a dream of her worst fear come to life or was he really in trouble?

It had felt so real to her she was not sure. Her heart was still pounding as she relayed it all to Carey, who had woken up hearing her sobbing a little. Large tears filled her eyes as well, as details about the dream came out and by the time Katherine had recalled it all a few had escaped down her cheek.

"But it was just a dream Kat. Like you said, just your worst fear come to life,"

"I know what I said but it felt so real. I could feel every punch...every bruise, like it was happening to me. I could almost reach out and touch him," her breath was caught in her throat as she remembered the brief yet troubling details of the night.

Hearing her sobbing had alerted the guards on duty outside their tent, who without her knowledge, had left quickly and fetched Calzar and Lanell. They entered the tent in a hurry just as Katherine was trying to compose herself.

Calzar quickly surveyed the scene. Katherine's sheets were soaked through with sweat while her face was a mask of utter sadness, her eyes were red from tears and complete heart break. Carey sat beside her with one hand on Katherine's shoulder and the other on her arm, trying to calm her. Her face also held an expression of deep concern. Calzar was immediately at her side next to Carey.

"What happened? Are you all right highness?" He asked hurriedly ensuring that she was not in any danger or physically harmed.

Katherine, who was both shocked and embarrassed that they had come to her because of a dream, was not sure on what to say. However seeing Lanell in her tent made her uneasy. If the dream had been or was in anyway real he would surely know something about it.

"Sorry to cause your distress Calzar, I simply had a bad dream," she mumbled quickly wiping the tears from her stained face. Lanell could tell his presence was causing a problem as her eyes kept shifting from the ground, to him and then back again.

"If that's all I'll just wait outside," he mumbled in response and left quickly. Once he had gone Katherine told Calzar in detail about the dread she had had. To her surprise he seemed concerned.

"Did you see anything around him showing where they may be?" He asked in the same hurried tone. Katherine was shocked by the question and paused for a moment to catch her breath. "Highness, please it is important. Did you see anything that would indicate where they would be?"

"I don't think so," she paused thinking for a moment, "But now looking back there was a faint dripping sound, like water was entering from above. So maybe a cave or dungeon," picturing the scene in her mind again made her stomach turn over. Breathing in deeply for a moment she nodded, "That's all I can get. I'm sorry,"

"I know it may be hard seeing these things, but you must concentrate on the images. We need to find out as much information as possible,"

"But it's just a dream," the worry clear in her tone, "A dream doesn't require concentration! One moment it's there and the next it's forgotten. It was just a dream, wasn't it Calzar?" He seemed to hold his breath for a moment as if afraid of speaking out loud the thoughts that were whizzing around in his head about her.

"You are right that is probably what it was. However we need to be prepared…just in case," he chose his words carefully as he responded.

"What are you saying? I might have seen something that really happened or is happening right now?" She stared at him with her mouth open and held her breath until he nodded slightly confirming her fear, "What? No, that's crazy! How is that even possible? It's just insane!" She yelled at him, expecting him to know every detail.

"I don't know and since we don't know whether it was a dream or something else, I feel we need to be prepared," he explained in a calm manner. Katherine could almost hear her heart as it snapped in two.

What if it had been Lance suffering at the hand of Staton again?

Even if he had been or was there was nothing she could do to save him. She had no home, no army and no idea on where he could even be. Large tears began to fall rapidly down her already red face. From what she had seen he could be dead within days, if not hours, depending on how long Staton wanted to play with him.

Carey had left the tent and had been obtaining water for them, yet seeing that her friend was in more distress had appeared quickly back to her side. Carey held her tightly at her shoulders shook and trembled.

Calzar took his leave of them without either of them noticing. As he was about to close the tent entrance he glanced back at them. He watch them sitting together on Katherine's bed, made up of blankets, holding each other as tightly as they could. With tears rolling down both beautiful faces of the young women he found himself fighting his own emotions that were threatening to overwhelm him.

The morning was gloomy and grey, reflecting the mood of the entire camp. The white mist still held a hint of the darkness that had been present only a few minutes before. The camp had already been packed up and the horses loaded up with their supplies. The swamp was dangerous to a human but for the horse it usually carried no threat, except for the pits filled with water. As the footing was unsure even as they walked around, they could no longer ride and forced to lead the horses around on foot. Like before Katherine and Carey led the way at the front of the group with Calzar, Lanell, Magel and the others right on their tail.

They started to follow the path around the swamp. Carey insisted on wearing her usual attire of light gowns, yet Katherine had decided that the remaining portion of the journey would require a less than lady like approach. She did not know why but she could almost feel trouble heading their way. She could sword fight in her dresses, but they tended to slow her down and cause problems with her foot work.

The Royal tailor, who had been sworn to secrecy at the time, had been given the task of designing training clothes specifically for her. They were shaped in the same way of the men's riding garb, while accommodating her womanly features. She had a pair of fitted trousers made of soft, dark brown leather along with a matching breastplate that fastened on each side and arm guards that were worn over a simple white, long sleeved shirt.

When she left the tent in her training attire no one made a comment, although she could see a few raised eyebrows mixed in with a couple of responsive smiles. Lanell just seemed to be impressed, which caused her to smile widely at him in spite of herself and the events of the evening.

Since they left the camp that morning Lanell had been trying to speak with Katherine, however Carey and herself had found perfectly legitimate reasons to avoid to him. Katherine knew that sooner or later they would speak again, she just wanted to postpone it as long as she could.

The opportunity came towards the end of their first days travel around the left side of the swamp. As the path was muddy, dark and covered in mist it was increasingly difficult to see so travelling had slowed to an almost crawl. Everyone in the company became irritated by the frequent stops, however it gave Lanell the chance he had been waiting for.

On one such stop Lanell handed his horses reins to another guard and was at Katherine's side before she had even considered him trying.

"Katherine, please allow me to speak with you for just a moment," he stated quickly making sure that his statement was said before she could find yet another reason to turn away from him.

"You're welcome to speak to whomever you wish," she replied simply looking over the ground to find the path again.

"I wish to know, why you don't want to continue travelling with me to the haven?" She paused at the section of the floor she was checking, took a deep breath and closed her eyes unsure for a moment on what to say. Standing straight up she came face to face with him.

"I just want you to tell me the truth," his voice was calm and sincere.

"Honestly, I don't know if I can right now," her expression was one with both sorrow and regret.

"I understand more than you think about what happened with the creature," he spoke in a matter of fact tone, "Do you have any idea how much I wanted to kill him myself? After what happened to Buletis and not knowing if my mother is alive or dead...all of us feel the same way. I'm more like you, than you want to believe,"

Katherine was shocked.

She had not thought about how the others would be feeling at all. It never occurred to her that seeing her over the Katzi with a knife to his throat had caused them to secretly begin cheering for her or that they had been happy that she had killed him herself.

"I'm sorry that I didn't ask you or the others how you felt about everything," she replied in almost a whisper.

"I know you're as upset, angry and frustrated as I am about this whole thing but I also know you are hiding your feelings from me on purpose. I understand that my father being who he is doesn't make you trust me. In fact I know it has the opposite effect on most people, but I still standby what I said by the camp fire that night. I'm honoured to be your friend, even if you don't trust me with your feelings," he spoke in a serious yet honest tone and Katherine had no idea what to say.

It was as if he knew her feelings on the whole matter. It sounded so close that he could have been listening to her conversation with Carey, a fact which did not help her in trusting him at all.

"I'm glad you feel that way Lanell. I will remain your friend, as I said before, however that doesn't mean that I need to share all my feelings with you," she responded simply leaving no hint of emotion.

"I thought that friends shared their feelings so they don't need to suffer alone," his reply was given along with a small smile. Katherine smiled a little at his stubbornness. He was in many ways like Lance.

"You think that every friend you have in your life should know all the thoughts and feelings you have? Only old, true, close friends ever receive that privilege. It takes time to build that kind of relationship, I hope you remember that." Lanell seemed on the verge of replying to her when Katherine quickly grabbed her horses reins from Carey and started walking in the continued direction of the path that just became clear once more.

The path started to turn right heading around the swamp, however still being so close to it caused the effect to be felt as they walked. The mist and a faint chill seemed to follow the group as they travelled. Once in a while the sun appeared briefly, which made Katherine smile if only for a moment. It gave Katherine a tiny sense of hope that everything would work out in the end, but when the thick mist would again plunge them into darkness, a dark shadow crept back into her heart.

The darkness grew and wrapped around her soul, threatening to drown her she could only hope she would come out on top in the end. Secretly the darkness told her that this few weeks had been nothing and the worst in her life were still to come.

The first night next to the swamp passed slowly as each small sound that was heard caused every person in the camp to place a hand on their weapons, even if it turned out to be only for a few seconds.

Katherine had been outraged at having her new authority challenged by Calzar. They had been setting up camp for the night when he insisted on placing the tents as close to each other as possible and stated calmly that guards would be placed outside the women's tent entrance each night until they reached the haven from then onward.

It had taken both Lanell and Carey to calm her down to the point that she could see the reasoning and not resist Calzar on the matter, even if she was not thrilled with the idea. Lanell had requested to be the first watch, making her certain he simply wished to speak with her again.

She had been right. Shortly after the tent torches were extinguished he asked to talk to her for a moment.

"I thought that putting out the torches meant we are supposed to be sleeping," she replied grumpily as she pulled the blankets up from her feet and wrapped up in them snugly. Her pale yellow night gown and leggings made certain she was not cold as they slept outside and out in the wilderness it was still improper to have a man see you in your night wear if he was not either your brother, lover or husband.

"Well, come in," she huffed, "What do you want Lanell?"

"I wanted to ask you something. It may be something that you get upset about, but I really want to see…to know what your answer would be," she sat up straighter in her blanket bed slightly intrigued.

"Ask me anything you want, although I'm not sure what you mean about my reaction," he walked close to her and sat down on one of the stools that surrounded the small table in her tent. He seemed on the verge of speaking for many moments, seemingly uncomfortable about what he had to say. Finally he spoke in a rushed explosion of words.

"Did Henry ever speak with you about becoming my wife?"

"No, should he have?" Her reply was sharp and shocked.

"Before we left to come to your palace I told you that I had been training non stop. Well, one night I managed to sneak away from my trainer so I could rest, but on my way to my cot I passed by my father's council room. I thought my heart would stop when I heard his voice...I thought he had me. The door had been left slightly ajar and I overheard him say my name. After a few minutes I realized that he was dictating a letter to Henry and he was...asking for consent to marry the two heirs so we could become one kingdom,"

"What?" She snapped back loudly. She was overwhelmed with this information. Her heart belonged only to Lance and she would simply refuse anyone else but him, "He never spoke of it to me I assure you. Do you know if Staton ever received a reply?" Her curiosity wondered whether or not her father would have agreed without speaking with her about it.

"Unfortunately I don't know if he did not or not. A week later we were heading to Maltesh and nothing was mentioned to me before he left me there. I was just wondering...out of my own curiosity really...if he had spoken to you about it, what do you think you would have said?" She sat still for a moment trying to gather her thoughts. After a short while she found her voice.

"I think I would have been furious. I hadn't even met you before the feast and even though I wasn't sure I loved Lance then, I certainly wouldn't have wanted to marry someone I hadn't even seen or gotten to know. I would've needed to at least know someone before I could have considered that," she paused and then continued, "With that being said I know now that I love Lance with all my heart and soul and nothing will ever change that fact,"

"I know that you have feelings for him, Katherine, and I'm in no way trying to disminish that. I'm simply saying that if you were not in love with him or if, the gods forbid, he were dead, would you ever even consider me as a potential husband?" He spoke quietly ensuring that the entire sentence was said before he caught his breath. He could not look her in the eyes as the words left his lips. Katherine seemed shocked by his manner. It was not like Lanell to act so unsure of himself. After another moment to think she sat closer to him looked directly into his eyes and spoke calmly.

"Yes, I would however let me be very clear about this," she added in a serious tone after seeing his eyes light up at her answer, "My answer is based on two things that I'm sure will never happen before myself and Lance are already married. I'm now and always will be in love with Lance so there will never be a time when I'm not. Dead or alive. Should he die for some reason either before or after we're married I wouldn't marry anyone else for a very long time to honour him, is that understood?" He seemed emotionless save for a disappointed expression in his eyes.

"I understand completely Katherine. Thank you for allowing me to speak with you so late. I appreciate your honesty with me," she smiled at him as he stood and turned to leave. At the last moment she called out.

"Good night my friend," smiling as he glanced back he replied.

"Good night."

Carey remained silent in her bed on the ground near Katherine's pretending to be sleeping as they spoke. Now that Lanell was leaving she was ready to talk to Katherine, however before she could speak they heard loud noises from the camp. They were jumping up out of the covers quickly and heading for the tent entrance.

REVELATIONS

Staring out of the tent entry way both women were shocked at what they saw. Each of them guards were being attacked by what appeared to be small, very hairy children with sharp teeth, wearing nothing but rags. Katherine was about to say something when one of them turned and stared directly at her.

The child was not human at all.

It had slightly pointed ears with no lops, skin with a brown red colour hint, bright yellow animal eyes and wore nothing save for a small piece of material that was wrapped around its waist to cover its gender. It carried a small axe made from what appeared to be a tree branch and a small chiseled rock.

The creature snarled loudly at her as she slowly bent down and drew her dagger from a small pocket hidden under her nightclothes, then with a glance of surprise the creature hesitated and suddenly covered its face with its small clawed hands.

Katherine noticed at that same moment Carey had appeared stepping into the camp fire. As Carey did not carry a weapon she was reaching for a log that was slightly ablaze to help fight off the creatures. From the expression on its face and its black hair Katherine thought that it had never seen anyone with blonde hair before, and maybe was surprised to find such a person in their camp. Lanell was close by fighting another creature and since he had a similar colour to her Katherine dismissed the theory.

The creature seemed bewitched by her. First it could not turn its eyes away after he removed his hands form his eyes to make sure she was still there, then it dropped the axe like weapon and at the very last moment it fell to its knees mumbling something that sounded like a chant of some kind.

Katherine had been so intrigued by the creature's actions that she had not noticed the fighting around their tent had ceased and that many of the creatures had begun copying the first, right in front of her and Carey. Lanell slowly came over to stand by Katherine's side, his sword still drawn.

"Do you know what they are?" She asked as he approached.

"No, do you?"

"They are the Tisna I told you about," Michael stated over hearing them speaking, "They are calling thanks to their god for delivering them such a beautiful creatures," he indicated towards Carey who suddenly realized it was not Katherine they were staring at. She dropped the log and moved backwards a little trying to hide from them, yet as she did so some of them mumbled. To Katherine their expressions were almost concerned, as if they were worried something was going to happen to her.

Katherine had an idea. Speaking in almost a whisper she motioned to Carey.

"Say something to them,"

"Like what?"

"I don't know anything. They seemed to be focusing on you. Say something to make them go away or find out what they are doing here,"

"We is come to kell bad ones in arr swamp," they all jumped back like they had been struck. The small creature who had spotted Carey first had stood up and started speaking directly to Katherine as if he had done so all along. His speech was thick with accent yet understandable if you listened close enough.

"You can understand us?" She asked surprised.

"Is dark one," it replied nodding in a male, matter of fact, tone.

"Dark one? Why do you call me that?"

"Yarr wave is dark thus are carred dark one," it pointed to

her dark curly hair. She thought it was odd that they were calling her by the colour of her hair but then she had never heard anything about these creatures before.

"What is your name?" She inquired

"I is Taza," his tone proud as he held his chin higher than previously.

"Why do you stare at me?" Carey found her voice and it came out scared and serious.

"Pees forgives, oh Golden one. We is no thinking that yar would be coming hiss way and wit suc peoples," his voice turned nervous at being addressed by Carey directly and was able to reply without keeping eye contact with her for too long. The way the Tisna said Golden One caused everyone in the camp to shiver. It was said in such a kind and tender way that it obviously meant something more to them than just her straight blonde locks.

"Just who do you think I am?" Carey asked rather hoping for no answer.

"Yarr the bless head Golden one. Princessa this well save us from da Meshi," his tone seemed to gain in strength and power by uttering the words out loud, yet spoke the demons name in a hushed voice as if it could hear him, "Is know, when yarr well faces the demon and is wenning. We is being frees by um you so we cans live wif no more servis to im,"

Carey smiled nervously at the creatures, unsure as to what to say in response. They expected her to face a demon and win so they can live a life free of service. Michael had spoken the truth. They were slaves to another creature. However she was no warrior and could not face anyone in a fight with or without a weapon. Katherine thought quickly in her silence.

"Good Tisna, the Golden One would be honoured to fulfil her destiny with your people as it was foretold, but first she must travel with us to help another people. It will take only a few weeks and she promises, faithful Tisna, that she will return as quickly as the wind," the creatures seemed to pause for a moment taking in everything that she had said. After a moment of mumbling between themselves Taza stepped forward again.

"Truth Golden One?"

"Yes, the dark one speaks the truth," Carey replied out loud understanding that Katherine was trying to ensure they stayed away from her.

"Hen we shell eave yarr to yarr journeyings. May Tisnameshi protectings yarr Golden One," he stated seriously. Muttering another one word to the others they all gathered up their fallen weapons, their dead and proceeded to leave the camp.

"What was that all about?" Carey uttered out loud still shocked by the whole nights events as they entered the tent once more.

"I'm not sure exactly but it didn't sound like something we want to get involved in," Lanell stated simply having followed them inside.

"I agree," Carey laughed, "I mean me fighting a demon. Can you imagine it? I'm certainly glad you spoke up Kat. I had no idea what to say. Thank you,"

"Well, I couldn't very well have them carrying you off to fight a demon without me, could I?" Katherine chuckled a little as Lanell wished them both a good night and left the tent as they slipped into their beds once more. Katherine smiled at Carey as they laid down although an uneasy feeling had come over her, giving her the sense that this was far from over.

Taza who had spoken directly to the women glanced back at the camp as his group settled back down for the night. He was not convinced by Katherine's words.

Despite the evenings events Carey feel to sleep quickly and slept hard, so much so that she did not hear Katherine leave fully dressed in her training clothes some short hours later. She strolled over towards the men, all of whom had decided to keep watch. Walking up boldly behind Lanell caused him to turn suddenly with his sword drawn in his right hand. Seeing it was just Katherine as she raised her hands up showing it was just her, he quickly lowered his weapon and smiled a little.

"I thought you were sleeping?"

"Can you sleep knowing that strange little creatures could be watching the camp as we speak?"

"Not really, but then I'm trained not too. What's your excuse?"

"I don't know. I just have this weird feeling that some things going to happen. Feelings like that make it hard to sleep,"

"I second that. Ever since our encounter with the Tisna I've had that same feeling," he agreed in a serious tone glancing around uneasy at their surroundings.

At night the mist seemed to get thicker and along with the sounds of the small animals scurrying in and out of the murky water holes or scratching the bark on the nearby trees made everyone in the camp anxious.

Before the Tisna had appeared no one in the group had been afraid of what could happen on the way around the swamp or confident enough that they were prepared for anything that it truly shook them to the core. Now the tension in the camp was at the highest it had been since the Katzi had been killed.

Katherine and Lanell had been talking for a while about the journey and the road ahead of the group, when loud rustling noises were heard in the dense, dark green bushes close to the left side of their camp site. Instantly Katherine, Lanell and the two guards on watch closet to the bushes were on their feet.

Lanell pulled out his broadsword to his left, while Katherine pulled out her dagger that he had given her. As one they started walking in the direction of the sounds. As they got closer the noise increased causing each person to be fully focused on the bush and what lay on the other side.

Katherine closely followed Lanell, a few steps, when her stomach lurched causing her to come to a complete stop, while the men continued towards the bushes. It was the feeling she got when something bad was about to happen, yet it had never been this strong before. Knowing her feelings were usually right she called out to Lanell and began running as fast as she could back towards her own tent.

Reaching the tent entrance her mouth fell open and the dagger feel from her now shaking right hand. Carey's cot was empty and her blankets were scattered on the floor along with her pillow, which bore a small patch of blood, where her head had been. A large, jagged cut in the back wall of the tent indicated that she had been taken from right under their noses while they had been distracted by the other sounds.

"Carey!" She screamed loudly, running towards the tear as she swept the dagger from the ground and her short sword that lay to one side of her cot. Lanell, Calzar and the guards appeared instantly at the tent entrance just as Katherine was seen running through the large opening in the back.

"Katherine no!" Lanell shouted after her as he tried to give chase.

Katherine ran into the darkness.

The thick mist quickly swallowed up the light of the camp and there was hardly any path from the broken twigs and damp leaves to see at the speed she was running, but she refused to slow even the smallest amount. She had already lost her father and possibly Lance, she would not lose Carey too.

Her anger, fear and determination kept her running as fast as she could after the large amount of small, childlike tracks she could barely see. As she ran her thoughts were flooded with possibilities. It made sense that in order for them to take Carey away the Tisna had relied on their knowledge of the swamp and mass numbers.

Her clothes were wet from the mist and her face bruised as wide thick vines whipped her while she ran passed them. She lost track of time running and her hope of finding Carey began to fade with each minute. It was then she saw a light a little further ahead passed some bushes and thick grass. Her speed decreased until she was almost strolling at a slow pace.

A slower pace enabled her to see small child like foot prints along the ground and a large patch of grass ahead that was trampled. She crept closer to the light trying to stay hidden behind the bushes when she heard Carey scream loudly.

Katherine's pace quickened until she came to the thick bush she heard the cry come from. The closer she came to the bush the more she could now hear chanting and Carey's loud voice calling out for help in between whimpering. Swallowing hard and taking a deep breath she pushed back a small portion of the branches to see a bizarre scene laid out before her.

There was a well trodden, winding path leading from the thick grass to her right down a steep incline towards what appeared to be hundreds of small round mounds that were coming up out of the ground. She could tell that the mounds had been there for a while as each one was covered in centuries worth of moss, grass and overgrown weeds. Each one had no windows but only the Tisna were busy coming and going through a tiny dark opening in the front of them. She assumed that these were where they lived because they appeared to be afraid of the large building on her left side.

This building was definitely out of place in the middle of a swamp. To Katherine its design seemed way too advanced for these primitive people and she had no delusions that they had any hand in making it, except to move the giant stones. No water or plant life grew within fifty feet of it so the walls still looked clean and crisp with a slight tint of light brown colour.

The walls were high and straight in a box shape and angled corners. Katherine did not blame the Tisna for being afraid of it as the large stone sculpture sitting on top was just terrifying. It looked to be a creature with a deformed lizard like figure, and huge claws that seemed to grip the top of the building. The monstrous status appeared to have more than five heads from what Katherine could see from her position and each one held an expression of hunger and rage. The teeth on each head seemed to have been made specifically larger than necessary to emphasize the danger and threat that caused the Tisna to obey without question.

In between the small huts and the large building was a huge dark hole in the ground, above which she saw Carey. Carey was being dangled over the huge pit by a system of wheels and a group of about fifteen Tisna standing close to the large building, all of which did not look comfortable there. Carey and the pit were around one hundred feet almost directly below the bush Katherine was hiding behind.

As each Tisna left their underground dwelling they gazed at the large building with fear for a brief moment and then joined the others. There were hundreds of Tisna surrounding the pit in a semi-circle by the time she took in everything. All of them were chanting and swaying as they had done outside the ladies tent earlier that evening. It was then that Katherine noticed that each mound and the building faced the pit, even though they were on opposite sides.

The contents of the hole could not been seen and Carey's hand and feet were bound together leaving her helpless. Katherine could see a small patch of blood on her left temple indicating that they hit her while she slept just hard enough that she would not alert anyone to the fact that she was being taken.

Tears ran down her face freely as she hung in the air. Her white cotton nightgown had been made thick similar to Katherine's to ensure it would help keep them warm during cold evenings. Katherine was relieved to see that it was not damaged, except for some dirt and ragged edges showing that she had been carried, dragged and then pushed to the edge of the pit before being tied up and hung over it. At the moment Carey was no longer shouting for help but sobbing both in fear and pain. Happy to find that she was at least still alive Katherine took a few moments to plan her next move.

Katherine had been sitting silently for only about a one minute or two trying to work out a way to save Carey when she heard a noise over the chanting coming from the thick grass behind her, up the path from where she had come from. Staying completely still, her short sword poised for action in her right hand while her left palm tightened its grip on her small dagger.

The sound came steadily closer yet Katherine was sure

that only she had heard anything as the chanting was beginning to get louder and increase in rhythm. For a moment everything around her, except the chanting seemed to stop and take in a breath until Lanell came into view. Katherine cursed under her breath. Seeing her he came walking slowly towards where she was kneeling closer to the ground still slightly hidden behind a bush. She was furious and whispered in an angry tone.

"What the hell are you doing here? I almost killed you!"

"What did you think I was going to do? Just let you run out of the camp and get yourself killed or caught," he replied simply taking up a position next to her. Viewing the scene quickly he continued speaking, "Four against, at least a hundred or two...hm, that doesn't seem to be good odds,"

"Four? What four?" As if Lanell speaking had delivered them straight to her, Calzar and Michael approached from the same direction he had just moments before.

"Well, its nice to see you gentlemen decided to come and back me up, but its not the Tisna I've got a bad feeling about. It's that dark pit and what they said the Golden One was supposed to do. Take a look at that statue," while the men glanced over her shoulder. Katherine's eyes could not leave the darkness that beckoned at Carey's feet.

Something was waiting, for what she did not know but whatever it could be Carey was about to be sent down to it.

"What I don't understand is how she is expected to fight something without any weapons?" She whispered curiously. Calzar spoke up in a hurried tone.

"Michael, you heard stories of these things before. Do you know anything about the prophecy they mentioned?"

"No, just what I told you already that they offer people up to a demon," his response was regrettable as his eyes glanced for a moment towards the large stone statue behind them.

"We have to do something. Any second they are going to send her into that pit to face whatever is in it. What can we do?" She asked in desperation.

Just as they began to discuss their options and a possible

rescue using a diversion, an ear splitting scream echoed around them. Looking through the bushes at Carey, Katherine gasped as she watched her being lowered slowly into the dark pit. Her legs were swaying back and forth quickly as she started struggling against the rope that bound her captive. Katherine admired her fighting spirit.

Suddenly the Tisna stopped their chanting and the only noises that could be heard were from Carey struggling and the wheels squeaking as she continued to be lowered. After a few seconds of silence an enormous roaring sound shook everything in sight.

Everyone, Tisna and human alike, froze where they were.

Katherine's throat constricted making it hard for her to breathe. Carey's screaming resumed with more vigor than before, the terror clear in her voice as the darkness reached her knees and crept higher the more the darkness engulfed her. A calming voice spoke in Katherine's mind, much to her surprise.

"*Drasio.*"

Instantly her mind was clear and she knew what she had to do. Katherine leaped up, backed up a little, ran to the edge and jumped high onto the rope and Carey, who was almost entirely covered in the blackness. She had been so fast and unexpected that none of the men or Tisna had time to react.

Lanell, Calzar and Michael could only watch in horror as both the women vanished into the darkness. Katherine holding tightly to Carey around her hands and midriff, who had been made silent by seeing her almost sister come to her aid. The men stayed in their hidden seated position unsure as to what to do next when Lanell nodded smiling a little.

"It make sense now. The prophecy!" The others looked at him blankly, "The Golden One. They said that she would kill the demon, but it didn't say how. What if the Golden One was not supposed to kill it herself, but to bring the person here that could? It would still make the prophecy true. She would still have been the reason the creature was killed," after a moment of silence Calzar nodded slowly. Michael still seemed confused yet smiled weakly.

"So what do we do?" Michael asked in an anxious voice. Lanell smirked a little.

"Calzar, you know Katherine better than I do. Nothing on this world will be able to stop her from rescuing Cary, not even a demon. She'll ne back and when she returns we'll be waiting for her,"

"You're right but may I suggest we move somewhere else before these things come to their senses," Calzar replied as the Tisna began to stir and mumble in concerned tones, "I would also recommend that we move the entire camp since these little fellows know where were are. I don't want to wake up in the morning to find we are all following the women down that hole tied up,"

"Sounds good to me." Michael semi-smiled, uneasy about the amount of activity coming from below them. Indicating to keep low and out of sight Calzar was the first to move out, closely followed by Michael who was happy to get away. Lanell could not help but take one last glance towards the black hole below them. He could only hope that he was right and that he would see them again. Though his concern surprised him as it wondered about one of the women above the other and not the one he expected.

Carey swallowed hard a few times. The ropes had started burning her wrists and ankles the moment she had begun struggling and now that Katherine was along for the ride she felt sure either the rope or her body would break. Through all the pain of the situation Carey could not help but feel a tiny bit of relief. She had known as soon as her eyes had opened to being surrounded by Tisna and tied to the rope that Katherine would come.

She also felt guilty about her pleasure of having Katherine with her. She would never wish any harm to come to Katherine and even though she was happy at having help, a part of her wished that one of the men had jumped so she would have been spared. Katherine took one last look at the torch lit ground as the darkness washed over them speaking in a whisper close to Carey's ear.

"As soon as we hit the ground I'll move away from you and search the immediate area. We don't want to be surprised." Katherine was listening to the changers in the air as she tried to use the rope above Carey's hands to relieve some of her weight off Carey.

Something big was moving and although she could not quite tell in which direction. She was sure it was heading towards them. The rope jolted a little as their descent began to increase and four small lights appeared below them.

The space beneath them was square and had a torch on each wall, one behind them, one in front, one on the right and one on the left. Even though they were still high up Katherine's eyes darted from light to light trying to see anything moving in the darkness behind them. All her senses screamed at her that something was hiding just behind her vision where the light could not reach, simply waiting for its prey to reach the ground. Slowly yet surely the dark brown colour of the ground beneath them grew bigger and after what felt like days Carey's feet touched the soft dirt.

Immediately after hitting the floor Katherine jumped away from Carey relieving some of her pain and check each corner for danger. The cave they landed in was small, around five feet in width, with only the opening they have come down through as the ceiling. Katherine noticed that it had three tunnels leading deeper into underground. One to the left, one to the right and one directly in front of them. Each was only big enough for a man to walk through and it seemed that the torch to their back was intended to be taken with them as it was the only one that could be removed. The appearance of the tunnels did make Katherine relax a little as any creature that could enter them would be small enough to kill easily. However walking through one of them she did not know what they would face.

"What do you think is down here?" Carey whispered as Katherine started cutting her loose.

"I have a few guesses but I think its best not to dwell on that. Let's just see if we can find a way out of this place," Katherine replied quietly, "Hopefully before we meet whatever lives down here," she added a few minutes of silence mumbling more to herself than Carey.

Once the rope went slack as she was set free Carey rubbed her wrists, which had become red, swollen and bleeding in a few places from her struggling. The Tisna must have noticed the weight was gone as they immediately retracted the rope and as the women watched it disappear into the darkness above them their decision was clear.

"I guess the only way out is through there," Katherine pointed to the tunnels.

"So which one should we take?" Carey asked standing next to her before the three archways. Katherine was silent for a moment.

"Left is for love strong that will last for an age, right is for riches beyond imagination and forward is for honour is all things,"

"What?" Carey voice curious.

"It's something I remember my father telling me. When I was choosing my room in the palace I was faced with the three final doors of the royal quarters and he said that when you are faced with a choice that is three fold this little rhyme will help you see the right path for you,"

"So which door did you choose?"

"I was a selfish child that thought of nothing but myself. Of course I chose the door on the right," she admitted sadly.

"You're no longer that child or selfish," Carey replied smiling at her. Katherine's eyes focused on the tunnel in front of them as she answered.

"Nor will I make that same mistake. We go this way."

The left tunnel was full of jagged rocks that stuck out from every angle on the walls, where as the ground was soft, dark brown soil on which Carey could easily walk through without hurting her pale bare feet. Katherine led the way with her short sword drawn in her right hand, even though she knew in close quarters, like the tunnel, it would be useless. Her entire body knew they were not alone and the only light they had between them was the torch that Carey had taken from the cave opening. The dark shadows that led the way in front of them did not ease Katherine's mind.

Suddenly Katherine paused raising her left fist over her shoulder indicating silence. She could of sworn she had heard a loud deep sigh coming from the tunnel they were in and it was not too much further ahead of them. Signaling to Carey, Katherine silently indicated that she was going to scout ahead and that Carey was to stay as far back as possible until she figured out what they were up against.

Creeping slowly forward slightly crouched towards the ground a little Katherine took a few steps closer to the sound. As she approached the place where the noise had been heard the tunnel came to an end.

Katherine found she was staring at the biggest cavern she had ever seen. Always one for exploring in the forest when she was able to lose her old maid, Mary, she had discovered several small caves with pools, which were made from drops of water that trickled down the walls once it rained. Each cave had both excited and worried her at the time as they could be dangerous, yet at that moment she just felt numb with awe.

She could not estimate the size of the cave she now stood in, as most of it was black, yet from the way the smallest sound echoed she predicted it was bigger than the entire palace. The portion that was lit up from the torches was immense. There were huge columns that spanned the distance between the darkness of the ground below and up above Katherine's head towards the ceiling of the cave.

Immediately at her feet was a crude stairway cut right from the stone of the cave. She almost called back to Carey to bring the light when her eyes adjusted and she could see more of the way down. The stairs seemed to hug the right side of the cave wall and a torch every fifty feet or so showed the way. Walking a little towards the end of the path in front of her, Katherine could see nothing but darkness over the edge. Seeing an opportunity she kicked a small stone lightly over the edge and tried to listen to see how far down it went. She counted slowly as it fell.

One. Two. Three. Four. Thud.

Katherine knew that anything over a one count was unreachable without rope and would cause serious injury or death should you fall. Most wells in the kingdom had been made only one count deep as they had lost children before. Katherine could not help but shiver knowing that their lives depended on the stability of the stairs to her right. After a moment to calm herself Katherine started to descend slowly.

Being no longer protected by the walls of the tunnel she was extremely cautious by double testing each stop before entrusting her entire weight to it and hugged close to the wall away from the edge. Carey had just appeared at the tunnel exit as Katherine had gone down about four steps when they both froze in place.

"You would leave a defenseless woman behind while you try to kill me. That is humourous. You know nothing about me, yet I know everything about you," the voice was male and deep but it echoed loudly, almost like it came from everywhere. Katherine quickly scanned the cavern seeking the owner, however even with the mass amount of torches leading the way down the steps they only thing she saw was herself and Carey. Snapping back at him she yelled loudly.

"You know nothing creature. The Golden One has come to kill you as the prophecy foretold,"

"Perhaps," he seemed amused, "Although you should give your dagger to Carey then, unless she had another weapon hidden under her nightgown somewhere. Either way I would not leave her alone for even a moment in this place. The Tisna do not know that more than one creature lives in this cursed place,"

Katherine was confused and shocked for only an instant at the creature knowing Carey's name, then a second later, she was signaling to her to come closer. Carey did not need to be told twice. In a heartbeat she was running as quickly as possible to be beside her sister. She was running so fast in fact that she almost knocked Katherine to the floor as she came grinding to a halt one step behind her.

"Sorry Kat," Carey spoke in a whisper closer to her ear, holding onto one of her shoulders to steady her.

"A nickname for Katherine? I was under the impression that servants called their masters by their title or highness. Have things changed so much?"

"Carey is not my servant. She is my sister in all but blood," she snapped back. Hatred and confusion towards the creature growing each second.

How did it know their names?

Why was it hiding and why was it speaking to them as they carried on walking down the stone steps together quickly?

The silence wrapped around them menacingly as they continued walking and finally reached the bottom step. More torches were lit up showing a crude path through the bottom of the cavern. This did not give them the comfort they had been hoping for. The new vast amount of light they now had showed bones of other humans and creatures littering the ground in every direction.

The torches that Katherine had seem from higher on the steps were a lot brighter, however they also made numerous and bigger shadows giving the creature many places it could be hiding in. A faint sound of water dripping could be heard in the distance somewhere to their left. As they stood huddled together with the steps behind them, Carey's eyes started to well up with tears. She could not stop her eyes from seeing all the torn, ripped clothing, piles of dirty and gnawed on bones of those who had come before them. The path laid out in front of them with torches on each side appeared to be made from skulls and the smell that now invaded their noses was nauseating.

"I can't walk on those," Carey gasped a little, "I'm not as strong as you Kat,"

"That is why you were chosen Katherine," the creature spoke once more causing them both to gasp and rush to the hard rock wall to their right, pressing their back into it as much as they could.

"What are you talking about?" She replied angrily. Her tone both suspicious and scared while her eyes still glanced quickly around every corner and into every shadow. Grabbing Carey's hand forcefully they started walking on the path of the skulls, making their way further away from the stone steps and the other bones.

"You really think that Carey was meant to kill me? She is an ordinary woman with no skills for fighting. She was taken as the Golden One to bring you to me. Your love for her made the prophecy come true as you risked everything, including your own life to save hers,"

Katherine was more confused. As the male spoke his voice seemed excited, not scared or arrogant about killing them. Standing on the spot for a moment she replied loudly.

"Your voice betrays you. I can tell you wish to die,"

"Die? Every creature dies. It is a part of life and nothing to be denied or feared. Yet you know me better than you think Katherine. I am Alador," at that word her heart stopped. The last dragon that was thought to be dead for hundreds of years, was alive and in that very cave.

Impossible.

"You lie! We know that he died centuries ago," she shouted back at him as fear gripped her soul.

Would she have to fight a demon that could appear as a dragon?

Suddenly the ground began to shake and groan as something large started to move towards them, then a flash of light shone so brightly that it caused both the women to cover their eyes with their forearms. After a few seconds the light dimmed, yet Katherine's breath would not come.

A tall figure appeared from behind a rock formation to their left. Before her stood the same man from her dream. Had the same long black ponytail and dark red eyes, he even wore the same light brown ceremonial robe.

"You!" She exclaimed, "It was you in my dream,"

"Yes, it was me. I was not sure that I had been successful. I had almost given up on you coming,"

"Are you really Alador? The last dragon?" He nodded smiling at them both, "How are you looking like that? I thought dragons were big with teeth,"

"I thought a large dragon in your dream may have been too much for you. I took this form as you see me now to ease your mind about me wanting to eat you," he chuckled a little, almost to himself as if the idea of eating her was utterly ridiculous.

"I'm so confused," Carey stated out loud looking at the handsome man and Katherine in turn.

"Do not worry Golden One, I will explain everything. Well, as much as I can," he simply stated as he turned and began walking away from them off the lit up path.

"Where are you going? The path is that way," she pointed as torches ahead on the path about two hundred feet away from them seemed to be blown out by a rush of wind from somewhere.

"You cannot leave this place that way. It is a trap for everyone who is sent as a sacrifice," he turned briefly to face them before continuing, "Would you like to speak in my private quarters with warm food and drinks or stay talking in here with them?" He pointed to many holes that were high up the side of the cave wall to their left. Katherine had been so focused on the lit path she had not even noticed them before. It was then she realized it was meant to have that effect.

The openings were large, shaped like a circle but rough around the edges giving the appearance of a pentagon. Suddenly a long, dark green, scaly snout started emerging from one of the holes near the top. It was closely followed by a forked tongue that was flicking in and out of a large mouth and showed several rows of razor sharp teeth.

As the creature got closer to the hole entrance long, thin and jagged claws could be seen coming out by each of its sides, creating a terrible scraping noise as it did so on the rock walls. Standing still in shock they continued to stare as a large oval shaped green head with a large fin at the very top and small beady little black eyes that were fixed on the two women.

"We're coming with you." Katherine stated as she quickly grabbed Carey and hurried after the human formed dragon, who had quickened his pace away from the holes as soon as he had pointed them out.

They ran after Alador as quickly as they could trying to catch up. The green creature's roar could be heard behind them along with a rush of air as large wings took to the roof of the cave. A loud flapping noise sounded from above as Alador turned left into a small opening and stood in the entrance to help Katherine and Carey through.

Only moments after he came through himself a loud thud shook the small tunnel they now found themselves in. The sounds of claws against stone were heard behind them as they turned their backs to it and followed him. They were in a small tunnel, very similar to the one which had led them to the cavern. Alador grabbed a torch seemingly out of nowhere and passed each of the women who were still catching their breath from running. After travelling a short distance they seemed to go downward and the small tunnel opened up into a large candle lit cavern. The cavern was huge, but small when compared to the one they had previously left.

Katherine was not sure what she expected from a dragons lair but human sized furniture had never even crossed her mind. A large wooden table and four chairs were in the center of the room. Looking passed the table they could see a four poster bed, small side tables on each side, candle holders with pure white candles in them and a medium sized wardrobe.

They had been so fascinated by the human sized things that it took them an extra moment to notice all the shining gold and jewels that filled the rest of the cavern. There were mounts of them everywhere, even smaller piles hidden closely to the human furniture. Only one pile seemed to be different and it was shaped into what appeared to be a bird nest, except this one was much, much bigger.

Their thoughts were interrupted as more clawing noises came from the tunnel entrance and the darkness that now filled it. Katherine spoke up first in a worried tone.

"Can that creature come through?"

"He will continue to try until you leave," he simply stated waving her question away like he was squatting a fly.

"So we're going to be leaving here then? I mean you're not going to kill us, right?" Carey asked in an almost relieve ton. Smiling slightly at Katherine he replied.

"That would depend on her,"

"Me? Why does that depend on me? It wasn't our fault that we came here. I'm not planning on hurting anyone, unless I have too,"

"We will get to that. For the moment we need to discuss the past," waving his hand slightly at the table a range of hot and cold food appeared on three sets of the silver plates that were laid out. Sweet aromas reached their noses and their mouths began to water at the feast before them. Roast pig, potatoes, steaming vegetables and a smoking liquid coming from the silver goblets that smelled divine.

"Please sit down ladies. Eat with me and everything will be explained," they all sat down and Alador sat at the head of the table with his back towards the tunnel opening.

Katherine seated herself between him and Carey as she was still weary of him. It was hard to shake off the feeling that she would still need to protect her. Both women were weary from lack of sleep and hunger since they had gone to sleep many hours before. They glanced at the amount of food laid out in front of them with excitement, yet neither of them lifted a hand to touch anything.

"Please be assured ladies that nothing you see before you in tainted," as he spoke he lifted his goblet, took a deep long drink and started cutting up the food on his plate.

"At least you understand our reluctance to trust you," Carey spoke up bodly, "Until today I had never heard of you, but it seems that you two are already friends,"

"I never said he was my friend," Katherine snapped back, being still on edge.

"Proper friendship and understanding take time. Unfortunately those are both luxuries, I am afraid, we will not have time for. With that in mind I have chosen understanding as in the coming battle you will need it," he spoke sadly looking down at his plate without moving for a moment.

"Battle? What coming battle? We just barely escaped an attack on Maltesh. What I want to know is why dragons are more than legends now? What happened and why are you hiding down here?" Katherine was both upset and shocked that another fight would be coming their way.

"Unfortunately the attack on your home was just the beginning or the middle depending on your view of time. Some of my history I will explain but I think in order to explain the coming events you must understand your destiny, which is far greater than ruler of a kingdom. Some of what I am about to tell you will cause high emotions, however I need you to remember that everything I say is the truth. Nothing you do now will be able to erase the past or the words I speak. Are you ready to hear what you must?"

"Yes," they both chanted together. Katherine and Carey were both intrigued about what he was going to say, yet Katherine was also scared. She was not exactly sure she wanted to know what her destiny was or how it could be greater than ruling a kingdom.

"First of all allow me to ease some of your comfort child," he walked over to Carey slowly so as not to alarm her, then waving his right hand over her head, hands and feet she appeared to be healed from the rope marks.

"Better?" He asked kindly.

"Much, thank you," she smiled a little back at him.

"Now," he walked back to his seat, "I should explain to Carey about your dream as she will not understand fully if I simply elaborate. Katherine dreamt of the past when she first saw me and not just a few months or even years before now. She saw the world as it was at the time of the beginning. It was a completely different world than what you know. This one was full of ancient creatures. Elves, Dwarfs, Wizards, Witches and Dragons. In the beginning all was perfect with good and evil living in harmony, however like so many things it was not to last. Eventually it came to an end,"

"The races started to know of greed, selfishness and the lust of power to rule over others. This caused the Desolation War. The war raged between each race for centuries causing the destruction and final devastation of the entire world. As the world became nothing short of vast deserts and marshland, humans came from another world though why it was never known, though most thought it was the will of the Gods as our punishment,"

"For ruining our world it would be taken from us and given to the humans to rule over. However as they were to be doom they seemed to also be the survival of each race as long as each could breed with this new race of begins. Sadly, this revelation caused even more hatred and resentments between them,"

"Some like the Wizards and Witches were extremely successful while others failed at every turn. It was not really surprising that the Witches and Wizards were one of the most successful as they, in fact, closely resembled humans in both appearance and manners before the breeding began. It is from them that we now have the Magi,"

"Magi? They are real?" Carey asked in a gasp.

"You can sit here with a mighty dragon and not realize that each story from your childhood is based, some parts at least, in fact,"

"Yes, but men and women who have enough power to move mountains...that's a little hard to come to terms with. Where are they now? If they are so powerful, why do we not hear about them?"

"Allow me to continue with the story and I will explain," he took a deep breath and continued, "Other races, such as Dwarfs and even the Elves were not as lucky. Some births showed great potential, possessing great power that was used for good, others created beings like the Katzi, who only wish to dominate the entire world,"

"When the Dwarfs and Elves discovered that their good hearted offspring, the Leludians and Carvians, may not survive in the new world they decided to leave. Thus leaving them to their fate. The Witches and Wizards, even with success eventually left the new world after coming to the knowledge that they no longer belonged here, but their offspring did," he paused for a moment glancing over the two women. Carey was completely taken in by his words, while Katherine held a gaze of interest yet was reserving her judgement for the punch line.

"We, Dragons, decided on a different approach. We had become rogues. Travelling alone and only coming in contact with each other for either blood or attempting to breed amongst our own kind. Because of this, it seemed that our race was doomed to fade out of existence. In the end all it would take was time,"

"Contrary to common myths or beliefs of others, Dragons can die of old age. However with a natural life span of hundreds upon hundreds of years it is not commonly known. Most were sought out and killed by a rather new group of humans before their time," Alador appeared distress as he spoke about the dragons being killed but did not elaborate.

"Finally after many, many years I heard through the birds and forest creatures that I was the last of my kind, so I started the rumour of my own death to stop the knights of the human race from coming to claim my hind. After a century or so I found a cave closer to your home, Katherine, in the northern mountains thinking that I was doomed to die there alone. I had accepted my fate and was waiting for death to claim me when I received a visitor," he paused again as a glazed expression quickly passed over his face as he remembered. Breathing deeply he continued.

"At that time our existence had become legend and many people worshipped dragon imagines. We were thought of highly, so much so that I had placed one such image outside the cave entrance where I lived saying it was the last place a dragon was known to have lived. People would come from miles around with offerings of fruits, nuts and livestock so my spirit could help make their lives run smoothly. They asked for guidance, good fortune, good harvesting, good weather and sometimes help with their relationships," he took a few long deep swallows of his drink before he spoke again.

"Honestly after a few hundred years I stopped listening and did not pay much attention to their worries. I would wait until they had left the area before leaving the cave and eating what they had brought for me. Yet even now I still remember every detail of the day she came…"

*****

It had been raining for almost three days straight and since most people stayed away from the caves during those times I slept to conserve energy. But even in my deep slumber and through the sound of the quiet ran that filled the morning air, I heard tiny footsteps running towards the cave entrance.

They did not slow as they entered the cave, then in almost a whisper deep mournful sobbing began to echo around me. I got curious and sneaked closer to the man sized dragon statue that stood at the cave entrance. As I looked down I saw a beautiful young woman sitting on a rock close to the statue crying into her hands. She had a slightly rounded face, long straight dark blonde hair and wide shoulders. She was wearing a soaked through dark, blue dress with a thin shawl pulled around her shoulders. After centuries of silence I instantly felt in my soul that I had to speak with her. I needed to heal the heart that broke in her chest each time she cried. So I did.

"Please tell me what is wrong?" My voice calm and echoed around the cave.

"Who said that?" The woman asked in a terrified voice looking into every shadow. Her voice sounded sweet yet she seemed to speak like a person from two places.

"Do not be afraid. I cannot hurt you as I am simply the spirit of the dragon that died in this cave many years ago," she glanced at the statue with a look of concern and I heard her heart rate increase, but she kept her voice calm.

"Forgive me spirit. I didn't know of your resting place I was simply trying to find shelter from the rain,"

"I will forgive you as long as you allow me to comfort you. Pray, tell me. Why does someone as beautiful as you have so much hurt in her heart?"

"I was betrayed by my family," she began to sob once more and my cold heart broke for her. After a few moment she gathered herself together enough to explain, "I'm from far away and was coming here to study this wonderful culture, but I overheard a discussion this very morning between the King and Queen saying that I'm to be married to the Prince in less than three days,"

"And you believe that your parents sent you to this place for the union?" My question came out as sad as I felt for her.

"I don't believe I know. I heard the Queen say she was disgusted with my parents for not telling me why I was really being sent here,"

"After hearing this news, you left the palace and found yourself caught in the rain. This cave is a nice place to rest while you collect your thoughts about this union," I was uncomfortable with the prospect of this woman marrying someone else, yet at the time I could not understand why.

"I was not sure what else to do. I can't run away for I have no money and can't face my parents again knowing they caused this,"

"What of marrying this man?"

"I'm not sure I'm ready to be wed. Least of all to a man I have only seen twice during dinner since I arrived a few weeks ago,"

"Begin a dragon I would not know much about the troubles of marriage so I would not be able to be of help to you. However I can offer a friendship from one lonely spirit to another," she smiled for the first time since her arrival and my heart soared.

Her teeth shone brightly and her entire face seemed to light up the world. It was in that moment that I had a strange thought. I was in love, and with a human of all races. With this news came terrible feelings of jealousy, hatred and sorrow as I knew that I could not interfere with her relationship or risk being hunted once more.

Yet as my heart sank, she picked it back up by promising to visit me often. And she kept her word. Five days later she came again telling me, her new friend, all about her beautiful wedding day and her new husband.

"Are you there my friend?" She called out sweetly and I could see her smiling widely and her face lighting up as she did so.

"Yes beloved, I am here,"

"You were right about everything but I'm sure that you knew you would be. I spoke honestly with him before we were wed as you suggested. He is so kind and understanding just as you said he would be. We were wed as planning although I'm still unsure if I love him,"

"Love does not always happen when we expect it to. Let your heart guide you and you will not falter," she smiled towards the inside of the cave and though she could not see me I returned it.

"Thank you my friend."

My heart ached to tell her the truth. To touch her, to hold her, to kiss her. But each time my feelings came, a warning entered my soul keeping me in the shadows. Every two days after that she came to see me without fail, no matter the weather. Never once did she bring anyone else with her.

For years I watched her grow older and yet she had never spoken of children. Finally after her wedding had been many winters passed I asked her when a child would be expected and her reply broke my heart into pieces.

"Each night for these many years we have embraced, but still I sit before you without a child. My husband loves and cares for me as I do for him, but I fear I will lose him if I don't have a child soon. With his parents now dead those seven years ago he has wished for an heir to be born to rule in his stead,"

"How do you feel about a child of your own?"

"I would willing die for a child of my own. Someone to care for, to cherish and to love without question," I sat silently for a moment before replying to her.

"Fear not beloved. I am able to grant you, one wish. On one condition,"

"Name it?" She pleaded.

"Should anything threaten you before the child is born, you will come to me at once without hesitation, and do I have your word?"

"My dearest friend, grant me this one wish and I will forever be your slave and will come to you whenever you have need of me. I will forever be in your debt."

That night when her husband lay sleeping she came to me at the cave and was placed into a deep sleep. She never recalled the events of the remaining hours and once she arrived back at the palace early that morning she was with child. She waited many days before informing the King that she was at long last going to bear a child, yet unexpectedly the King was furious.

He claimed that another man had tainted her as they had not conceived for all the years before. She begged and pleaded with him that the child would be his but he would not listen. It was then she told the King that if he did not accept the child, the she could do nothing but leave. It was on that day, a few days later, that she came to me. Her world falling apart because of the gift I had given to her.

"I am sorry for this terrible gift I have given to you," I pleaded for forgiveness.

"Be not sorry for his anger. It is to be expected. I can feel great power in the child growing inside of me and I will not allow her to be harmed in anyway,"

"Her? How do you know it is a female?"

"I do not pretend to know how but I'm certain." She replied smiling.

We spoke for hours as I tried to calm her emotions. She returned to the palace reluctantly that evening to fulfil her promise of leaving and the King sick with heart break. The thought that she would leave, taking the child that was part of her caused him more grief than he had realized and upon her return begged for forgiveness, just as I had done for my gift.

She gladly accepted and continued to visit me every few days all the while the child grew inside of her. She rejoiced in telling me everything that had happened with the unborn and that her husband had felt her move inside the stomach causing more love to be poured out towards her.

One evening months later she came to visit me again with an expression of pure sadness on her face. She sat in her usual spot completely silent, not even greeting me for what seemed like a life time so I spoke first.

"Beloved, what causes you so much grief?"

"I'm afraid I will not be able to come and see you every day as I once promised, my dear friend," I felt panic in my heart.

"Why? What has happened?"

"I now know that this birth will end my life, but I feel that she will grow to be an old woman with grandchildren of her own,"

"Are you not afraid to die?"

"I once said that I would die for a child of my own and I was afraid. Then I received comfort from my only true friend, whom I shall never forget. I never told him that I would die. I promised myself I wouldn't until the end was near,"

"Are you saying that you are close to death dear one?"

"She is strong and will come in the next few days. At the time she arrives I will die but don't feel sad for me. I know I go to a better place full of peacefulness, happiness and unconditional love. I come to you tonight, my friend, to say goodbye," my heart was crushed, however in my soul I knew my gift would be her death. It was in that moment I told her the truth about her friend and her reaction was not the one I could have predicted.

"Thank you for your honesty, my dearest friend. But I must also confess I knew all along you were not what you seemed,"

"All this time you never once spoke of it," I was bewildered.

"I immediately understood, why you wanted to keep your existence a secret. You are now and will always be my greatest friend in the world. I would like to ask one request, before I leave,"

"What would you wish of me?"

"To see you in your true form."

I did not have to debate at all if I would grant her request. I finally came out of the shadows for just a moment in my great form for her and her alone to see. Her smile once again made my heart sing. She did not cower away from me or run, she simply remained seated smiling up at me. We both had tears in our eyes as she spoke.

"My friend is truly a great thing to behold." At that she stood, turned and left without saying another word.

***

"A few days later word reached me that a healthy baby girl, had been born but my beloved friend had died as she foresaw she would," tears began welling up in his red eyes as he recalled the day he received the news of his beloved passing away. He glanced over at the two women who were both crying silently. After a few moment of silence the women gathered themselves together.

"It's a sad but lovely story. I just don't understand why you're telling this to us?"

"Katherine," her name was spoken so sweetly it was a shock, "Did you not think anything about the story was similar to your own? The woman, my dearest friend, came from a faraway land and died giving birth to a daughter,"

"Wait? What are you saying?"

"My beloved's name was Arianna De Manshena,"

"You lie!" Katherine jumped out of her seat bringing up her sword instantly level with his throat as tears began rolling down her face. Alador did not flinch, move or lose eye contact with her.

"Remember my words child. I have told you nothing but the truth and nothing you do now will change the past,"

"I don't understand," Carey asked quickly standing between them, "Who was she?"

Katherine took deep breaths to calm herself before finally lowering her sword She sat back down hard fighting back large tears that rolled freely down her face.

"Father couldn't pronounce it so he nicknamed her Anna for short. The whole story was about...my mother," Carey had only ever heard the Queen be called Anna so it was a surprise to hear that her name had been changed and no one outside the palace had known.

"Oh Kat," Carey was instantly by her side with her right arm around her.

My mother.

Katherine could not comprehend the fact that the memories she had just heard about were about her mother. She had been beautiful, just like she had thought from the pictures in the palace, yet she seemed to be a wonderful person on the inside as well.

"It was not only about her but about you as well. Now you know why you were treated differently. Why you had the dream about the past with me. It is also why you are here now with Carey. You are a human with Dragon heritage and the only person who can save your world from the same destruction that killed ours," it was then a sudden realization struck her.

"You're my father," she mumbled out loud, almost to herself, "Did father, I mean, Henry know?"

"Yes, from what I was able to find out moments before her death, your mother told him everything about me, except my true form, as she knew telling him all may have caused harm to me or worse to you,"

"He knew...the whole time, that I wasn't really his daughter and yet he never loved me any less than one,"

"He was a great father and King. He will be missed by more than just his kingdom,"

"Are you saying that he is dead then?" Katherine spoke lookgin at him with tears continuously rolling down her crimson cheeks. Alador moved his eyes betraying his feelings, "Though nothing is for certain I fear you will never again touch his hand while he lives. He fell during a huge explosion at the hands of the Katzi several weeks ago,"

"How do you know that?" Carey asked.

"It is one of my many gifts. I can see the past, present and some future events. Just as you have come to see as well," he gestured at Katherine, who had turned to look at the table once more.

"What are you talking about? I don't see anything,"

"The visions are different for every being that experiences them, but it seems your manifest as dreams," she took in a quick breath as she realized what he was saying.

"Lance!" She gasped shaking her head briskly from side to side. She would not, could not, believe it had been real.

"Your instincts grow strong. Yes, I speak of the vision you had involving the man you have fallen in love with," hearing the words Katherine could not raise her head to see his saddened eyes. However Carey spoke up boldly.

"And how did you know about that?"

"I have to admit that I was planning to visit you, child,

in your dream some way to help you come here, yet when I attempted to do so the vision began to appear. Curious as to what your first vision would be about I watched with you, experiencing all the same sensations,"

"You saw?" Katherine gasped out loud again. Her gut twisting, causing her physical pain from the emotion and thoughts as she saw the images in head once more.

"Is there anything you can do for him?" Carey asked hopefully as Katherine could not yet speak. Alador shook his head slowly.

"I sincerely wish I could but my time on this world grows short. However his fate as yours, mine, Carey as well as all the other worlds in the heaven, rest with you beloved,"

"I'll do anything to save his life and the people I love," she stated turning her emotions quickly inward, into hatred and anger once more.

"Even though I have only known you a short while, I understand this about you already. But it may prove more difficult than you think. What if his life means sacrificing your own?"

"Then I would give it," she wore an expression of pure determination.

"Do not be too hasty to answer my beloved. There are indeed worse fates than simple death,"

"Do you know what will happen to him?" Carey's voice emotional as well.

"No, the future is unpredictable as our choices dictate the path we take. This can make the future unclear or if once clear it can shift. I can however see some hard choices are in both of your futures. And you my beloved, your choices will depict not only your own life, but everything on this world as well."

Katherine took a deep breath.

In the past few weeks she had lost her home, her father, her new found love, discovered a new friend or potential enemy, killed for the first time, found out who her real father is and in turn what she is. Now it seemed that she was somehow going to have the fate of the world in her hands. Her mind raced with thousands of questions and emotions.

"Surely, this is too much for one person to bare." She thought to herself.

Gathering herself together as best as she could she glanced around the huge room again. Eventually her eyes rested on the mighty dragon in human form sitting close by. She was tempted to speak but really did not know what to say or where to start. Before she could form words Alador spoke to both of them in a calm, soft tone.

"I understand more than you know. You have dealt with many things the last few weeks, more than anyone should have to shoulder. Please take rest. You will be safe here. I will keep watch while you sleep." He indicated with the sweeping of his left hand towards the bed a few feet away. In that same moment Katherine and Carey both suddenly realized that they were exhausted from having been up all night.

They decided without saying anything out loud that they would rest for the night here with him. Taking the same bed they settled in for the night wearing the same clothes they had on. Katherine paused for a moment to take off her shoes and looking over to her left at Carey, saw she was instantly sleeping beside her. Before she could close her eyes Alador was sitting on the edge of the bed close by.

"I am sorry you had to find out about me this way. After everything you have experienced over the course of these few weeks you will probably have trouble getting to sleep. I can help with that. If you wish," he seemed unsure of himself and Katherine could not help but feel sorry for him. He had lost his beloved and gained a daughter that had not known about him.

"I'm not sure how you could,"

"Magic, of course. I am a dragon," he smiled a little.

"Honestly I haven't slept well since we left the kingdom. Anything that you think might help," she smiled back at him. It was hard for her to imagine that this man was really a dragon, but even more so her father. Alador spoke in a voice that seemed to grow softer with each word.

"Once you awaken you will feel refreshed and ready to face the darkness ahead. Sleep deeply my beloved, and dream of nothing but love and happiness." With a slight wave of his right hand over her face the world went dark, as Katherine feel instantly sound sleep.

Carey rode a beautiful horse through a wide open field. Reaching a small brook at the edge of a dark forest she took rest and let the horse drink to its heart content. Dismounting Carey turned her back to the trees and stared in awe at the kingdom in the distance and the rising sun. Her beautiful blue gown moving slightly in the breeze beside the only white rose in the entire field. Suddenly the horse screamed and fell to the ground hard spraying blood all over the yellow flowers that were all around her. Her eyes bulged in horror as she turned and saw something moving quickly towards her. Before she had time to react a creature was on top of her ripping her clothes down the arms and legs. She screamed loudly as blood splattered over the white blooming flower.

"Carey!" Katherine was instantly awake sitting upright shouting with all her might.

Looking over to her right hand side she saw Carey and Alador were seated at two of the three places that were set at the table. They had been eating breakfast when she had shouted. Without being asked or requesting permission to leave the seat Carey was immediately running to be by her side.

"I'm right here Kat. What's the matter?" She took several deep breaths and refused to meet Alador's gaze as she responded.

"Nothing, just concerned you weren't next to me," Carey did not completely believe her, yet quickly dismissed it. She knew all to well that it would not be easy to get the truth from her. Alador, of course, knew it had been something else. When Carey strolled back to her seat after a few moments he appeared by Katherine's side.

"Another vision my beloved," it was more of a statement than a question or allegation, yet she could do nothing except nod, not wanting to say what she had seen. However her eyes betrayed her by the pained expression she had glancing over at Carey.

"If she is in danger you should warn her,"

"No, it would only worry her further," she explained while moving her feet out from under the covers and leaving them hanging down over the right side of the bed.

"You should know that not all the visions you see will come to pass,"

"How can I tell which ones will and which will not?"

"You cannot,"

"Why do we have them if we can't do anything about what it is we see?" Katherine raised her voice at him in frustration. Both the images of Lance and Carey forced themselves into her memory.

"They are to help you in the coming battle. Knowing how the enemy will try to manipulate you will help you fight him,"

"You're saying that the people I care about will be targets for them to get to me?" As she grew louder Carey left the table and was again standing close by.

"Did you, yourself, not study warfare? It is the only logical choice that they will be used against you. You said to me not hours ago that you would give your own life for theirs without thoughts,"

"You said 'him' just now. Do you know what enemy we'll be fighting?" Carey inquired seeing that Katherine was trying to come to terms with the fact all the people she loved could be a target, including herself.

"Very little, but I know his name. He is called Barberus,"

"And you know what else?" Carey continued.

"After all my years of searching very little," his head hung down disappointed in himself, "Once I found out about your powers I knew that sooner or later an enemy would arise to claim you. At first I was content as I knew only a few people knew of your true nature, then I heard rumors of a dark force that was set on world domination and destroying everything in its path. From what I heard he had a part to play in the battle of BloodHene but Henry protected you. You may not remember but you had power long before your first vision,"

"What?" She could not help but yell loudly, standing up again, "What are you talking about? I would have known,"

"Not if everyone who witnessed it had been sworn to secrecy or death," he simply stated.

"Wait, you're saying that people saw her use power, like real magic, and no one said anything?" Carey remarked curiously as Katherine seemed on the verge of screaming.

"When you were almost five years old I was visited in the same cave your mother came to, by some servants of Henry's palace. There had been an incident that had caused many of the staff to come running to my hiding place with offerings or protection, both for you and themselves. From what I heard there had been a quiet dinner with Henry, his counsel members and you. Everything was going great until the end of the meal. Suddenly objects, such as candle sticks and plates, lifted off whatever surfaces they were on by themselves and started swirling around the room. There was a shock, screaming and running from the room. Everyone was in a panic, but when the King glanced over at you instinctively for protection you were sleeping. As soon as he grabbed you, waking you, the objects stopped flying and fell with a loud crash to the ground,"

Katherine lowered herself back down to the bed slowly trying to take in each word he muttered.

"It was you. You caused the magic. You had been dreaming and being so young with no idea of your true potential were channeling it into your reality. The servants and all those present witnessed the objects stop when you awoke. They all knew in that moment that something was different about you, although most made up their own stories,"

"So what happened?" Carey asked the question that Katherine could not bring herself to to.

"Once everyone had calmed down the King called a meeting in which, every person who had seen your gifts were told never to speak of them or die. Only some knew you were different from birth, others witnessed that day the truth, but most do not realize to this day how truly special you are. I now know that Barberus somehow discovered what happened that night and wants to use your power to take over this world and countless others,"

"That is utterly ridiculous," Katherine blurted out, "I've never been able to move anything and I only just now started having visions,"

"Really?" He could not help but smile at her, "Have you ever woken to find things in your room out of place? Have you ever gone to sleep with your quarters tidy and clean, only to wake up to a complete mess?" Katherine was lost for words. As he said the words several occasions sprang to mind where those exact things had happened.

"Would you like to try it now beloved?"

"What do you mean?"

"I am thirsty. Without moving passed me my goblet please?" The large grin on Alador's face was starting to annoy Katherine, yet she was intrigued.

"So what do I do just say come?" Katherine was half joking and thrust out her right hand towards the goblet as she said the word Come. To both her and Carey's surprise the cup immediately lifted off the table and began floating a little shakily towards him. After a few moments he was holding it in his hands smiling.

"Kat," Carey had a huge smile on her face, "That was amazing,"

"How?" She was looking at her hand like she had never before seen it.

"It is not the word but the thought," he explained, "You wished the cup to come to me and it did. And if I say so, extremely steady for someone who had never consciously done so before. When discovering magic and power it is usually by accident when the person feels threatened or in love. Since you have never used your power it is extremely powerful, but unstable and may be released at the wrong times. You must learn to control it and to do so you will find the Magi,"

"Where do we find them?"

"They live in a hidden city to the north-east. A place called Mantagoria. Though I feel you will not reach them in time. Barberus is already searching for you and I fear with you travelling with little protection away from the kingdom, it may be his opportunity to obtain you,"

"But after all this time, why now? Do you think he just found out about her?" Carey wondered out loud again.

"Who cares? This meeting is over. We are out of here once I've eaten," Katherine stood up pushing passed Alador and seated herself at the table. She did not meet either gaze as she began putting food onto her plate in a hurry. She was excited about having powers, yet scared that someone could take control of them but using her friends.

"I cannot say why he is choosing now to strike, but I know it will be soon," Aladan answered Carey's question, then spoke louder looking directly at Katherine. "I know how hard this is for you, my beloved, but you must understand. You are in great danger, even more so now you have discovered some of what you can do,"

Katherine almost choked on the food she had begun chewing as his words cut deeply into her heart. Placed the bread back onto her plate and swallowing she turned once more to face him. Taking a few deep breaths to calm her emotions her tone was clear and angry.

"You just told me to use my powers?"

"So you could see what you can do? See the truth,"

"You just said that now I've discovered them..."

"He does not care if you are an apprentice or master with your gifts. He simply wishes to use you to obtain what he wants. I know this is hard for you, but nothing I have said can be taken back. It is the truth,"

"You don't know anything! In the past weeks I've lost everything. My father. My love and my entire life. And while you sit there telling me that regardless of what I see or how powerful I'm to become I can't prevent anything bad from happening to the ones I love, Lance is being beaten, probably to death. And now since all of this can't possibly be enough for one person to deal with, someone called Barberus knows of my existence and wants to use me to dominate the entire world. Somehow I doubt very much that you know what I have to deal with or how hard it is for me to resist the urge to simply crawl back under those covers and stay there for the rest of my natural days!" She shouted at him as her voice cracked with emotion in places.

"How could he know her feelings? A dragon he may be, but even if he could read minds, no one would understand her pain and strife." She thought to herself.

"Listen to me closely, both of you, with each passing moment my time here grows short. You have great strength that will help you in the events to come. To help your friends in the coming days you need to learn true, real deep true courage and the most important thing. To love through all hardships, not matter how heart breaking they seem to be,"

"What do you mean by your time grows short?" Carey asked quietly giving Katherine time to calm down.

"A dragon is cursed by knowing when their life will end,"

"You're dying?" Katherine stated in an almost sorry tone, "Are you not well?"

"No, as I said dragons will rarely die from illness or old age. You need not worry yourself about me. I have lived longer than most of my race and have been granted my one wish,"

"What was that?" Katherine asked almost holding her breath.

"I only ever wanted one wish for myself. To see you before with my mine own two eyes. It may be vanity of being around humans for thousands of years but I am so very proud of you. I know you will be a great leader, a wonderful wife and in the future a power beyond any I have known, which is more than we could have ever prayed for. Were your mother here in this moment I know she would feel the same way. Speaking of which," Alador seemed to produce, out of nowhere, a piece of bron cloth, which contained a necklace.

The cord was simple, made of what appeared to be twine and the center was a small stone about the size of a fingernail, which was bright white with swirls of black woven intricately. It was the simplest necklace she had ever seen, yet it was also the most beautiful.

"This is a gift from your mother that she left in my possession. Should you feel lost or sad just rub it slightly and you will be comforted. It does contain power but none that will work for anyone, except you," he softly placed the cord over her head so it lay flat against her chest.

"Kat, your mother." tears of sorrow and joy ran down both the women's faces.

After a moment or two of silence a faint scratching noise started to be heard, like an echo, from the tunnel they had entered through the day before.

"What is that?" Carey asked as they were pulled from the place of happiness and thrown back into a place of uncertainty.

"That is the sound of the prophecy regarding the Golden One coming to pass. My death and your freedom," he simply stated smiling a little towards the tunnel.

"The creature from the tunnel, is trying to get in here?" Katherine walked closer to the entrance and placed a hand on the right side of the tunnel opening feeling the vibrations.

"They have waited a long time and this time the Meshi shall succeed,"

"They? What do you mean them? We only saw one," Carey replied as her breathing and words came faster. She took many deliberate steps away from the entrance.

"How many of them are there?" Katherine's voice came quickly feeling the increasing force being used on the rocks with each passing second. Carey looked towards the black opening and muttered.

"It sounds like hundreds,"

"Not that many child, yet enough to wreak havoc on the world should they get released from here. From what I can tell only fifteen remain from the fifty that were here when I first came. Did you not see the other holes? They travel in flocks and depending on their food source they have been known to turn on each other. From the lack of sacrifices the Tisna have had the past few decades the original flock has decreased dramatically,"

"There are fifteen of those creatures waiting outside in the cavern?"

"Trying to get in, not get us out," he replied simply. Sounds of flapping wings, scraping claws, breaking rocks and screeching could be heard growing louder and louder.

"What did you mean by if they get released?" She exclaimed in a horrified tone.

"The Meshi are creatures from ages past. Their existence spans more life times than even my own. They come from a time when hunting was the only thing worth doing. They would hunt for sport, not just to feed, and when that happened the very ground opened up under their nest. The mightiest world shake there has ever been swallowed their entire race deep into the ground never to reappear," Aladorpulled Katherine away from the tunnel entrance gently by turning her to face him.

"After all my years of living I am saddened that we did not have more time together. But I must tell you one more thing before you go. The past few weeks have been harder on you than any you have known, up to this point in your life. Remember that this war will not be over quickly. People will be hurt and some even killed, yet believe in yourself and the people you love and nothing will stand in your way,"

"Alador!" Carey whimpered hearing the noises continuing to increase in volume and sounding closer and closer.

"You, you must go now. I have packed some provisions

for you in these packs," he handed them each a brown, cloth back pack and a matching cloak that seemed to appear out of nowhere, "These cloaks were made by the Leludians a long time ago and given to a dragon that helped them rebuild their homes after a most dreadful tragedy. They will help you in the weeks to come,"

"How are we going to get out of here?" Carey pulled on the cloak quickly following Katherine's example while trembling in fear. She glanced at the tunnel entrance they had come through praying they would not need to go back the same way.

"There is another way but we must hurry," he lead them quickly through the high piles of gold to the far back, left hand side of the cave where a small breeze could be felt.

"Once they break through the archway, this doorway will open but it will only be so for a few minutes. You must run and do not look back once it does. Katherine, do you understand?" His expression was so full of sorrow as they stared into each other's eyes. Even though they had just met, he could sense her need to protect him and the loathing she felt as she had to watch yet another door close behind her with a father on the other side.

"Yes, I understand," she replied.

"Wait, I thought that I was meant to kill you. Not that I would," Carey inquired hoping she could not need to stay to fight with him.

"No, the prophecy stated that the Golden One's coming would slay the demons but it did not say specifically that it was by your own hand," Carey seemed upset until he continued saying, "Your coming here symbolizes a great deal more than just my death. It signifies a new beginning. Katherine's. A hard and treacherous road lies ahead of you, both, which in turn will bring you enemies and friends," looked at each of them in turn carrying a look of pride and sorrow, "I do not know how long I will be able to keep the door open, but I will hold as long as I can,"

"We can help you," she insisted pulling her sword up as

Carey added another suggestion.

"Can't you just come with us and pretend to be human?"

"Your maternal instinct to protect me little ones is heartwarming to an old soul such as I, but if you were to stay it would surely be your end as well as mine. That is a risk I will not take," his eyes glanced over Katherine carrying a hint of underlining menace that left no question. She would not win this argument.

"How can this be?" She wailed suddenly as the selfish child she had once been, "I just found you and now I'm expected to just walk away...again...leave you to die in this place...alone?"

"It is my time. My destiny,"

"I can't lose you too," a silent tear crested over her eyelashes, escaping down her cheek as she remembered Henry. Alador cupped her face in his warm hands, kindly and spoke in such a calming manner she could not help but feel comforted, even though the words he said brought a warning.

"We shall both be with you, to guide you in the trails to come. Our bodies may die and fade into nothing, as everything does, but you shall always be guided by those you love and who love you in return,"

"I can't lose you yet," she begged almost alarmed by his tone of urgency, "I still have so many questions,"

"Alas the time for questions has come to an end. It is time for you both to leave, to be free and save the world from evil and darkness."

Everyone froze as loud cracking sounds could be heard coming from the other side of the cavern. Without seeing it, they could all feel the wall around the tunnel entrance starting to give way from the large amount of pressure on the other side. Large chunk of rock crashed loudly to the ground, some even bouncing and hitting objects close by causing rock on gold sounds. Each passing second caused the cracks to become larger and the terrifying shrieking hurting their ears. The more spaces appeared in the rock the more Katherine realized she would have to continued wanting. Alador had been right. There was not enough time for everything that needed to be said.

"Father," she asked quietly unable to hold his gaze as the words left her suddenly dry mouthed, "May I ask one last wish before we leave?"

"You do not need to ask it my beloved. I have already predicted what you would want and I am prepared. It is my honor to share it with you both."

For a moment the air stilled.

The loud noises and ground trembling from the tunnel faded into the distance as a brilliant red light suddenly filled the cavern. It was so bright the women were forced to hold their arms over their eyes for a brief second.

When the light finally dimmed a large shadow was cast over them. Glancing slowly upwards a huge, dark red dragon stood towering above the high piles of gold. Every inch of him sparkled as he moved as thousands of gold coins were reflected onto apart so they could see a deep black color complementing his other beautiful shades.

Small spikes trimmed his face around the eyes and down the nose slightly and his long face, smiled showing the shine extended to his dark red eyes. Both women were speechless but before either of them could speak aloud, a thunderous cracking sound snapped them all back to the lurking danger.

"Father, you truly are a sight to behold," she smiled as a single tear rolled down her face. Looking over at Carey, who was also crying Katherine could see even though she was extremely emotional about the situation she held her head high in respect to the mighty dragon.

"*The door will open soon. Stay here and leave when it does. I love you now and forever, beloved and I will speak to you again, when the time is right.*" He spoke in their minds as the large figure turned carefully to face the tunnel. His long spiked tail waving high above their heads as he appeared to lower his head so it was level with the tunnel opening. A sudden roar and blast of hot air rushed towards the women and they both realized at the same time that Aladon had blown fire into the opening entrance to slow the Meshi's progress.

It was not enough.

Within minutes the cracking and banging resumed louder than before, as if they had been more enraged by the death and destruction of Aladors fire. Finally there came a thundering crash and a large ball of dust covered the entire cave. For the briefest span of time the world stood still and silent, then once the dust had settled Alador roared with so much might and power that the entire cave shook.

As Katherine and Carey were looking up at his figure a sudden warm breeze was felt on their backs. Turning they saw a stone man sized doorway had opened where they had previously felt the slight breeze. Looking through a distant sunrise could be seen beckoning them.

"*Go now!*" Alador yelled in their minds, snapping them out of their daydream.

They quickly ran out of the doorway. Katherine could not resist glancing back for a moment as the floor shook and a loud screeching could be heard answering the attack call of Alador. She could see flashes of red under a mass amount of dark green claws, wings and teeth as the Meshi swarmed over him.

With the knowledge that it would be over within minutes she forced herself through the doorway following Carey, yet as she only within a foot of the entrance she heard a noise and stopped in her tracks to stare at the doorway in horror. A large Meshi, who had seen her enter the tunnel locked eyes with her as its long snout entered the opening towards her. She could see the hatred and hunger in its small black eyes as it glared at her.

Before she realized what she was doing, the creature screamed and clawed at its own head, making it appear it was trying to claw out its own mind. It was then Katherine sensed the anger she had forced into its head and the creature gave out a final cry of pain before falling to the ground dead, green ooze spilling from its open mouth.

"*I am so proud of you. Thank you beloved.*" Alador's voice

sounded weakly in her mind for the last time. To emphasize the fact he was being worn down the doorway began closing behind her, blocking the view of the cave. Carey came running back to her side.

"We must go now!" Carey did not wait for permission and put an arm under Katherine's shoulder seeing she was also weak and started the climb upwards towards the light and out into the sunrise. As they left the dark tunnel and felt the sun on their faces a large stone appeared out of thin air and moved into place blocking the exit they had used. One final roar was heard echoing in the tunnel but the stones edges glowed brightly and removed all evidence that any type of tunnel had existed there.

The next thing Katherine knew the sun was high in the sky, almost directly above their heads and she was laying on her back surrounded by fresh, green grass, beside Carey. Opening her eyes and seeing Carey sleeping soundly, had her instantly nervous that they were vulnerable to attack. Instantly Katherine tried to sit up in a fast motion and then changed her mind just as fast. Her head felt like it had been slammed into a rock and just sitting up a little, made the world spin and her stomach lurch.

She felt something on her upper lip but when she removed her fingers after touching the area under her nose she saw it was dried blood. Her nose had bled but why she was not sure. She decided to try sitting up and maybe standing, yet slowly this time and the pain in her head eased quickly as her eyes remained steady.

Checking Carey to ensure they had not been attacked, it made her feel good to see that she had slept without any further signs of harm. Since the Tisna attack Carey still had a bump on her right temple and other small bruises along with cuts on her arms and legs that had occurred while she had been carried through the foliage on the way to the Tisna village.

Katherine noticed after her examination was complete just how high the sun was, and glancing at the stone that now covered the tunnel they had used for the escape, she knew their experience had caused them both to just collapse in exhaustion, once they had tasted freedom. The more she thought about it the more she came to the conclusion that using her gift on the Meshi had caused her nose to bleed. She silently counted on her fingers, one levitation and two, somehow, the power to kill a Meshi with her mind.

"Well," she chuckled to herself, "*I always wanted to be different to all the other princesses and I guess I am. But at what cost?*" She ended up scolding herself for being almost hysterically happy about her gifts, when they had cost her everything she had ever known and could still cost more.

Making a quick decision Katherine decided to use the time while Carey slept to test her new abilities and go hunting for food so they could fuel up before heading towards the camp. It did not take long to find some rabbits and after a few attempts she had a little too much fun lifting them out of their holes in the ground with her mind. So much so that she had pulled up an entire family of them and had them hanging in the air, in a row about five feet off the ground in no time. She quickly selected the ones she wanted and gently set the others back in their home without harm.

Approaching where Carey still slept after collecting firewood to cook the rabbits on and started building a fire when the log in her hand caught fire. Instinctively she dropped it to the ground afraid it had burnt her hand. Checking her hand quickly, she noticed that there was no cause for the fire to start and that she had no marks anywhere. Shocked at the possibility she was thinking, her hand reached down towards the fire and though it felt warm to her palm, the heat did not harm her, no matter how close to flames she reached.

By the time she was touching the piece of wood right in the middle of the blazing fire she was certain that she had somehow created the fire. Using her hand that was in the flame she lifted her hand out closed, opened it away from the log and the bright orange flame still shone brightly from her palm.

Quickly she lifted a rabbit a foot from the ground with her mind a few feet away and pointed at it with her index finger close to the flame, instantly the flame disappeared from her hand and appeared along the body of the creature, cooking it while away from the other logs or wood of any kind. The shock was clear on her face and she added in her mind.

Three, creates fire and four, can manipulate it.

Over confident about the level of power she had, Katherine decided to try removing the now crisp skin from one of the rabbits with her mind, but instead made it twitch and move in such a way that caused her skin to crawl instead. Not being a person with a weak stomach was one thing, yet seeing the little dead creature move on its own added to her uneasy feeling and a shiver rolled up her spine and immediately she ceased doing it. Her gift were useful in some respects, but she decided to never try such a thing again. Surely they did not need to be used for every little thing.

The smell of the now cooked meat was enough to wake Carey from her dreaming and not long after they were both eating with enthusiasm, since it had been many hours since their last meal. Neither of them could speak nor move for a few minutes while they devoured the rabbits and the things that were discovered during their ordeal washed over them. Katherine was the first to speak.

"I need to ask you something that may seem strange," they had eye contact instantly as she spoke.

"Ask me anything Kat,"

"I need you to swear that you won't tell anyone what we found out…especially about Alador,"

"I swear Kat. And I understand why you needed to ask," she replied in a calm matter of fact tone, "So what do we tell the others about what happened to us in the cave?"

"The truth for the most part but don't worry. We'll have all the details worked out long before we see the camp again," she added to herself, "I hope."

SUSPICION

Their new save-the-world mission gave them a sense of purpose, yet the food and warm sun kept them from moving longer than they both knew it should. At the same time they both stood and found themselves seeing the mountains. In every direction they could see the tall, snow covered tops.

They were high enough from the ground to see over the mist that covered the swamp and from their view it was beautiful and felt completely different. Clean crisp air, birds singing and the sun shining along with the light blue sky. Katherine tried to remember how awful and afraid she had been of the swamp and now the feeling of warmth on her face was almost impossible.

"Carey!" She exclaimed excitedly, "Over there," pointing down to their left they could see what appeared to be the Tisna village. Their confusion was clear.

"How far do you think it is from here?" Carey asked unsure her eyes were seeing it correctly.

"I'm not sure…maybe four or five miles at the most," even as the words left her mouth Katherine did not know if she believed it herself.

"Did we really travel that far back around in such a short time?"

"We must have but I don't feel like we did. If we came out where we should have, we wouldn't be facing the village. I mean we've been walking away from it since we entered the first tunnel. We should be only about one or two miles away, but on the other side of the mountainside,"

"I think Alador had something to do with this, don't you?"

"He must have. I didn't see the village while I was hunting, only after we had eaten. I'm pretty sure I would unless some kind of magic was involved,"

"Do you think we were moving without knowing we were?"

"That would be something now wouldn't it," Katherine could not help but gaze in wonder at the village. Alador really way a marvelous creature. Placing a hand on her throat where the necklace lay under her shirt she smiled. Even though she had lost him she would always have something to remember both her parents by.

"Well," Carey stated bringing her out of her peaceful moment, "It shouldn't take us long to get back down there,"

"I just hope the men found somewhere to stay and wait for us,"

"I'm sure that they're fine. It's us I'm worried about,"

"How can you say that?" Katherine smiled a little, "We just defeated that great cave demon, Meshi, and lived to tell the tale," a small laugh escaped her bitter lips as she held back tears. Taking a deep breathes she simply continued.

"We must put our feelings aside and make it seem like we killed the demon. The Meshi is what we killed and we're glad of it. Which we are, in a terrible way," she took another deep breath forcing all her emotions deep into her soul. She would deal with them but not now.

"Really that's nothing to pretend about Kat. You did kill a Meshi..with your mind," Carey sounded both proud and a little nervous about the fact.

"I know. It's hard to describe what happened. My anger just took over and I thought about killing it, then I was in its mind. I could hear its thoughts, although I didn't know what it was saying, and without being told I knew exactly what I could do. I started to push on its mind and then it screamed out in pain. It was the strangest feeling to realize that I could control it, manipulate it and force it to do whatever I wanted...even to the point of killing it. But when we find the mend, we should probably leave the mind part out of the story,"

"For now we probably should."

During their conversation they had begun walking slowly down a dirt path that seemed to head in the direction of the village. The path they had chosen started descending at a slow rate, of which both women were extremely grateful for. Their fast exit from the uphill cave tunnel had caused the muscles in their bodies to ache all over, even after resting as much as they could.

Katherine walked slightly ahead holding her sword at the ready as Carey followed closely behind being careful not to fall on any rocks in her new flat traveling shoes. Aside from her new shoes, Carey, had been given a similar outfit to Katherine by Alador. He thought it would not do to have her travel in the wild with only her nightgown and bare feet, and so gave her proper clothes. She now wore tight, dark brown leather trousers and a form fitting leather chest plate.

Carey's movements were stiff in the new clothes as she tried to keep up with Katherine's watchful stances. She secretly marveled at the fact that it was second nature to the ruler of the kingdom and yet to her, a commoner, it was something she had never given much thought to as she always wished to wear dresses and take part in the court side of the palace life. It was at times like this that Carey realized how very different they were and how perfectly they complimented each other being best of friends.

As they traveled Katherine thought more about her gifts. She had come to realize that when she attacked the Meshi her power had been triggered by her emotions, specifically her anger and feeling that wanted to protect her new found father and Carey. She also decided that it was simply too hard to concentrate with everything they had been through and keeping her eyes on the surrounding areas at the same time as they walked. With this thought in her head she made the goal to practice any time they stopped to rest and eat. Not being able to practise more made Katherine uneasy. Since they walked a feeling of dread had been building up in the pit of her stomach. Something bad would happen very soon, but she could not place where it would come from or how it would affect them.

They had been walking for hours when Katherine heard voices coming from the path just ahead of them. Indicating to Carey to take cover, they both sidestepped behind one of the medium sized bushes they had been seeing near the path for the passed ten miles or so. They had just found the right hiding place when two men appeared. Neither were known to either of the women but Katherine instantly recognized the uniforms they were wearing. They were the same as the men who arrived with Staton, the night of the ball.

The feelings of hatred and resentment immediately came back to the front of her mind as they continued heading up the path slowly towards their hiding place. The men paused just a few yards short of the bush they were hiding behind and glanced around the area. Anger stirred in Katherine's mind and barely resisted the urge to kill them both, when suddenly she was surprised to hear their voices.

She was shocked.

Neither of their lips were moving yet she had clearly heard them...in her mind.

"I hope we can go home soon. I hate this creepy place," the man standing the closest to her said.

He stood around six foot two inches tall with ear length brown curly locks. The brunette appeared kind in the face and although he carried a long sword, a mercenary, he did not seem in the least bit threatening or intimating. The other man was the exact opposite in the fact that he was indeed completely terrifying. From their position in the bushes Katherine thought he was about the same height as the first but bigger in build and had short black hair.

His face was a mask of seriousness and the three scars on his face gave him a scary appearance. He had one scar through his left eyebrow that started at his eyelid and stopped one inch above his eyebrow. Another scar caused a white line in his thick black beard from the top of his right cheek that extended to his chin in a diagonally line. The last scar was close to his left ear and gave the impression that someone had tried to take it off and failed.

"*I will not die for something as stupid as a being unable to find a Prince. I'm not a child watcher damn it!*" The second man mumbled to his own mind laughing slightly as another thought came, "*Well, one things for sure, I'd like to see Staton try to kill me. He'll have one hell of a fight on his hands,*" his face turned menacing as his mind rolled over all the details on how he would kill Staton. Listening to his thoughts intrigued she got the distinct impression that these fine gentlemen were not sent by Staton to help them, nor that they were particularly loyal to him.

"*We shouldn't go back, even if we find him. We know too much. We're on borrowed time, that's all. Borrowed. Time,*" the first one thoughts only confirmed what she had suspected and came up with a quick plan. She smiled to herself as she tried something she had never dreamed possible before today.

"*Stay here no matter what happens.*" Carey instantly grabbed her left arm.

Katherine had spoken to her with her mind and simply smiled at her triumphantly as she picked up her short sword and started to move away from Carey. She moved slowly keeping low from their hiding place, using the trees and bushes around to disguise the direction she approached from. As Katherine stepped out from behind the finally tree on the other side of the men they looked like they had seen a ghost.

"Where the devil did you come from?" The brunette asked in shock at her sudden appearance.

"I think the questions should be, where are you coming from and who sent you?" Smiling at them both she started swinging her sword playfully, while watching the larger of the two men closely. If either of them would give her trouble it was bound to be him.

Katherine had been right.

"That's none of your business bitch!" He snarled at her while his expression was one of seeing an insect walking across your meal. "Now be a good little bit and clear off!"

"I was so hoping you would say that." A humourless smile appeared on her face as she leaped into the air. Before he had time to react the larger man had been knocked to the floor by the impact of her entire body weight. Of all the things he had seen over the years, never once had a seemingly harmless woman jumped towards him using her own body weight as a weapon, this was the only reason a seasoned veteran like him was caught completely by surprise.

Once the shock wore off he still could not move as Katherine's sword was level with his throat making it almost impossible to force her away without causing damage to himself. As the dust from the ground settled from her leap Katherine felt a small tap on her right shoulder from the other man.

"Ha," the larger man boomed, "Dumb bitch thinks she can kill us both," Katherine was tempted to release him just from the stench of his breath. It smelled like rancid ale and more than a few rotten teeth. Instead she just returned his smile.

"Who said I can't?" Without releasing her sword, grip or glare from the larger man beneath her she forced herself into the mind of the brunette.

Instantly she could feel his reluctance to hurt anyone and his high emotions that told her he was concerned for her safety from the other man. He seemed to doubt his own skill in the way of protecting himself and feared for her life should the other man become free as his skill rivalled anyone else he had ever met.

Not wishing to dwell on these thoughts she began pushing as she wanted to show them both she was more than capable of dealing with them. As the brunette started to scream she felt the larger man freeze and his breathing slow to almost a stop. The brunette continued screaming and fell to his knees, gripping his head with both hands as the Meshi had done. Before he could fall unconscious Katherine released him quickly. After a few minutes the brunette stopped rolling around the floor and his breathing became normal. Standing on his feet he was a little shaky, had a small amount of blood coming from his nose but otherwise was unharmed. He walked towards the nearest tree, away from Katherine, and leaned on it for support.

"Now are you lovely men going to answer some questions for me or not?" She asked sweetly smiled at their new fear of her.

"How can you trust them? They belong to Staton," Carey walked at Katherine's side once more as both men walked slightly ahead.

"Were Staton's men. Now they are mine. Trust me. They understand I'm powerful and I used their doubt about Staton to make them join us instead. Anyway, I can read their minds so if they even think about betraying us I can kill them...just by thinking it," her tone was serious yet held a hint of amusement as she realized that she could kill a men twice as big as herself so easily.

"You must be careful with this power. It takes a toll on you every time you use it. What if you push yourself to far? And what if they manage to lose us and tell Staton about your power?"

"I appreciate your concern but I'll be fine. So I get a beating head for a few minutes every time, I've had a lot worse. And I already told you, they already doubted Staton before we showed up and I used it to help turn them to our cause. And from what he told them I think Staton may already know what I can do. I mean think about the facts for a minute. They were sent to find Lanell and capture me by using specifically made shackles. What would a normal, stuck up Princess needs to be held captive with special restraints for? They could just use rope,"

"I see your point but I still don't see why he wants you? Unless its something about Maltesh,"

"I don't either and I don't like the idea that he knows about my abilities, especially since I just found out about them myself. All this is why we need to find the camp and get some answers as quickly as we can,"

"Well either way I'm positive that Lanell had nothing to do with this,"

"How do you know that? He could have been the one to tell Staton our location. Its not the first time he would have given his father information,"

"Kat, he left the tent before you told Calzar about your vision remember,"

"Yes, and tent walls are so much thicker than stone castle walls he could not possibly have overheard us,"

"If Lanell was able to hear us then so were half the camp. Listen I know this new information has made you upset but please promise me you're not going to take it out on Lanell. At least until we can prove he knew something. He could be innocent,"

"Well at least reading minds will be useful in this situation, I'll be able to tell if he is lying." Katherine mumbled to herself.

Over the course of next few hours Pete, the large tall dark headed man, had told Katherine that they had passed signs of their camp on the way up the mountainside. Daniel, the brunette, had told her all the details about their mission including a rendezvous with more of Statons men near a cave three hours ride from the haven.

"How did he find out about the haven?" Carey wondered to herself.

"I really wish I knew," Katherine answered out loud.

"Stop that it's creeping me out," she replied out loud laughing a little.

"Oh sorry, I can't seem to stop. The thing that concerns me most is that all the clues so far, point to someone who is travelling with us. Knowing about me, about the haven location that I only put on the map a few days ago and that we would be coming out of the pit somewhere in this vast area," she thought out loud and grew heavy hearted with each word as if saying the words out loud made it real.

They both became quiet as Pete and Daniel had stopped slightly ahead of them and had crouched down low to the ground. A lot of noise could be heard just in front of where the men were and as they approached Daniel spoke.

"It sounds like Staton's men. It must be one of the patrols he sent behind us," he observed speaking in a low tone while glancing over at Pete. Pete sat as still as stone listening intently. Suddenly Pete whispered in a fierce tone.

"We need to leave now. Follow me this way," Katherine was about to object when an animal like male voice penetrated her mind.

"Flesh, flesh hows I like the human flesh. Lean and fatty meat, me likes a lot this creamy bright red eats," her stomach churned over at the delight she could sense in the creature's mind and the realization of what he was singing to himself about. Carey looked at her with concern as she whispered out loud.

"Katzi!"

They moved as one backwards about a hundred yards and to the right of the large group they could now hear being sure to keep as low to the ground as possible. They remained quiet and low for what seemed like a lifetime until finally Pete stood erect and spoke out loud.

"We should be able to continue on as normal from here but at a faster pace. Just make sure whoever is on watch stays extra alert. I don't want to wake up with one of things chewing on my favourite body part." Even Katherine, who had not known a man intimately before, knew Pete was making a sexual reference and tried her best to appear unaffected yet she thought she saw a look of humour on Daniel's face as he caught a glimpse of her reddened cheeks.

"How did you know the Katzi were there without looking?" Carey asked curiously as she had not seen either man look through the bushes they had been hiding behind to check what was going on.

"Let's just say years of hard experiences on the front lines of most Staton's battles. Once you have seen what they do as close as I have, you pick up a few extra skills," Carey was still curious but she decided to leave the subject alone as he seemed reluctant to speak about it further.

"It should not be far now. Our camp was about a mile up that path," Daniel stated quickly breaking the awkward silence.

"Great. What provisions do you have at camp?" Katherine asked trying to find something to take her mind off the Katzi's voice she had heard and the embarrassment that followed.

"Only the basics really a few biscuits, dried fruit and dried meat. We were to get more when we met up with Staton's troops." He added the last portion with a weak smile. Katherine smiled back reassuring him as she knew he was now on her side without question and she did not need to read his mind.

She was, however, still keeping a close eye on Pete. Although she knew he would not betray them out of fear of the consequences and the fact he hated Staton for reasons other than what he had yet revealed. He was reserved to trust her without seeing for himself if she was deserving of it and she could respect that as it was an expected response in their current situation. She completely agreed it was the best course of action for all of them.

Once they reached their camp it was nightfall. The camp consisted of one tent, a small campfire and two horses, who seemed a little uneasy but well rested. Daniel had explained when they arrived that a second tent was available but stored in the saddle bags and that the horses were secured for their cause as they did not know if her camp had been given horses of their own they could have stolen when collecting her. Both women were tired and hungry after the long day they had had except that Pete had other ideas of what to do next.

"We should eat quickly and be gone before all the stars are out. And don't light any fires,"

"What? We're not staying here?" Carey asked wearily.

"I'm sorry but if those damn creature's catch our scent they will swarm on this camp within hours. We need to get as far away from here by then," Pete replied in a sorrowful yet serious tone.

"I agree with Pete. We have wasted enough time here. We need to find the others as quickly as possible. If I'm in danger then they will be as well," Katherine nodded at his plan, even though her body was exhausted her mind raced. She needed to find out what was going on with all these events and quickly as her entire being felt they were all connected somehow.

"Carey, you double with Daniel and I shall ride with Pete."

If the men questioned her choice they did not voice their concerns either in their minds or out loud. Katherine was still sure that neither man would turn on them, however she knew Pete would be the biggest threat, of which only she would be able to deal with as Carey did not know how to use a sword. Mounting behind the enemies turned allies seemed strange to both women, yet neither complained as it was a welcome break from walking.

As the stars began to disappear above their heads as they rode they halted to rest only once more. At the new location the single man tents were not made to house two fully grown people but no one complained. The men used Pete's which was slightly bigger and cleaner since it had been exposed to a recent rain, while the women had Daniels that smelled like old pipe smoke and dried meat. Once they were pitched and the entire camp was sound asleep before the first rays of sunlight began to crest over the mountainside, aside from the current person on watch, Pete.

Staton laughed loudly and it echoed around a large, dark room. Lance shouted over him from his position shackled against a large grey wall.

"Burn in Hell You Bastard!"

"The righteous walk through the fire to be cleansed and

so I shall still be the better man," he smirked with a glint of evil in his eyes as he walked towards his helpless victim, "Do you really think she will send someone to rescue you? You? A mere broken soldier from her father's court. She is royalty. A Princess. Someone who will rule one of the biggest kingdoms in all of Talveon. How could she ever care about you?"

"I don't need to justify her to you,"

"It's true you don't but you worry about her love, don't you?"

"She loves me,"

"So you think but how can you be sure. From what I've heard she has an ability to get whatever she wants clothes, exotic fruits, fabrics, close friends and most importantly information. She has manipulated men in many ways, ways you can not imagine. A similar soul to my own if you ask me. Yet you really feel she will settle for someone with no rank, no riches, a destroyed body and a twisted soul,"

"I'm not the one with a twisted soul!" He spat back.

"You misunderstand me. I'm trying to help you Lance. Save you from the devastating heartache that is bound to come. I wished to spare you the details but now you force my hand. She has already forgotten about you. Moved on as they say,"

"You don't know anything about her,"

"Don't I?" He screamed back at Lance so loud the room almost shook, "The truth is far more fun. She is to meet someone else very soon and she will not be able to resist his..charms. You know as well as I that she is still selfish under her new forgiving posture. When faced with a choice between an arranged marriage or dying slowly after watching you have your skin peeled from your bones...which do you suppose she will pick?" Movement out of view and Staton taking a deliberate step to his left caused Lance's eyes to bulge and take in a deep breath of shock.

"No!" Lance's scream cut the night with a dagger of pain and heartbreak.

Katherine woke up with a start.

She immediately sat upright breathing quickly as her heart raced. Had she seen the future? It had to be something she could change. Of one thing she was completely sure Staton did not know her. She would never choose anyone over Lance whether that meant dying quickly or slowly. She had to admit to herself that he was right about using them to get to her, just as Alador had said. She would face challenges involving them and soon. Carey had known instantly that she was woken up by another vision and asked the obvious question out loud.

"Are you alright?"

"Certainly, it's nothing. You know dreams are always so dramatic," she replied out loud yet in Carey's mind she informed her of the vision in detail.

"Yes, I have those kinds of dreams myself," came the strained automatic answer out loud while in Katherine's mind a more detailed conversation took place.

"What do you think? Could you tell if it was past, present or future?"

"It has to be the present as Staton said I'm going to meet someone else soon and we haven't met anyone new except these two and I don't think he meant them. Although Lanell did mention something about an arranged marriage with him before,"

"You said that Lanell understood about that so there is still a chance you can prevent it,"

"True, but Staton was happy. I mean really happy. Anything that makes him happy makes me extremely nervous. He was there with Lance chained to a wall, he knew what reaction Lance would have when he was told of the arranged marriage. I could tell from his face." Katherine knew her anger swelled due to her vision and tried to control it.

Knowing her emotions were connected to her powers as Alador had said made her worried as she just considered something. What if she got angry while having a vision? What if she hurt someone close by mistake? What if she hurt Carey or someone sleeping in the next tent over? Her mind was made up. As a group they were vulnerable from outside forces and herself.

Alone she could kill them all.

As nightfall once again came Pete indicated that he was waiting outside the tent for them. Unable to go back to sleep after her vision Katherine had been planning their next move, packing up their things ready to move out and devising her own plans. Due to this the men only had to wait a few minutes while they finished packing the outside of the tent away before they were again on the road. Even though they were still heading towards the haven, Staton's troops and their old camp, Katherine had not yet figured out where they would end up and was so mentally exhausted she did not want to dwell on it.

It only took a few hours to reach Summit Peak. Summit Peak looked over the entire valley, if you climbed high enough. The cave that they chose to rest in was only up enough to see about three or four miles in each direction. Crouched at the entrance to the cave Pete pointed to a camp fire that could be seen up the path about a mile ahead of their location.

"That is your camp there and that is the Katzi camp following us," he pointed back up the way they had come down to another camp. It was about two miles from their current position.

"I see now why you didn't want to lit a fire. We would be easily spotted from up here," Katherine nodded towards him somewhat impressed by his experience. He had already saved their lives twice and had not asked for anything for return.

"We should rest a little and head down to the camp. It would help having more swords handy if they catch up to us," Pete continued as Katherine shook her head slightly.

"I agree, but I think before we join the others we need to talk more," both men sat next to each other on the hard, damp cave floor in front of her as instructed while Carey laid down in the back only a few feet away. They had both agreed to help her and seemed willing.

"I want you to be honest with me. I give you my word that anything you say will not make you countable. I will never harm you for honesty. What do you know about the attack on Maltesh?"

"I don't know anything about that," Daniel spoke quickly and honestly.

"I heard something about it. While we were waiting for Staton to give us directions to follow you out here, one of the soldiers mentioned that there was a rumour floating around that one of your own set it up,"

"Did they say why or who?" The question came out hurriedly and Pete continued.

"I hate to say it highness but I'm guessing it was you. The guy told me another rumour had stated a child was born in your kingdom with...special talents and it had been kept a secret as to the child's name or when it was born. A major attack was set up to draw the child out as they thought the child would either come out fighting to protect the kingdom or be too young to stop it and die in the process. The only problem is, as I said, they didn't know when it was born or how old it would be. The child could have been a little baby for all they knew but someone inside didn't think so and said the attack should take place now,"

"Me? They destroyed our home to find me. All those people died because of me," Katherine spoke quickly in Carey's mind. Her devastation clear as Carey instantly replied.

"No, those people died because someone wants to find you..for who knows what..and they were willing to take innocent lives to do it. Everyone died to protect you and I'm sure they would be willing to do it again. I know I would," Katherine looked over at Carey, her eyes giving away her overwhelming feelings of emotions for her closest friend. She focused her attention back to the two men, who noticed the exchange and Katherine's sorrow but said nothing.

"Only a few more questions before we leave and please tell the truth, even if you think it will hurt me. Does Lanell know about you coming for him and capturing me?"

"He may suspect that we were coming to claim him, but he knows nothing about you..yet,"

"Yet? What you do mean?" She asked in a dangerously quiet tone.

"Last we heard Staton planned to give you to him as a present. A way to earn forgiveness for killing his adopted mother, Mischelle," both women gasped. The one person in the world that Lanell truly trusted had been killed by his own father.

"How do you know this? Why would he have killed her?" Her tone suspicious.

"When Staton's personal guard told us about the assignment I asked him where we needed to bring you. He told us the rendezvous and that we would not need to bring any of your belongings as the Queen's things were being brought for you. I joked with him about the Queen being mad when she realizes some of her things were missing and he says to me, it won't be a problem as he had killed her that very morning. From what he heard Mischelle had discovered what was going on and tried to stop him, something about hurting children once before and letting it slide but she couldn't ignore it again. He heard it was over very quickly. She didn't suffer, like most,"

Both men looked down towards the stone floor of the cave embarrassed that they had continued the mission after discovering that the man behind it had killed an innocent woman who had only wanted to do the right thing. Forgetting that the men did not know she had been talking to Carey in her mind Katherine spoke out loud carrying on their previous conversation about Lanell.

"He really doesn't know anything about this, does he?" Her voice was shaky and sorrowful for her new friend.

"No, but now you know for certain you can trust him as I do." Carey thought knowing that Katherine would hear the same sadness in her voice at being right.

Lanell, Calzar and two of the guards on duty were armed with their swords drawn as they heard footsteps approaching the camp.

"Wait!" Lanell shouted quickly as Carey, Katherine, Pete

and Daniel appeared from behind a bush to the right of the camp fire leading two dark, brown horses.

"Glad to see you survived," Lanell spoke in jest to Katherine as she got closer.

"Glad to see you were worried," she laughed back. He suddenly noticed the two men that were by her side and seemed to recognize the uniform instantly just as Katherine had. However before he could say anything about it Katherine spoke up.

"Calzar, Lanell, we must speak privately...right now," after they had moved away from the others and entered the women's tent that had been set up on their behalf Lanell could not stand the suspense.

"Can someone tell me what the hell is going on? They are from my father's troops?"

"Please sit down this is going to be hard for you to hear," Katherine indicated to the cushions on the floor. Looking a little shaken by her serious yet sorrowful tone he sat down slowly suddenly unsure if he wanted to hear what needed to be said. His gut told him that something was very wrong.

"Pete, please tell Lanell why you came here to find us," she indicated to him slightly by moving her head in Lanell's direction.

"Sire, we were sent here by Staton to take you to the haven where he waits for you," he paused slightly as Lanell seemed happy and was about to speak when Pete raised his right hand a little indicating there was more to be said.

"Please highness, I must continue before my words fail me completely. We were also instructed to kill all the other guards and ensure that her highness was captured. We were to bring both of you to a rendezvous close to the haven to enable someone else to take you further on," pausing again for a brief moment. Pete never looked up as he took a few deep breaths and continued,

"Before we left on this mission we were told by one of Staton's personal guard that he had killed the Queen as she discovered his plot to capture her highness and was trying to stop him. She did not suffer,"

Lanell sat still as stone. His face a mask of pain and confusion. Katherine knew that if she wanted to she could read his thoughts but decided against it. She motioned with her right hand to the tent entrance indicating that Pete and Daniel should leave them. To Calzar she raised her hand showing he should stay a moment.

"Lanell, believe me I know this is hard for you but we really need to discuss our next step. I would really like my new friend to be here when we do, but if you need some time?" Katherine motioned towards the tent entrance sadly. His eyes glanced upwards for a moment. He held a glazed look yet his eyes were still free of the tears except they were close to the surface. He nodded slightly at her, stood and walked out of the tent quickly without looking back.

"Why do I feel like there is more to this story than we were told?" Calzar smiled out of the corner of his mouth.

"Have any of the men been away from the camp alone since we began our travels?" Ignoring his remark Katherine started her questioning. After everything that had happened she needed to be careful whom she spoke with.

"Highness, you know that everyone away from the kingdom travels in pairs. No one ever goes anywhere alone," Calzar replied in a serious uncomfortable tone.

"Sorry Calzar, I need to ask these questions," her reply was quiet yet firm, "What is the longest any pair stayed away from the camp?"

"Michael and myself scouted ahead when we left the Tisna village. We were gone for most of the day,"

"Who watched over the camp while you were gone?"

"I left Magel in charge as he was watching Lanell,"

"I need to speak with him immediately," she demanded to one of the guards standing close by.

"What is all this about highness?" His impatient tone about being left in the dark was clear.

"You heard for yourself that men were sent here to capture me. Is that not reason enough for my line of questioning?" She snapped back upset that he would challenge her.

"I apologize highness. I understand your reasons for questioning us but if you are in danger it is my job to protect you and I need to know all the information before I can help you,"

"I thank you for your concern and your protection. But I will question anyone and everyone necessary to find out for myself what is going on before deciding what our next step will be. The quicker we sort out this mess the sooner we will all know what is going on,"

"Of course your highness," he turned and left the tent without saying another word. Carey could not hold her feelings in any more. Staring sternly at Katherine so her intent was clear Carey thought her upset feelings.

"What the hell did you do that for?"

"We can't trust anyone until we're sure," Katherine read her mind instantly and responded in a quick calm voice.

"It's Calzar. He has been with us since we started on this journey and has been a close friend and guard to the King for decades. Do you really think that he would be the spy?"

"We can't risk it. Remember when I had my first vision he said we needed to prepare in case it wasn't a dream. He was the one who said it might be something more. Why would he think that? And he would have been there in the room when I was a child and made things float around the room, right? He would have known I wasn't a normal child, right?"

"I'm not saying it's not possible, certainly but the truth is we just don't know and we need his help. Can't you just ready everyone's mind in the camp and see who the traitor is?"

"It has crossed my mind, but for one I don't know the range of my power, two I think it's wise to watch how many people know about it and third it weakens me. If I use my power to hear everyone we have no idea what it would do to me and the last thing I need right now is to draw more attention,"

The sound of footsteps approaching quickly made both women mentally silent. Katherine was both surprised and pleased to see both Magel and Lanell enter the tent.

"You asked to speak with me highness?" Magel asked in a serious tone as Lanell simply walked in and sat down on a pile of cushions next to Carey. His eyes stared at the ground avoiding all contact with anyone else. It was clear that since he had left the tent he had been crying. Carey silently placed a reassuring hand on his right shoulder, yet did not make any other movement towards him. He smiled a little towards her but then faced the ground once more.

"Yes Magel. Thank you for coming so quickly. When Calzar left you in charge of the camp, did anyone leave alone or did a pair leave for an extended period of time?"

"Only Mened and Carboz left during that time. They were gone until almost sundown,"

"Which direction did they come from when they returned?"

"From the east," he added quickly, "They were scouting ahead in the opposite direction of Calzar and Michael,"

"Why did Calzar not mention that they had been gone for a long time?"

"He didn't know highness. By the time we realized how long they had been gone, they were spotted walking towards the camp. Calzar and Michael came back a few hours later and when they arrived everything was packed up and ready to move out. Sorry, highness it was forgotten once everyone started walking," Magel lowered his head ashamed that such a critical thing would be overlooked while he was left in charge.

"Don't feel bad Magel. It could be nothing," Carey piped up reassuringly.

Over the course of the journey Carey had begun seeing Lanell in a new light and she liked the view. Sitting next to him while Katherine questioned Magel some more the urge to lean over and hold his clenched, white fist, forcing it to relax became overwhelming. He was in ruins. Any hope he had embedded in his soul that he would see her again had been shattered and Staton had been the cause.

A thought that had not occurred to her before edged its way into her mind as she watched his bottom jaw clench as tight as his fist. She had been defending Lanell to Katherine, swearing his innocence, protecting him from her potential anger and watching him develop a friendship with someone she considered to be a sister. She had watched him go from being an outsider, to life saver, to friend and now ally. Lance would never have approved of her choice and yet without realizing it she felt that the decision had already made. In trying to convince Katherine to give him a chance she had allowed herself to feel for him and now she did.

"Katherine?" Lanell spoke up quietly bringing Carey out of her own mind and into the tent again, trying to control her shocked face at her recognition for her new feelings towards him. "Does this have anything to do with my father?"

"That will be all, thank you Magel," Katherine indicated that he could leave now. Once he had closed the tent opening Katherine shocked Lanell by speaking in his mind.

"Don't speak out loud just think and I will hear you,"

"What's going on?" His thoughts confused as he instantly stood as his wide eyes stared between Carey and Katherine, *"You can hear my thoughts?"*

"Yes, I've discovered over the past few days that I'm more than just the ruler of Maltesh. I have special gifts that only a few people know about. Because of these powers my kingdom was attacked and your mother killed,"

"What?"

"I found out from Pete and Daniel that Mischelle found out about me and the plans that Staton made to capture me. Lanell, she tried to stop him. She was protecting me, since she couldn't help Lance and the others. She was killed for trying to help me," Katherine sorrow was felt in his mind as her expressions on her face changed. Being unable to hold them back she spoke with large tears rolling down her face, *"Believe me if I could have saved her I would have,"* Lanell remained silent for a few moments then he spoke slowly.

"I don't blame you for what happened. I always knew my father was capable of terrible things. I just thought that my mother and I would never have to be any part of it," shaking his head from side to side as he muttered, *"I was naïve,"*

"We can still stop him. He knows about my powers and he knows the general direction of the haven. He has his men waiting a few miles from the haven for us and he understands all of this because someone from our own camp is helping him. We need to find out who it is and fast,"

"Agreed. Who did you have in mind?"

"I suspected everyone until Magel mentioned the situation with Mened and Carboz. Did you see them leave or return?"

"Yes," he paused in his thinking, *"Now that you mention it, I remember thinking it was strange that they didn't look tired or dirty from travelling so far,"*

"Really?"

"Yes. Honestly they seemed well rested and I noticed their boots had hardly any mud on them. I'm sorry Katherine, at the time I just thought they had been lazy and just fell asleep under a tree or something," Katherine spoke out loud.

"Magel, send in Mened and Carboz please," she stated quickly as Magel appeared at the entrance to the tent without thinking. He did not say anything yet his expression was one of confusion as he turned around to fetch the men.

Minutes later Magel returned in a hurry. Bursting into the tent he exclaimed loudly, "They're gone!"

"What!?" Lanell and Katherine both shouted in unison as Lanell sprang up again from the cushions. Merely seconds later both Pete and Daniel entered the tent. Daniel had been beaten so badly that Pete half dragged him into the tent. Instantly he was surrounded by people trying to help him. Carey ran from the others as quickly as possible to gather bandages, clean water and vinegar as Lanell ran to his side helping Pete carrying Daniel to the cushions that he had been sitting on moments before. As they began lowering him Katherine exclaimed.

"What happened?"

"He can't speak highness. His jaws been broken, probably on purpose so he can't say who it was," Pete's tone quietly obviously ashamed that he had not been there to help his friend.

Katherine felt so sorry for Daniel and the pain he had suffered. His right eye was almost all the way closed showing colours of black with purple parts. She could also see blood on his face in many places and he held his right side with his left hand indicating that some ribs may be broken. Pete was right about his jaw, there was extensive bruising on the left side of his jaw line, which held colours of yellow, blue, purple and black.

Taking in his wounds made Katherine all the more furious with the spies in her camp and she was determined that she would find them and make them pay dearly for the pain they had caused. She nodded at Daniel in a reassuring way before speaking to him in his mind.

"Daniel, don't be alarmed. I have the ability to hear your thoughts. Please tell me what happened and who did this to you so I can stop them?" She spoke in his mind as gently as she could so as to not scare him. In doing so she also tried to enable Lanell to hear what he said, which seemed to work as his voice came to them in a scared yet determined tone.

"Mened and Carboz. They heard that you were asking questions about everyone who had been away from the camp while you were gone. I saw them leave heading east and I followed them. I didn't realize they had seen me before it was too late...they grabbed me and dragged me into the bushes covering my mouth...I tried to yell but they threw me down and stomped on my face..." he paused as he mustered the strength to keep explaining, *"I thought they were going to kill me,"*

"Thank you for telling me. You are a brave man. I swear to you they will pay dearly for this," Katherine tried to soothe him as best as he could, but his sorrow seemed to drag his thoughts into a dark and lonely place.

"I found him when he fell out of the bushes to the east. He was barely crawling," Pete continued explaining not knowing about the conversation that had taken place during the few minutes of silence.

"It was Mened and Carboz the whole time!" Lanell mumbled out loud in a furious tone, "They will pay dearly for this! I swear to you Daniel!" Lanell firmly grasped his left shoulder with his right hand as he declared vengeance.

"Mened and Carboz? Who said it was them?" Calzar had entered the tent unannounced hearing all of the commotion.

"It's not obvious. I'm asking questions about those who left camp, they suddenly decide to leave and Daniel is found almost dead on the same road they were checking to the east. He must have gotten in their way somehow and this was his punishment," she simply responded in a calm, logical tone.

Katherine had decided that she was still not one hundred percent sure that someone else was not part of the whole scheme so she would limit the amount of people who knew about her gift. Confirming her words Daniel nodded slightly, wincing trying to say that was correct in her supposed assumption. Katherine could not help but smile widely at him. He knew without being told that not everyone knew about her gifts and he felt great pride knowing that she had chosen to share it with him.

"Pete, take Daniel to his tent, set his jaw and sort those cuts out," Carey entered again carrying a basket of supplies to help him with the damage the others had caused so Katherine continued, "Oh good, Carey please go with them and help as best you can, won't you?"

"Certainly highness," Pete replied immediately.

Carey simply nodded with her face white with strain of seeing so much blood and pain. Although she was trained to help with injuries she had a hard time around blood. It would take a while to clean up all the blood from Daniel as she would need to take frequent breaks to breathe fresh air, however Katherine knew she would be one of the best at helping him heal quickly.

As they left Katherine felt sadness and rage at what had been done to Daniel. The realization that it could have been anyone in the camp including Carey, haunted her thoughts.

"Calzar, double the guard at once. If we are attacked I want us to be ready!" On hearing her orders he appeared ready to object but he did not mutter a word as he left the tent quickly. Lanell was the first to speak once they were alone.

"When did you discover you had powers?"

"From what I found out I've always had gifts. It was just hidden from me to ensure that I or my loved ones were never in danger. Yet now, thanks to Mened and Carboz, Staton knows about me and wishes to capture me for that reason,"

"I could never imagine anything that like being real before now," Lanell looked shocked that he had never heard of any human having powers before, except for Magi but they were not really considered to be entirely human.

"Well now you know as much as we do. We just need to find out what he needs me for, although I'm not completely convinced I really want to know,"

"That may be harder than it sounds. With Mened and Carboz on the way to him, we have no idea when or where they will strike or even how many of them we'll be up against,"

"True, we do have an advantage though. They don't know the extent of my powers. This, at least, means that if we are able to get close enough I'll be able to read their minds...hopefully before they see us,"

"So what is the plan? You do have a plan, right?"

"Of course," she smiled, "The plan is simple. We head east in the direction of the haven,"

"Are you crazy? They will be waiting for us!" Lanell exclaimed loudly,

"That's just it, they won't be. They will probably be thinking that since we know about Mened and Carboz we would have decided to go another way to avoid them, right?"

"If I know my father, and sadly I do, he would probably cover all directions to be safe," Lanell spoke up calmly this time as he looked up at Katherine. She could tell he was still having a hard time with the entire situation but nodded a little adding,

"Yes, he would ensure that all possible exit routes would be cut off. He may even send someone to scout the camp since his spies are no longer among us. We really should leave as soon as we can," he muttered more to himself than to her, then glanced at her as she nodded in agreement quickly about leaving.

"I think we can all agree on that," she demanded as she opened the entrance to the tent for a moment, "Magel fetch Calzar and Pete immediately."

The men appeared quickly as they could tell Katherine was in the most foulest of moods and action was needed to be taken.

"Yes highness?" Calzar asked quickly.

"Gentlemen, it appears that we have a plan so let's ensure we are as far away from here as soon as possible. We leave as soon as everyone is ready," Calzar seemed upset as he had been left out of the planning yet due to his training he simply replied before leaving with Magel and Pete in a hurry, "As you wish highness,"

By the time the men had gone from the tent, Carey appeared once more. She was still pale, covered in blood and sad, except she was smiling a little.

"How is he?" Katherine asked before Lanell could.

"Better. He is extremely lucky they just wanted to silence him. Had they not been in a rush to leave camp..." she left the sentence unfinished aside from it was clear what they would have found when they packed up the camp and continued on, "Michael's taking over his care for a while so I can catch my breath,"

Katherine could not help but smile at her. It was her faint heart when it came to blood which made her leave to taste fresh air. There were times such as this that she was noble in the way that she made a perfectly sound excuse to leave someone else in charge for a few moments.

During their exchange Lanell stood still indicating that he wished to speak with Katherine and since the silence wrapped around the tent as Carey retreated to the cot area to change her red stained clothes behind a screen Katherine started the conversation.

"Did you need something else Lanell?" Smiling a little he glanced up at her with an expression of both happiness and sadness in the same eyes. Slowly he spoke.

"I wanted to thank you for allowing me some time earlier to compose myself," he stood erect except for his eyes refusing to focus on hers for more than a few seconds at a time.

"I have to admit I was surprised to see you come back in when Magel did. I thought we wouldn't see you again until we broke camp,"

"Believe me," he laughed a little nervously, "The idea that I shouldn't come back in crossed my mind more than once before I did,"

"I know this is going to be harder on you than the rest of us but I want you to know that I'm glad you're on our side," she smiled at him with tremendous pride.

"Thank you. Out of all of this I am glad of one thing,"

"Really? What is that?"

"That you trusted me enough as a friend that you would reveal such an amazing thing. I mean with my father being the enemy we face and all,"

"But you still don't understand why?" She asked in a shocked tone. As he nodded she smiled wider.

"Even hearing your own words you don't know. You said the enemy We face, like it was never even a question that you would be beside us,"

"Well, what do you know. I never even notice that's what I said," he laughed out loud for the second time since they had left the kingdom.

"I feel that I need to apologize to you Lanell," she glanced down ashamed as she spoke.

"Whatever for?" he asked surprised.

"From the moment you were left with us I have been suspicious of you and guarded all my feelings. It was only recently when a wise person told me to give you a fair chance that I truly have seen who you really are. My newest and close friend,"

"I'm honoured Katherine. But you must tell me who thought so highly of me so that I may thank them," without saying a word Katherine's eyes darted to their left a little to where Carey was now fully dressed in one of her travelling gowns and wrapping up her blood soaked clothes, pretending she was not listening to them.

"It seems I owe you thanks Carey. Although I don't know why you of all people would give me a chance?"

"What would make you say that?" She turned with a serious expression on her face.

"Not being a fool I naturally assumed that with you knowing the history between me and Lance you would hate me for even talking to Katherine, probably as much as he would,"

"You would be right there. At first I thought the worst of you, even more than Kat did. Truth be told I thought this whole friends idea was just a plot to gain her affection..." she paused looking anywhere but Lanell then slowly she said, "Then came the day she almost fell off the cliff. If you had not been there I don't know what would have happened. You saved the only sister that I have ever known and in my mind that was reason enough to give you a chance. I gave you a chance on that day and thought Kat should do the same," her eyes welled up simply thinking of how worried she had been that day.

"Oh Carey I had no idea," Katherine stated in a shocked tone walking over to her sister-friend giving her a tight hug.

"Well, I appreciate your honesty with me and after everything that happened when I lived in Maltesh before I understand why you would think badly of me," he stated in a matter of fact tone, "Although it was not only Carey who I had reservations about..." Katherine did not miss the emphasis on the word I and started to laugh out loud.

"Heaven knows what you thought I would be like,"

"I had heard stories of you but I was not sure what to expect. From all accounts they were good things, except maybe for your temper and having already witnessed that first hand now I don't believe it to be as bad as people made out,"

"You think you have seen my temper," she could not help but laugh again, "Sorry to disappoint you Lanell but you haven't seen anything yet," a playful smile touched her lips yet Lanell was certain her eyes held a hint of unpredictability.

"We should make ready the others will be leaving without us if we don't hurry," Carey interrupted quickly as sounds of tents being dismantled filtered in from outside.

"Tonight we'll stay at Hunters peak. It's about four or five miles up the way but it will depend on how close the Katzi follow behind us," Katherine was muttered more to herself than anyone else, however hearing the words Lanell's demeanour changed to one of seriousness and anger.

"Katzi!" His tone increased, "What Katzi?"

"The ones that have been following us since I killed one. As we were trying to find you we saw them about two or three miles back. If we continue to stay ahead of them, they may simply give up and turn back...maybe,"

"When were you going to tell us that we are being pursued by Katzi?" His tone now one of anger. At his words and tone Katherine's eyes began to burn as the same anger rose within herself. Her voice raised as well when she spoke.

"I thought with the situation as it was, we had more pressing things to figure out, like who is trying to get all us killed,"

"Magel!" Lanell ignored her and yelled as loud as he could, "Bring Calzar at once," Magel stuck his head in and out of the tent again before Carey had enough time to turn around to see his shocked expression. Within seconds Calzar came running into the tent.

"What's the matter highness?"

"Her majesty failed to mention that we have Katzi trailing us. They are about two or three miles behind us," Lanell spoke up before she could say a single word and her anger increased at the same rate as his tone, saying her majesty almost sounded like he was making fun of her.

"That is the last thing we need right now. Do you know how many were there?" Calzar asked quickly turning to face Katherine. Pete stepped into the tent and answered for her. He was not asked inside yet still he came in and stood directly behind Katherine showing his support for her and her alone. She could not help but smile at him as he spoke.

"Anywhere from twenty five to fifty from what I could hear. They were spread out while they partook of their meal,"

"We need to dispatch them before we continue on. If we don't they'll be set on our trail the entire way and we don't want to be fighting anyone ahead, only to get caught in the middle of two enemies," Lanell stated simply.

"Agreed. The women are to stay here while we take them out. Magel, you remain and guard them,"

"What?" Katherine could not help but yell in shock. After everything she could do she was still being treated like a little child.

"Highness, no doubt you are skilled with a sword but it'll be better in this situation to let the men take care of it," Pete spoke up as he placed his right hand on her left shoulder gently. A small moment of silence passed, then she slowly nodded in defeat.

"You're right Pete, thank you,"

Carey seemed on the verge of speaking yet refrained. The men knew better than to discuss their plans anywhere near Katherine or her tent, as she may just follow without permission, so they decided to simply leave and plan as they headed back. While the men gathered up their weapons, the others gathered the tents and packed away everything to continue on.

In Daniel's condition he was unable to walk or ride so the men had searched the surrounding area and luckily found an old two wheel hand cart, with one broken wheel close by that was easily fixed. It was decided without any conversation that the tents would go down first, then Daniel would use them to make it more comfortable for his healing wounds. The women, Pete, Daniel and Magel were to carry on up the path to the east until they were about five miles from the haven, there they would wait for the others to catch up.

"Lanell, please be careful," she smiled at him as they prepared to move out.

"You too. Try not to be a hero, if something happens," he smiled back knowing she would try to win any battle herself if she could.

"Take care Lanell," Carey added quietly as he followed the others back, westward, towards the Katzi camp. As daylight shone from behind the mountains Lanell glance back only once and seeing the straight blonde hair waving in the air still looking at him, made a large smile spread across his face. Carey watched Lanell's back until he was nothing but a small brown speck on the path.

Katherine helped Pete lift Daniel into the cart on top of the tents and bundles of belongings, while Magel started hooking up one horse to the front of it. They worked in silence until Carey, hating that she was being kept in the dark once her eyes left the path had to speak up.

"Can someone tell me what is going on?" Her voice was frustrated and emotional.

"Whatever do you mean?"

"You know very well, what I mean Kat. Why didn't you argue with Calzar about going with them? I know you. You wouldn't take defeat so quickly,"

"Believe me I had no intention at all to let them leave without me, but then Pete touched my shoulder. I instantly read his mind as he suspected I would and he told me that I may be a good idea to keep my power hidden for a while longer. He figured out that I had somehow spoken to Daniel and found out who hurt him but knew to keep my secret to himself,"

"Yes, but why keep your power a secret. Mened and Carboz have already gone and you can help them kill the Katzi,"

"We've already spoke about this Carey. What if they were not the only ones working for Staton?"

Pete interrupted suddenly, "You forget highness, we were

scouting the camp for days before we realized you were not there and came looking for you. Daniel and I saw many people leave the camp, alone and in pairs, and each were gone for several hours at a time. Mened and Carboz were simply the only ones seen by an honest guard," he glanced over at Magel with a look of great pride on his worn face as if respect had been earned many times over. Magel was still too far away to hear what was being said and continued his work without knowing how much respect the others had for him.

"If that were true why would they leave us?" Carey wondered out loud.

"I was thinking that myself. It does leave us vulnerable to attack as we are now limited to how many people we can have standing watch at one time. Also if there are other traitors among them it would be easy to kill one of our own men and make it look like they were just killed while fighting the Katzi. It may also prove a problem in regards to direction as we will be expecting to hear movement coming from the west, since that is the way they will be returning from. If an enemy somehow knew that, it could be our undoing." Katherine was ranting to herself as they began walking towards the haven once more.

"I wonder what other powers you have?" Carey thought to her after a few minutes.

"The thought is intriguing isn't it?" She chuckled a little back as she replied.

"When we stop to wait for the others you should try some things,"

"I think that is the best idea I've heard all day." Katherine smiled widely at her.

DEEPEST BETRAYAL

They had been riding for hours. The sun was close to setting when they finally decided to stop and rest. The women had been taking turns riding on the back of the wagon with Daniel all day, when after a while Katherine chose to ride one of the spare horses after she saw Carey's eyes closing against her will.

It soothed Katherine's heart a little watching over her best friend as she slept peacefully surrounded by men who give their lives for her. No matter what trouble they had faced or would in the future, watching the relaxed expression of her sister caused Katherine's soul to settle in a calm state, if only for a few brief moments.

"We should rest here for the night," Magel spoke in a serious, deep tone, pulling his horse alongside hers.

"I agree. Have Pete help you setting up just two of them. I want us all close by out here. No one goes anywhere along, is that understood?"

"Yes highness," was the chanted in response by both Magel and Pete.

"Carey," Katherine's reluctance at waking her clear in her changed tone as she pulled up at the side of the now stationary wagon,

"Kat?"

"While the men set up camp, you and I will collect wood for a small fire. I'm not willing to let you out of my sights." Carey nodded and smiled at her knowing her over protective nature was not likely to decrease while they were away from the kingdom, and even then she was certain neither of them would be so carefree.

Searching around the dirt for broken twigs and branches that they could burn was a quick and easy task as it had not rained since they had left the palace. They split up for only a moment when Carey saw an abundance of little twigs at the base of a steep incline to their left. Carey was so busy picking up the smaller pieces she did not notice a large hollow log resting above her head a few feet. The more pieces she gathered the more the log shifted slightly.

Movement above caused her to glance up, yet seeing nothing out of the ordinary she continued her task, smiling widely at the large amount she had. Suddenly the log came loose and began to roll right towards her, gaining speed as gravity gripped it tightly and pulled with all its might. Hearing the increasingly loud thudding and crashing noises as the log impacted the ground, other branches and leaves heading into Carey's direction, Katherine screamed out.

"No!" Instantly the log was yanked off the dirt covered floor and thrust up into the air, along with several other twigs and other smaller items.

In surprise of what had happened both Katherine and Carey stood as still as stone watching the large piece of wood hang, a hundred feet off the floor, slightly spinning, hovering silently above their heads.

Hearing the scream Pete had ran as fast as his legs could through the woods. As he turned a corner to see them, he also could not move. He watched in silent awe as Katherine began flipping the log slowly in the air by moving her right hand in a circular motion.

He smiled as she did caught in shock by her display of power and yet the child like face of joy she held in that moment. Pete was reminded that even though she was considered a woman in most things, in others she was very much still very young and inexperienced.

Katherine had recovered from her shock quickly and while she liked moving the log she had a thought. She carefully aimed her left hand at the log and large orange and red flames erupted on the surface from nowhere. A gasp from Pete caused her to jump and she did so the floating wood exploded into a thousand pieces with a large bang.

"What the...?" Was all Pete could muster when she came over to see if he had been injured.

"Are you hurt?" Carey asked loudly, both relieved that she had been saved and that Katherine did not hurt him in anyway. Before Pete could respond his sword was drawn and he turned within a second at the sound of footsteps approaching. Seeing the others approaching he quickly lowered it.

"I should have known you'd get into trouble without me," Lanell spoke as he lead the others closer. Katherine was so happy to see the men walking over towards them with their swords drawn, yet each of them were unharmed after fighting the Katzi.

"When did you return?" She asked quickly in an embarrassed tone.

"Just now..then we heard you call. Seeing the log floating, well, we thought something strange was happening and boy, we were right," Michael exclaimed still in shock from what they had seen.

"When did you discover you could do that?" Calzar asked suspiciously, yet he scanned the surrounding area at the same time as if checking it really was Katherine.

"The same time you did. I saw it rolling towards Carey and I reacted. I saved her life," she simply stated in an angry voice due to his accusing tone. Carey nodded in agreement. She was pale in the face and carried a look of shock similar to the men.

With all the excitement the fight with the Katzi had been forced out of their minds so on the way back to camp all the questions were asked and answered.

"Pete was right. There were around twenty five of them following us. They had many torn, blood soaked uniforms that were from Staton's guards," Calzar explained, "It looks like they were following us and the Katzi were on their tail for a long time,"

"They were all dead by the time we got to them, but the Katzi were so full and unaware that they didn't expect us to just walk right in their camp. The element of surprise was all we really needed," Lanell added proudly.

"We should all turn in for the night. We have a long day tomorrow." Calzar stated still glancing at Katherine in a way that seemed out of place, yet feeling the moment of curiosity about her would pass she discarded it.

Katherine slept deeply. As the tent was shrouded in darkness she knew she was dreaming but the picture that appeared in her mind was clear to her, as if she saw it with her own open eyes.

It was morning and the sun blinded her for a moment as she stepped out of the dark tent. The small table used for viewing the map had been brought out and placed close to the fire that still smoldered from the previous night. The mountainside to their left was darker than it should have been and before her eyes a large shadowy hand stretched forth its long clawed fingers, reaching towards them.

Walking slowly, against her will, towards the table Carey laughed and smiled at her, while sitting next to Lanell on the left side. It was clear their hand were entwined. Everything appeared in slow motion as Calzar passed over the bread to Magel, on the right side, smiling up at Katherine. Lanell raised himself slightly to reach one of the pieces of dried meat that were in the small basket as he too smiled up at her.

Suddenly everything started to shake, although those at the table did not react as if they did not notice any difference. A deep rumbling could be heard from the woods at the base of the mountainside causing Katherine to turn away from her friends. A loud deep growling voice entered her mind and spoke with pure malice as the tips of the shadowy fingers reached them.

"We come for you. Chosen one!"

Katherine awoke screaming, sitting straight up in fear of what she had seen. Carey was at her side wearing a concerned expression. Removing the cover quickly Katherine grabbed Carey and hugged her like she would never let go.

Lanell woke up startled at the outburst as it echoed around the camp. He was up in a second and was forcefully entering the tent before she had time to compose herself. He calmed down slightly seeing the two women holding each other. Calzar, Pete and Magel closely followed him.

"Are you alright?" Lanell gasped catching his breath from sprinting over as he sat down on the corner of the blanket next to Carey, so he could look at Katherine in the face. Carey spoke for her.

"Kat, just had a bad dream. That's all," covering for her without a second thought was a given.

"Yes, but it wasn't a dream this time. I'm sure it was another vision," as much as Katherine appreciated the attempt to hide the truth she could no longer lie to Lanell, even though others that were close by were not all in her good graces, she still let the cat out of the bag. She quickly recapped the entire vision in detail as everyone was silent, hanging on her every word. Once she finished Lanell sat quietly for a few minutes thinking.

While he contemplated what he had heard Calzar tried to dismiss Magel and Pete, yet Katherine indicated they should remain. Carey just remained silent occasionally glancing over at Lanell. When Katherine described them holding hands Carey had realized that in his haste to come to their aid Lanell had entered their tent with no shirt. She could not help but admire his soldiers physique but she knew the attraction she was feeling for him extended passed just want she could see.

"I'm guessing this isn't the first time you've had one of these...visions with me there right? That's why you hide it from me,"

"No, I've never," she could not hide her fury at being reminded.

"In that case it must have been my father?"

"Yes," she tried to fight the vile that rose in her throat thinking about the vision with Staton in them, "It was him. And I can't explain how much I wish I'd been there in person with a sword,"

"I see. I'm sorry Katherine. Do you know what this vision could mean?"

"I think that finally the true enemy is about to reveal itself,"

"My father? We already knew he was behind the attack?"

"No, I have a feeling that Staton is just a part of something much, much large than even he might know. He is a pawn as much as we are. Another 'force' called Barberus has been searching for me longer than him and I think that this thing is using him to find me,"

"Who told you about this thing that is supposedly searching for you?" Calzar asked with a curious and concerned expression.

"A close friend." Was all she would say about the matter. As it was still not dawn Calzar insisted that everyone but the guards on watch go back to their tents to rest. The next day they would continue up the trail towards the haven despite the threat so they could regroup and figure out their next move.

With her power coming to light Katherine was selected to pick the wood again the next day for their breakfast, mainly it was voted so she could practise to control it away from the others. However Lanell had insisted on going with her regardless of the potential danger. She only agreed when he promised not to be standing over her shoulder the entire time and that Magel would stay close to Carey while she was gone.

"Just promise me you'll stay close by?" He had argued.

"Fine, but don't be my shadow. We already have one. Calzar." She had replied playfully back. Katherine could not help thinking to herself as she collected the dead branches from the dirt floor.

"Men. He knows that I can protect myself. Of course I've seen the way he glances at Carey so keeping him close by will help me watch his intentions." She smirked to herself.

Lanell was out of sight to her left somewhere when she heard a twig snap behind her. At that same instant a small sting struck the right side of her neck. Taking a huge breath of air from shock she reached up and pulled out a three inch blue dart from her throbbing throat.

Panic erupted from the pit of her stomach as she opened her mouth to scream and nothing came out. Katherine started to feel weakness spreading through her knees and legs and her head felt fuzzy and her eyes unable to focus.

Horrifying thoughts bombarded her mind and she could do nothing to stop them.

How would you capture a being that could set you on fire or throw you into the air? You could not approach directly and even a stealthy attack was risky. There was only one sure fire way to get close enough.

She glanced down at the dart in her hand barely able to make out the small two inch shape.

Asleep. They would have to be asleep.

Fear mixed quickly with the panic rising up in her throat as she tried in vain to call out for help. Tears came to her blurred eyes. Unsure of what to do she thought of her friends, Carey, Lanell, Calzar, Magel and even Pete and Daniel, all the people she had come to adore on their travels. Her legs finally buckled under her sending her knees into the dirt, leaves and twigs.

"*Help!*" She almost did not recognize her own voice. Even in her mind she sounded like she was already drowsy from too much wine. Asking for help drained her of the strength she had left. Falling forward on her hands trying to keep her head away from the ground was a battle she knew she would lose soon enough.

Footsteps. Someone was coming closer. Trying to see who it was, was almost impossible as her eyes were now passed the point of seeing anything but blurred shapes of color. Without a target she could not use her power and she was too weak to reach for her weapons. Then out of nowhere a thoughts came to her mind.

"*It's true. Its her. I never really believed.*" A male voice. Terror gripped her as she did not know who they were. As impossible as the thought was she felt more fear rise up in her stomach along with bile.

Katherine could now tell there was more than one person near by. She was being surrounded and without being ale to use her powers or weapons she was helpless. She heard the thoughts of someone close by and they were not human. In fat it was making fun of the human girl, who had been so easily taken by a single dart. A shout sounded over her left side far off in the distance as a human male voice rang clear in her mind.

Then something worse happened.

"Quickly, she alerted the others. Take her now while I send them the other way!" Recognition fell on Katherine like a wall of stone. She knew that voice. Very well. He was the spy. But why?

It made no sense to her and yet it could not have been more clear. Feeling someone standing near her head, she fell into unconsciousness wishing she knew why he had done it and wondering what would become of her and her friends.

Her last thought was a single name.

Calzar.

Will Katherine be able to escape her new prison?

What plans could this new enemy have for her?

Find out in the next installment.

Hertiage: Choice

Coming Soon!

Acknowledgements

This book has been many years in the works and to say it is now ready for publishing is incredible. There are so many people that I want to thank it would fill a new book. However, there are a few people that I feel need to be recognized the most.

Firstly, myself for not giving up and for always keep on fighting. I ignored the naysayers and pushed through to make this happen. I am beyond proud of myself for that.

Second, my beautiful daughter, Kaylee Pliley, for whom this book was written. Before this I was a writer, every chance I could, however, I never had such inspiration until she came into my life. This is all your fault, in a good way. I love you my precious.

Third, my wonderful husband, Josh Pliley and son, Nation Piley, who both put up with me as I struggled through my writing until early hours of the morning and gave me extra hugs when I needed it. You are my foundation. I love you both so much.

Fourth, my wonderful family both near and far who supported me in anyway they could. From my nephew, Harry Redfern, who created the Maltesh family crest, to my younger sister Angela Wheat, who listened to me rant about the characters and helped with feedback. My older sister, Anna Stevenson, who always knew I would achieve whatever goal I set for myself and my wonderful brother, Adam Redfern, who is my hero and idol just for being the truly amazing and spiritual person he is.

Fifth, it has to be my wonderful friends who believed in me through all the ups and downs. They also helped me by reading my work, editing, late night writing sessions, book clubs, writing groups and writer meltdowns. I can't express enough how much you mean to me. Laycie Jensen Bowers, Bonnie Foy and Jennifer Ruiz.

Sixth, is to my incredible patreons. Without this generosity self-publishing is an even longer, harder road. I honestly can not thank you wonderful people enough. You have made this final product a reality. I am completely serious when I say that every little bit helps. You are amazing.

Without each of you, and the others I did not mention by name, this book seris would never have made it into the public eye. Each of you has made me be a better writer and overall person on this journey. I will never be able to express in words how much you mean to me. I will be forever grateful.

Printed in Great Britain
by Amazon